The South Pacific Murders

A Mia Ferrari Mystery

SYLVIA MASSARA

License Notes

This novel is entirely a work of fiction. The names, characters, and incidents portrayed in it are the work of the author's imagination. Any resemblance to actual persons, living or dead, events, or localities is entirely coincidental.

Published by Tudor Enterprises
Australia
(61) 419 492 623

Revised edition 2016
First published by
Tudor Enterprises in 2014

ISBN-13: 978-0-9875475-4-5

Copyright © 2014, 2016 Sylvia Massara

Sylvia Massara asserts the moral right to
be identified as the author of this work

Dedication

To Mia, my naughty ankle-biting kitty;
and to the handsome officers of P&O's Pacific Pearl.
You guys are hot!

Titles by Sylvia Massara

Romantic comedy:

Like Casablanca
The Other Boyfriend

General fiction:

The Soul Bearers

Mia Ferrari mystery series:

Playing With The Bad Boys
The Gay Mardi Gras Murders
The South Pacific Murders

Sci-fi romance:

The Stranger

For more information on Massara's novels, both in eBook
& paperback editions, plus participating retailers;
or for latest novels or to contact the author, please visit:

www.sylviamassara.com

CHAPTER 1

I tried very hard to control my temper as I fixed my work colleague and friend, Guy Dobbs, with a look that could vapourise a planet in a millisecond. "Who the hell invited Smythe along?"

Dobbs winced at my enraged tone and did his best to give me a placating smile. "Now, Mia; you know you agreed to be good where Smythe's concerned. Don't forget he saved your life."

I banged down my cup on his desk, making the items on it rattle. We were having coffee in the security office of Rourke International Hotel Sydney, where Dobbs was the security manager.

"Honestly, I can't believe you're standing up for the guy. It was his friggin' job to save my life," I exclaimed indignantly. "Besides, I was the one who once again had to solve the case for the cops because they were too stupid to listen to me in the first place!"

Dobbs did not respond immediately but regarded me for a while, until I had time to settle down. He knew me too well to try to push a point when it concerned my archenemy, Detective Sergeant Phil Smythe of the Kings Cross police.

I took a deep breath in order to calm myself. There was no point in losing my temper with Dobbs since the whole thing was now a fait accompli. I therefore remarked after a few moments of silence, "I just don't understand it, Dobbs. What made you invite him on the cruise?"

Dobbs's large dark eyes gazed back at me from a chocolate brown crinkled face topped by grey frizzy hair. He spoke carefully lest he should provoke another outburst from me. "Mr Rourke told me I should invite someone in his place seeing as he couldn't make it," he explained in his deep voice with a marked American accent. "The reason I thought of Smythe was because he managed to keep the press off our backs after the drag queen murders. When I suggested this to Mr Rourke, he agreed it was a good idea in order to maintain a cordial relationship with the police."

I sniffed and felt myself relent, albeit reluctantly; but I wasn't about to admit it to Dobbs. He should suffer a little longer for what he'd done, even though it was a good move on his part to invite that prick, Smythe. I had to take another calming breath to remind myself that Smythe had cut me a lot of slack during the gay mardi gras murder investigation.

Taking another sip of coffee, this time I put down my cup gently to rest on its saucer. "Very well," I answered begrudgingly. "I guess we all have to sacrifice in the name of professionalism." I felt more than saw Dobbs's sigh of relief at my comment.

Dobbs ventured an encouraging smile. "I'm glad you see sense, Ferrari. The boss will be happy to hear it."

I turned questioning eyes on him. "How come David isn't coming with us anyway?" I secretly felt regret at the fact that David Rourke, CEO of our hotel group, wouldn't be with us on the trip. Although I'd had a thing with him in my youth and he was now my employer, nonetheless, the attraction between us had never completely disappeared.

"He's tied up with the project in Waikoloa," Dobbs informed me, unaware of my thoughts. Then he added, "In any case, Chris is coming along."

Chris was David's twenty-year-old son and my little helper whenever I became involved in solving a mystery. Not only was Chris like a pseudo-son of sorts, but he was my personal computer hacker—something Smythe had silently agreed to ignore during our last case, when Chris's contribution to the investigation had been invaluable. Yet another reason why I had to swallow my pride and stop protesting about Smythe joining us on the trip.

"Well, I only hope David's arranged separate cabins for us. There's no way I'm sharing with anybody," I remarked as if I wasn't too happy about going on the trip in the first place, which was not exactly the case. I really looked forward to some much-needed rest and relaxation.

Dobbs shook his head and threw me a look of amusement. "Don't be silly, Ferrari. Of course you'll have a cabin to yourself. You don't think they're going to make you share with one of us, do you?"

I shrugged. "If I had to share with Chris, I'd manage it," I returned with a grin. "But not with you. Eileen tells me you snore in your old age."

Dobbs's solid frame shook with rumbling laughter. "Don't let

Eileen fool you. She might complain, but she still thinks I'm hot in my sixties."

I replied with mirth, "If she can say that after so many years of marriage, then you're onto a good thing." My mind briefly flashed on my own broken marriage of eighteen years, but I forced my focus back to the present. I hadn't thought about my ex in almost a year, so I wasn't about to go down memory lane now.

The telephone on Dobbs's desk rang and he picked up. "Security, Dobbs speaking."

While Dobbs talked on the phone, I cleared our empty coffee cups in preparation for returning them to room service.

I had been in the middle of my rounds when I'd dropped by Dobbs's office for coffee, and now I planned to check on the kitchen before I carried out several random room checks to ensure housekeeping maintained the hotel's high standards. As a duty manager of the hotel, my job was to ensure things ran smoothly during my shift.

"Trouble in the garage," Dobbs announced, hanging up the phone.

"What now?" I queried, coffee cups in hand.

"One of the valets accidentally scraped a guest vehicle when trying to park it." He shook his head in annoyance. "It never stops with these young ones who think they can play car racing with someone else's vehicle."

We walked out of the security office together and made our way toward the service lift.

"Don't get me started on the Gen Y'ers." I rolled my eyes. "They have no respect for anybody. Plus with them, it's always *me, me, me.*"

"What's the matter, Ferrari; you've gone off the younger men for a change?" he teased with merriment in his eyes.

"Buzz off, Dobbs." I grinned wickedly. "You know there's only one thing that can stop me from a dalliance with a younger man."

"And what's that?"

"Death."

Dobbs roared with laughter at my response, and we entered the lift when it arrived. He was still trying to recover from his outburst when we stopped at my floor and the doors swished open.

"This is me." I threw him a look of amusement. "I'll catch you later, my man."

He nodded, still unable to speak, and the lift doors closed shut. I turned toward room service, my good mood restored.

~~~

"Counting the days before we sail?" Chris crept up behind me in the room service kitchen, almost making me drop the crockery in my arms.

"Shit, Chris!" I rounded on him. "Don't creep up on me like that. I hate it."

He appraised me with the same green eyes as his father's, and his dark good looks. "I bet you Dobbs just broke the news to you about Smythe joining us on the trip."

I placed the cups and saucers on a dishwashing rack and then threw my hands up in the air with irritation. "Does everybody know about this except me?"

Chris grabbed hold of my jacket sleeve and pulled me out of the kitchen before we could be overheard. I followed him to the service corridor and we proceeded to make our way toward Reception in the front-of-house area.

"Dad told me last night at dinner. So aside from him and Dobbs, no one knows about Smythe coming along," Chris reassured me, and then commented, "I didn't even know we were going on this trip until then. I thought I'd be working right through semester break."

When Chris was not attending university, where he was studying for a degree in IT, he worked as a casual waiter in the functions department of his father's hotel. Although he didn't need to hold down a job, he had a good work ethic, which made me like him all the more. I couldn't abide some of today's youngsters who simply sponged off their parents because they were too lazy to get off their butts and get a job for spare money.

"I'm still not sure why your dad even invited us on this trip in the first place," I remarked.

"Don't you know? Dad's financial partner in the Waikoloa project is also the owner of Columbine World Cruises. They plan to introduce cruise packages incorporating accommodation on arrival in Hawaii."

I raised an eyebrow and regarded him with interest but didn't say anything.

Chris went on. "Anyway, the guy gave Dad a few complimentary tickets for their upcoming Hawaiian cruise."

"I didn't know any of this," I uttered. "Your dad simply told me we were going on the cruise as part of a famil."

"Yes," he conceded. "In a way it is a familiarisation trip. After all, we're going to be accommodating guests that travel between Sydney and Hawaii. Plus once Waikoloa's finished and we expand to the island of Oahu, we're going to have even more business coming through. I think the deal is to eventually offer cruises from Sydney to LA and San Francisco via Hawaii—that is, once Rourke Hotels expand into the West Coast."

This made sense seeing as David Rourke owned hotel properties in every major city in Australia and New Zealand. He had visions of expansion in the Pacific Rim and eventually into his native homeland, the US.

I felt proud of my one-time love. When I'd met him, he had only been twenty years old and attending hotel school. Now, at age thirty-nine, he was a renowned hotelier with multiple properties and on his way to international expansion. Meanwhile, I was ten years older and I hadn't even been able to make the police force.

It had been my lifelong dream to follow in the steps of my father and his best friend, Dobbs, but due to circumstances concerning Smythe, and later marriage to my idiot ex, time had run away from me and I ended up in the hotel industry instead. I had to admit, though, that I enjoyed my present job despite the fact I never became a cop. The good thing was that being placed in the hotel world, I was daily exposed to all sorts of insidious activities such as drug deals made in guest rooms; prostitutes being sneaked in by male guests; suicides galore; and the list went on—and though I was the hotel's senior duty manager rather than a detective, I had gained the reputation of being the *informal* investigator among the staff, especially since two police cases had unfolded within our hotel over the past year. Rourke Hotel Sydney was located in the city's red light district, also a big tourist area. So we were never short of drama.

"Well, I guess it makes sense to send us on this experience. I suppose this is also a big 'thank you' from your dad for all the hard work we've put in. It's a shame David can't make it. Instead, we're stuck with Smythe." I frowned.

Chris cocked an eyebrow at my tone of discontent. "Hey, you should look upon this as a good thing."

"How so? I mean, what can possibly be good about having Smythe onboard a ship for fifteen days, and having to socialise with him in the middle of the Pacific?" My voice dripped sarcasm.

Chris wasn't put off by my manner and said, "Don't you get it? Smythe will be sweet once he gets to know us better. So next time we work a case, he won't threaten to lock us up for interfering."

I nodded at this veritable fact. "Hence the reason I'm putting up with it," I informed him with a big sigh. "Hell, if it wasn't in our best interests to keep Smythe happy, I'd throw the bastard overboard for the sharks to dine on."

Chris laughed and draped an arm around my shoulders as he drew my slight five-foot frame to his six-foot athletic body. "See? This is why I like you so much, Ferrari. You're such a selfless and caring person."

I pulled away and punched his upper arm. "Don't be a smartarse, Chris Rourke. And you'd better get back to work."

He rubbed at his arm. "Man, you still pack a good punch," he stated with a grimace.

I stood as straight as I could to try to add a couple more inches to my height, but the top of my head just made his shoulder. "I may be older these days, but I haven't forgotten my martial arts training," I remarked with pride in my voice.

"Yes, I know," Chris agreed. "As for being older, I hear this doesn't stop you from being approached by younger men."

I scowled. "Get away with you! I see Dobbs has been opening his big, fat mouth."

"Don't be too hard on the man—he's only being protective of you. You know he loves you like a daughter."

"True," I concurred. "He was, after all, my old man's best friend on the force. But this doesn't give him license to go around talking about my taste in men." I threw him a warning glare to signal the subject was now closed.

Fortunately for Chris, he got the hint. "Well, I have a function to work, so I guess I'll see you later."

He walked off in the direction of the functions department while I walked up a flight of stairs that led to Reception.

CHAPTER 2

The Ocean Star stood gleaming in the sunshine at the White Bay cruise terminal as we waited in line to check in.

"It says here the ship has the capacity to carry twelve hundred passengers," Chris commented while he read from a fact sheet that had been added to our ticket folders when the Columbine people had delivered them to the hotel the day prior to embarkation.

I took a look around the huge check-in hall and observed hundreds of people lining up at different counters, all waiting to check in. There were families with children of all ages, couples, elderly people, and quite a number of disabled passengers.

"The ship was built in France in 2005 expressly for the Columbine line, which has a fleet of twenty-nine ships covering the world," Chris continued, sounding like a tour guide. "The port of registry is the United States. The gross tonnage of the ship is fifty-nine thousand, with an overall length of eight hundred feet and a breadth of one hundred and ten feet. There are thirteen decks onboard, and the height of the ship from keel to mast is one hundred and eighty one feet. Wow, this baby's large!"

I rolled my eyes. "Thank you for the commentary, Chris. Now, can be have some quiet?"

"Ouch, Ferrari," Chris exclaimed in mock hurt.

"Relax, will you?" Dobbs whispered in my ear. "You could cut the tension in the air with a knife."

He was right. The fact that Smythe was standing with us as part of our group raised my hackles. If only I were travelling with Chris and Dobbs exclusively, I thought wistfully, we'd have a grand time.

I frowned at Dobbs but didn't trust myself to speak. It seemed Smythe had also decided to stay silent, I noted, as I threw a furtive glance his way. He was standing next to Chris, looking very smart in khaki shorts and a navy blue polo shirt, listening to more of the ship's statistics while Chris read on in a lower tone.

I turned quickly away, despising myself for finding Smythe

attractive despite my antagonism toward him. He reminded me of my ex-husband in terms of looks and stature—yet another reason to hate his guts. Moreover, it didn't help that his appearance was similar to Tom Selleck minus the moustache. Smythe was close to his mid-forties, only a few years younger than I. And a deep instinct told me that Dobbs got it into his head that because I was partial to younger men, Smythe fitted the bill.

A sudden burst of laughter caught my attention and I gazed toward a large group of men and women standing a few feet away from us, queuing at the "Groups" check-in counter. The group looked to be in the age range of late thirties to somewhere over sixty.

"I wonder who they are," I remarked to Dobbs and pointed with my chin in their direction.

Dobbs followed my gaze and took a few moments to assess them. "Probably some kind of convention."

"Hmm," I returned, soon losing interest. Our line was slow in moving and I fidgeted with the luggage tag attached to my suitcase.

"Try to have some fun, Mia," Dobbs implored, picking up on my mood of despondency. "Look at me; I've started already." He pointed to himself, wearing a big grin on his face, and I smiled.

He looked every bit the relaxed tourist with a loud Hawaiian shirt, which was a tad too tight around his widening girth, and white shorts.

Before I could comment, he interjected, "Yes, I know I've put back all the pounds I lost last year when I went to Hawaii to visit my daughter, but I intend to lose them again on this holiday."

I regarded him with amusement. "And how do you propose to do that? We're about to go on a cruise ship that's full of restaurants, buffets, cafés and bars. The temptation will be too much for you, Dobbs."

He winked at me with confidence. "I'll be walking a lot. They have a jogging track onboard for exercise. That's what I'm going to tackle every morning before breakfast. I'll walk two miles every day and soon this," he patted his belly, "will go back down."

"I'll hold you to that," I answered doubtfully. "But I bet you'll welch at the first sight of the desserts on offer."

Dobbs started to say something in his own defence, but the line moved forward all of a sudden and we were next to check in.

~~~

Our cabins were located on Deck 9. Chris and I had a cabin next to each other, with Dobbs and Smythe across the passageway.

"Too close for comfort," I whispered to Chris before inserting a plastic key to open my cabin door.

Chris winked with a grin and went into his own cabin.

"The luggage will be dropped off and left outside our doors." Dobbs, whose cabin was directly opposite Chris's, announced. "Why don't we go and explore together in the meantime? We've got two hours before departure."

Smythe, whose cabin was opposite mine, opened his door and replied, "Good idea."

I frowned, not wanting him to tag along with us, and inspiration popped into my head. "Dobbs," I addressed him without even glancing Smythe's way. "You and Smythe go. I need to discuss a few things with Chris."

Dobbs went to open his mouth to speak but seemed to think better of it and turned to Smythe instead. "Give me five minutes, Phil, and we'll go."

He and Smythe disappeared into their cabins just as Chris's head popped out of his. "I heard that," he remarked with a cocked eyebrow. "I hope you're not going to carry on like this for the entire trip." He admonished.

I pushed my way into his cabin and closed the door behind me. "Don't be a smartarse, Chris Rourke," I chided. "We're not here to play happy families, or I should say 'happy friends'. If Dobbs was dumb enough to ask Smythe along, let him hang out with his cop buddy. I certainly don't intend to."

Chris regarded me with surprise in his eyes. "Whatever happened to being more civilised in the spirit of keeping Smythe sweet?"

I scowled. "I hate it when you're right."

Chris laughed and patted my shoulder. "You're something else, Ferrari. C'mon; I'll hang out with you for now, but you have to promise to have dinner with us this evening, okay?"

I nodded with my bottom lip sticking out like that of a petulant child. "Oh, okay."

We decided to meet up after Dobbs and Smythe left on their

exploration. Meanwhile, I returned to my cabin to look around. I had a queen-sized bed in what was a smaller version of a hotel room with a rectangular window, or porthole, as they were known in the old days. There was a writing desk; a couple of plushy chairs flanking a small round coffee table; a flat screen TV attached to the wall opposite the bed; a mini-bar fridge; a walk-in robe equipped with hanging space and drawers, plus a small safe for valuables; and a smallish bathroom with all the amenities. The cabin was cosy and had all the comforts of home.

A fruit basket rested on the coffee table and I picked up the small white card attached to it. It read: *"Compliments of the Captain and Columbine World Cruises."*

I put down the card when I heard a soft knock at my door and Chris calling, "Mia, you ready?"

We went for an exploratory walk around the ship. Deck 12 was the busiest, with two restaurants and a café as well as an outdoor grill, which made mostly burgers and steak sandwiches. Opposite the grill were two swimming pools; one for adults, where one could swim to an open-air bar; and another for children.

Deck 13 was the highest deck on the ship and it contained the gym and spa; the jogging track Dobbs had told me about; and the entrance to the nightclub. The interior of the ship, from Decks 8 down to 5, consisted of an atrium filled with shops of all kinds; a casino; a theatre; the reception lobby, with an entertainment area and piano bar; a small café that sold hot drinks and cakes; an a-la-carte restaurant; and a series of theme bars.

"My God," I exclaimed, looking down at the atrium from Deck 8 and shivering in remembrance. "I hope we don't get another jumper landing on the baby grand like we did at the hotel last year."

"Don't even mention it," Chris stated soberly. "This is our holiday and we don't want anything to spoil it." He looked away from the atrium and toward the café, where we spotted several tables with computer terminals on them. "Great! They have an internet café plus Wi-Fi here; the same as on Deck 12."

"I thought you brought your own laptop."

"I did. But I still need a Wi-Fi hotspot."

I smiled. "Well, my dear boy, you better have loads of money because I hear internet access on ships is super expensive seeing as they have to use satellite."

Chris regarded me with an excited gleam in his eyes. "I knew this already, and that's why I told Dad to fix it with his business partner for me to have complimentary internet access."

I shook my head in wonder. "Trust you to think of that."

"Hey, Ferrari, I can't live without the net," he protested.

"Well, I can," I replied. "And if I don't see another computer again, it'll be too soon." I wasn't really into the internet, but I used computers at work every day when updating the duty manager's log or to generate reports for different departments.

"So it's a good thing you have me onboard." Chris smirked.

I threw him a suspicious look. "What's that supposed to mean? I hope you're not thinking of hacking into anybody's computer for a prank."

"Nothing of the sort," he assured me. We started to walk down the stairs of the atrium, toward Deck 7; otherwise known as the Promenade Deck. "I was thinking," Chris continued, "that if there should be a murder investigation, I'd be on hand to help."

I stopped walking abruptly and turned on him, causing him to bump right into me. "I thought you said to not even mention this kind of thing."

He gave me a sheepish look. "I did, didn't I? But then, I forgot wherever you go, trouble follows."

"You're mad." I resumed walking with him in tow.

"You think?" he challenged. "You're a magnet for trouble, Ferrari."

I sniffed dismissively. "That's what Dobbs always tells me." Then, I opened a door, which led to the outdoor deck area, and stepped out, only to come upon the group of people I'd seen earlier at check-in. They were drinking, smoking, or both, while engaged in loud chatter that ended in bursts of laughter. I backed away and returned inside. Chris followed me.

"That's the smoking side of the Promenade," I stated and headed across the floor, past the lifts, and to the other side of the ship. "I wonder who those people are. There must be like sixty of them."

"They're a convention of doctors," Chris answered.

"How do you know?" We reached the exit to the non-smoking side of the deck and stepped out to admire the view of White Bay with its little boats bobbing up and down in the water and the Anzac

Bridge in the distance.

"I checked the passenger list."

I cried out, upset with him, "You what! Why are you hacking into the ship's computer?"

"Hey, calm down." He tried to placate me with one of his charming smiles, which reminded me of his handsome father. "I was only checking to make sure my internet access worked through the ship's Wi-Fi."

I shook my head in disbelief. "But you were with me most of the time we've been onboard. So where did you do this?"

"In my cabin, while we were waiting for Dobbs and Smythe to go. It seems I can pick up the Wi-Fi from there, which is great."

"You're a shocker," I said, and then added thoughtfully, "but it's good to know we can check out who everybody is."

Chris grinned. "I knew it! I knew you'd be expecting trouble."

I frowned. "I'm not expecting trouble at all, Chris, but in life you never know. Now, let's enjoy the rest of our walk and then go back to see if our luggage's been delivered."

~~~

The ship sailed at 5.00pm and most passengers stood around the top two decks, taking in the September sunset while sipping on welcome cocktails, compliments of the ship.

I broke away from our group and went to stand toward the bow of the ship as we started to make our way out of White Bay and into Sydney Harbour. The ship sailed on, under the iconic Harbour Bridge, and then headed for the "heads". This is a cliff-like landmark with a massive gap in the middle, where the harbour waters give way to the Pacific Ocean. With a cliff on either side of the water, the heads, as they are known, form a dramatic entrance to the deep blue beyond.

Music blared in the background and loads of excited people yelled out in excitement when the ship emitted three blows of the foghorn to signify our departure from port. The sound was so loud, it reverberated inside my chest, bringing up a certain kind of bittersweet emotion I could only attribute to the fact that I was now single and had no-one with whom to share this special moment.

To avert the danger of sinking into melancholy, I headed for the small bar the crew set up for the welcome cocktails and picked up a fruity concoction laced with rum. Then, I returned to my spot near the bow and huddled into my windbreaker while I sipped my drink.

It was the beginning of spring in Sydney, but it was still quite cool out on deck. I looked forward to getting into the warmer climes of the Pacific Islands, especially when we neared Hawaii, which would bring us into the tail end of their summer.

I stood at the railing for a long time, lost in my own thoughts and missing the passing scenery, when someone accidentally bumped into me. "I'm sorry," said an elderly man sporting a black walking stick. He looked like Colonel Sanders, except he wore a safari suit with khaki pants, matching jacket, and Akubra hat instead of the colonel's famous white ensemble.

"No problem," I returned with a smile.

"I didn't spill your drink, did I?" he enquired with concern when he saw me dry my fingers with a tissue. "I'm happy to get you another one."

I shook my empty tall glass so he could see it. "The cocktail's long gone. I was simply wiping my fingers from the condensation on the glass," I reassured him.

He seemed relieved. "Well, I'm still happy to get you another one if you wish."

I declined politely. "No need. This one was strong enough for me. If I drink any more, I'll fall asleep before dinner."

I went back to watching the approaching heads and the Pacific Ocean beyond, and zipped up my windbreaker all the way to my chin as the wind whipped up, making me shiver. From the corner of my eye, I noted my companion, who stood beside me leaning on the rail. He lifted the collar of his jacket to ward off the cold ocean breeze and held onto his hat with one hand to save it from being blown off his head.

"This is the part I like best; passing through the heads and straight into the deep swell of the ocean," he remarked as he took off his black-rimmed glasses, wiped the lenses with a handkerchief, and put them back on while still managing to hold onto his hat.

I turned to him with interest. "You've cruised before?"

"Many a time," he replied with a smile that crinkled his rose-cheeked face.

He wore a white close-cropped moustache and a beard that only covered his chin. His cheeks were clean-shaven. I tried to work out his age but couldn't make up my mind. From the white beard and thick thatch of white hair, which peeked from under his hat, he could have been anywhere between late sixties to somewhere in his seventies.

"I'm Mia Ferrari, by the way." I extended a hand toward him.

He took it in his and gave it a firm shake. "Professor Benjamin Tully."

"And on a much-needed holiday, I imagine."

"Yes." He let go of my hand. "Time to get away from all those pesky students," he stated with humour in his voice.

"Where do you teach?"

"Sydney University."

"Well, it's a small world," I remarked. "One of my travelling companions goes to Sydney Uni. He's studying IT."

Professor Tully turned to look at the ocean ahead of us as the ship passed through the heads. "Breathtaking, isn't it?"

I nodded. "The ocean's always majestic."

"I teach physiology."

"Huh?" I was temporarily thrown off at the change of topic. "Oh, you mean at uni."

"Yes," he responded. "Therefore, I wouldn't know your friend unless he's taking medicine."

"Makes sense. It's a big university," I commented.

Professor Tully held the collar of his jacket a little closer to him. "Excuse me, my dear, but I'm going to go back inside. It's getting a bit too cold out here for an old man like me."

"It was nice to meet you, Professor," I replied. "I'm sure we'll run into each other again."

He gave me a parting wave and lost himself in the crowd while I turned back to drink in the awesome sight of the Pacific Ocean with its endless horizon.

~~~

Our group met for dinner at Horizons Restaurant, which was the ship's a-la-carte venue on Deck 7. I would have preferred the more informal and quick buffet-style bistro I'd espied earlier on Deck 12, called The Anchor, so I could make a speedy getaway from

Smythe's company; but it seemed I was destined to suffer his company for longer than I expected.

We were seated at a window table for four, with me and Chris side by side and Dobbs and Smythe sitting opposite. Dobbs was directly opposite me; and for this small mercy, I was incredibly thankful.

"Who's having wine?" Dobbs asked when the drinks waiter approached our table.

"Red for me," I answered, looking forward to obliterating the evening in an alcoholic haze, hence forgetting Smythe's presence.

The others opted for light beer, so Dobbs and I ended up sharing a bottle, half of which I consumed by the time we were into our first course. I felt Dobbs's disapproving glare at my behaviour, but I didn't care. What with all the rum in the cocktail I'd consumed upon departure and now the wine, I started to feel uninhibited and looking forward to begging off early so I could go to la la land. And I wasn't referring to LA, either.

I had no idea what kind of conversation ensued around the table or what I ate. I was only aware of Dobbs's grumpy manner toward me and Chris's amused gaze. Smythe was simply a blank—which suited me just fine.

When the waiter came by to ask about dessert, I took the opportunity to stand up, none too steadily, and announced, "I'm full, so no dessert for me. If you'll excuse me, I'm off to bed. It must be the sea air."

"More like the alcohol, I'd say," was the smartarse rejoinder from Dobbs.

I let it slip. "Well, goodnight everybloody... I mean... everybody."

Chris stood and took hold of my arm. "Let me walk you back to your cabin, Ferrari," he remarked with mirth in his tone. "If the ship should lurch, you could fall and break your neck."

Someone added a sarcastic comeback in answer to Chris's comment, but it was just as well I didn't take it in for I was sure it had come from Smythe.

~~~

I tossed and turned in my alcohol-induced sleep, thinking how noisy it was on the ship. How the hell could anybody sleep with all this racket going on? I was sure someone was playing the drums, and I had to fight my way back to wakefulness so I could go out there and tell them to shut up. Surely, the entertainment was over by now, I thought as I glanced at the clock on my bedside table with one eye. It was 2.11am.

I sighed and managed to push myself into a sitting position. It was then I realised nobody was playing the drums, but someone was knocking quite forcefully on my door. My temper flared and, with both eyes open and a tongue that felt as though it had fur growing on it, I climbed out of bed and shuffled toward the insistent sound. I pulled the cabin door open with so much force that the handle hit the wall behind it, making a loud bang.

"What the fu...." I uttered in a loud voice before I focused in on Chris standing there in his pyjamas, a serious look on his face.

Fully awake now, I ushered him inside. "Let me splash some water on my face and I'll be right with you. I don't know what you're playing at, waking me at such an hour, but it had better be good."

I turned to make my way to the bathroom, but Chris's hand shot out and grabbed hold of my arm. "Wait," he urged. "Get dressed, Mia. The captain wants to see us."

I shook my head in annoyance. "That bloody Smythe! I bet he ran to the captain with tales about my drinking at dinner." I knew what I said made absolutely no sense whatsoever, but neither did Chris's appearance at this hour.

Chris turned me gently around to face him. "You don't understand," he stated rather forcefully. "The ship's stopped its engines, and we more than likely have a death on our hands. A passenger's gone overboard."

CHAPTER 3

We were met at Reception by the ship's security officer who led us to the Bridge where Dobbs and Smythe were already in deep conversation with the captain and another officer.

After Chris had come to wake me, we each took a few moments to dress before making our way to the ship's control room. I threw on a pair of jeans and a white tracksuit top while Chris wore old khaki cargo pants with a black long-sleeved T-shirt. Although I'd had time to brush my teeth and smooth down my short blonde hair, I still looked like I'd just woken up, with bits of my hair spiking up here and there. Not only this, but I felt almost naked without a touch of make-up. At my age, a woman needed to look good in any event, even in an emergency. Chris, on the other hand, looked young and fresh-faced despite the fact he hadn't even attempted to comb his hair.

As we approached the others, I took comfort in the knowledge that Dobbs and Smythe looked as bad as I felt; with clothes thrown on in a haphazard fashion, a well-after-five- o'clock shadow on their faces and with Smythe's brown hair needing a good combing. At least, Dobbs was lucky with his short frizzy hair, which always seemed to remain neatly in place no matter what the occasion.

Unlike us, the captain looked very smart in his whites and I wondered whether he was pulling an all-nighter or if he was used to dressing in haste. His salt and pepper hair was neatly combed back from a good looking middle-aged face.

"Mia." Dobbs motioned for me and Chris to join them. "This is Captain John Wilkins."

"Mia Ferrari, Captain. It's a pleasure to meet you." I shook his hand firmly and then introduced Chris, who also shook the captain's hand.

With an American accent, the captain introduced the two men

standing on either side of him. One of them was the security officer who had escorted us to the Bridge. "Jerry Garcia, Chief of Security. And this is my First Officer, Mark Evans."

We all shook hands. Jerry Garcia looked like a Mexican version of Dobbs; late fifties to early sixties, with a short black moustache and a paunch to rival Dobbs's own. He stood at around five-foot-ten. In contrast, Mark Evans stood at six foot plus. He looked to be in his mid-thirties, fit, and he sported short blond hair that framed bright blue eyes in an attractive tanned face. I noted a twinkle in his baby blues as we were introduced and wondered whether he was the "bad boy" type.

"Please, let's all have a seat." The captain pointed to a round table away from the gleaming control panels of navigational instruments.

Mark went to make a quick phone call before he rejoined us. "I ordered some coffee," he announced and sat down next to the captain.

"Thank you all for attending so promptly," the captain began. "And my apologies for having to wake you so early."

We acknowledged this with a nod.

The captain turned to Chris. "Seeing as you're all special guests of your father's business partner and our CEO, Mr Edward Teppler, I made the decision to contact him about further investigating this unfortunate incident."

I looked puzzled as I directed my question to the captain. "With all due respect, sir; what can we possibly do about a passenger overboard when I'm sure your ship has a set procedure to follow?" I noticed my companions nodded their heads in agreement.

There was a knock on the door and a steward entered carrying a tray with a coffee pot, milk, sugar, cups and a plate full of Danish pastries. He set the tray down on the table while Dobbs eyed the pastries with anticipation.

"Thank you, Victor," Mark Evans said. "We'll help ourselves."

The steward nodded and left us. We didn't need any prompting; and while I poured coffee for everyone, Chris passed the cups around, and we all helped ourselves to the pastries.

"In answer to your question, Ms Ferrari." The captain glanced my way. "We are carrying out the standard procedures even as we speak."

"Please, call me Mia," I invited.

Smythe threw me a glaring look as if to tell me to shut up and let the captain finish what he had to say. I ignored him, but waited for the captain to continue.

"The thing is," the captain explained, "as soon as we had the report come through about the passenger going overboard, Officer Garcia and his team immediately checked the CCTV footage around the area where it was reported the person fell." He then nodded toward Garcia. "I'd better hand over to him to explain."

Garcia looked around the table at us, his gaze finally settling on Dobbs. "We have approximately four hundred CCTV cameras around the ship."

Chris let out a whistle. "That many?"

Garcia nodded. "This is a big ship, young man."

"So what did you find?" I skipped past all the preliminaries and went straight to the point, earning myself another glare from Smythe.

"Let me show you," Garcia responded and left the table to return momentarily with a laptop, which he set down in the middle so we could all see the screen. "Watch carefully," he directed and pressed the play button for the footage.

The image that came up was grainy, especially because it was dark outside when the camera had filmed this particular segment. The time at the bottom right hand corner of the footage displayed 1.15am.

I recognised this section of Deck 13, which was not too far away from the bow of the ship and near the entry door that led to the nightclub. The area was rather dark, but I could still make out the outline of a dark figure leaning against the wall, smoking a cigarette even though this was a non-smoking deck. Then, in the space of about twenty seconds, another figure appeared, startling the smoker. The two on camera went on to exchange a few words and almost immediately, the smoker was shoved toward the ship's railing with a hard push from the other figure. A struggle ensued between the two and the smoker was swiftly pushed overboard. The culprit then walked off camera with their back to the lens.

"Shit!" I exclaimed.

"And so we have a murder," Chris stated in a voice devoid of surprise.

Dobbs and Smythe were still glued to the screen, with Smythe asking Garcia to replay the footage. We watched it again in silence.

"As you can see," the captain addressed us when we finished watching, "this isn't a run-of-the-mill-man-overboard situation."

"What's being done at present?" Smythe spoke, his tone serious; the look on his face official.

"We stopped the ship's engines as soon as we knew what had happened and reported the incident to the authorities in Sydney. We're closer to them than our first port of call, Noumea," the captain explained. "We then spoke with Mr Teppler, who discussed what happened here with Mr Rourke. Mr Rourke suggested we make use of your investigative services until we ultimately hand over the case to the proper authorities."

"Dad wants us to investigate the murder?"

Chris's tone of excitement interrupted my train of thought, and I found myself asking at the same time as Smythe, and with the same words, "Who called in the report?" Smythe and I looked at each other in surprise. Great minds think alike even though I hated to admit it.

"We had an anonymous caller almost as soon as it happened," Garcia told us.

"Do we know who the victim is?" I jumped to my next question.

"Not yet. My officers are making enquiries and going through the passenger list. This will take a while, though," Garcia informed us, "seeing as most passengers are asleep and we can't blare this over the PA system and frighten everybody."

"Meanwhile," Mark Evans took up the conversation, "we're expecting search helicopters and divers from the Australian authorities. We're fairly sure the victim's dead. Unlike what you see in the movies, if someone goes overboard they're usually sucked under the ship almost immediately and it's near impossible for them to come back up. Then, there's the matter of the lifeboats. From where the victim fell, they could have easily hit one of the lifeboats on the way down, rendering them unconscious. So I can pretty much confirm that our only hope is to recover the body."

"The victim looks like a male, but we can't be absolutely sure on that," I uttered, almost speaking to myself.

"The anonymous caller referred to the victim as a male," Mark Evans informed me.

"Do we have a recording of the call?" Smythe followed my train of thought; and again, I had to look his way with newfound respect. We were definitely on the same wavelength.

"No," Garcia answered. "The call was made to Reception rather than the security office so they didn't have the facility to record anything. Besides, the caller only stayed on the line for about five seconds; not giving anybody enough time to do much else but listen."

"So where was the call made from?" Dobbs beat me to the next question.

"The caller used one of the public phones on Deck 12; the one at the Deck Grill to be exact," Garcia returned.

Could this have been the murderer? If so, why would he make the call to alert us? I asked myself. "I take it the caller was male?"

Garcia nodded. "The receptionist seems fairly sure it was a man's voice. However, we can't be one hundred per cent sure as it all happened so fast."

"Hmm. I think it was the murderer who placed the call. And he's definitely male because it takes quite a lot of strength to lift a body and shove over the side," I observed and noted the merest of nods from Smythe. For some reason, I blushed at his obvious approval.

"We made good time sailing from Sydney," the captain informed us, bringing me back to focus. "Therefore, we can afford to wait a few hours until daylight, by which time the helicopters will arrive to help in the search for the body. Meanwhile, we can identify who's missing from our passengers."

Chris turned the conversation back to what I had been saying. "What makes you think the murderer called it in?" he remarked with interest.

Before I could reply, Smythe stated, "Who else could it be? We didn't see any other people on deck at the time."

Now it was I who nodded approval his way; then something occurred to me. "Is it possible there could have been any witnesses from the nightclub?"

"We close the club at 1.00am," Mark Evans replied.

"But what about the employees left behind to clean up? Surely, someone must've seen something," I insisted.

"We already questioned the barman and the waiting staff," Garcia informed me. "They cleared up and went straight to bed. No one had the need to go out on deck in order to get to their cabins. Besides, we would've seen them on the CCTV."

"True." I leaned my chin on one hand, looking pensive, and brought the coffee cup to my lips with the other.

The captain turned his attention to Smythe. "You're a police detective, I believe?"

Smythe nodded. "Yes. And I'll be happy to work with your people."

My head jerked up at this; but before I could say anything in protest, the captain continued speaking. "Mr Rourke assured me you'd all make a very good investigative team; and Mr Teppler's given us permission to involve you if you're willing."

I caught the look of delight on Chris's face at being included in the team. "Well, I'm pretty sure I speak for all of us when I say you can count us in, Captain," I remarked.

There were nods all around from our group; and I thought how ironic it was that for once Smythe and I would be working on the same side, without him becoming enraged at my interference in police matters. I was beginning to enjoy the situation despite the fact that some poor soul lost his life.

Dobbs spoke, "Captain, when you said we'll eventually report to the authorities, I take it you meant at our final destination seeing as the ship's registered in the US. I'm an ex-detective with the Honolulu police so I'll be happy to liaise with the authorities if you're okay with that."

The captain looked visibly relieved. "Thank you, Mr Dobbs. I'm not yet sure what we're going to find, but we'll also report the incident to the New Caledonian police in case the body ends up washing up somewhere on their shores. Then, we need to resume our trip. Mr Teppler's a powerful man, and I'm sure he'll be happy to get clearance from the police in Hawaii for you to lead this investigation until we arrive at our destination."

"And in the meantime, we might just catch ourselves a murderer," I chimed in.

Dobbs shook his head at me to be quiet, and I went back to my pensive silence.

"My department will work closely with you," Garcia stated. "Anything you need, you've only to ask."

"Thank you, Officer Garcia," Smythe said and looked across at Dobbs. "I think the first thing we need is to plan our strategy. As for shore leave, we'll need to confiscate everyone's passports. We don't want the murderer to disappear."

Garcia nodded. "That's not a problem. We scan every passenger's passkey so we know exactly who goes on and off the ship at anyone time. So if someone suddenly goes missing, we'll know about it as soon as we sail, and we can report it to the local authorities to deal with."

Who named Smythe as officer in charge, when the captain had just announced Dobbs would lead the investigation? I felt my hackles rise for a moment, but then told myself to calm down. We were all in this together, and I wasn't going to be the first one to rock the boat—no pun intended.

CHAPTER 4

None of us wanted to go back to bed after the meeting with the captain and his men; therefore, Chris suggested we find somewhere to talk.

We went to The Mariners' Hub, a café that served coffee and cakes on Deck 5. The café, currently closed, was located to one side of the reception's main lounge, facing the windows, and carved into a small and private nook for privacy. This made it the perfect place to meet as it was both cosy and it offered expansive views of the ocean; except at this time of night, the ocean and sky were a black void. The four of us sat in comfortable plush sofa chairs around a small square coffee table.

"Mia," Smythe referred to me by my first name, which was another surprise seeing as he always called me "Ferrari". I certainly had no intention of relating to him as Phil. To me, he would always be "Smythe", my archenemy. Right now, however, I decided to call an imaginary truce with him so we could work together on the investigation.

Totally unaware of my thoughts, Smythe waited to get my attention. I glanced his way. "Yes?"

"You're good with getting information out of people, so I suggest you have a talk to the receptionist that took the call plus any other crew member or passenger you think may be able to give us relevant information." His official tone of command got to me despite my earlier intentions to keep the peace between us.

"Who made you the boss, Smythe? On this ship you're a civilian, like the rest of us," I uttered with annoyance. "Besides, the captain asked Dobbs to lead the investigation."

Smythe frowned; and if looks could kill I'd be a dead duck. Before he could speak, however, Dobbs interceded. "Hey, you two, cut the crap right now!" Dobbs's American accent always became more pronounced when he was upset. "Ferrari, for once try and co-operate."

I practically jumped out of my seat. "Why is this *my* fault all of a sudden? And why are you letting Smythe take command?"

I noticed Chris's look of amusement when I crossed my arms and pouted. Dobbs sighed with frustration and tried again in a cajoling tone. "Mia, we are all working together. I'm not going to pull rank on anybody. Phil's the real cop here and I'm happy to listen to any suggestions he might have."

I shot Smythe a furtive glance in case he dared to look smug, in which case I would have reached across the table to throttle him with my bare hands. I was disappointed. Smythe sat in silence, his eyes trained on Dobbs.

"Very well," I muttered reluctantly. "For the time being, I'll do what Smythe says."

There was an almost imperceptible sigh of relief from the others and after a few seconds of silence, Smythe continued. "Chris, please help Mia in any way you can. Dobbs and I will work with the security team and review every piece of footage from all over the ship to see whether anyone was about."

"That's like four hundred bits of film," Chris exclaimed at the immensity of the task.

"We'll obviously eliminate any areas we think are irrelevant," Smythe replied.

"Actually, Smythe, everything is relevant," I put in forcefully. "You should be tracing the path the killer took prior to arriving on deck. The same goes for the victim."

Smythe regarded me thoughtfully with his blue-green eyes, and I felt colour rush to my face. I prepared for battle, but he took the wind out of my sails by saying, "Thank you, Mia. That's exactly what Dobbs and I intend to do. I'm glad we're on the same wavelength."

Damn! The man must have read my earlier thoughts about us being on the same level and now he used exactly the same term I had—being on the same wavelength. Lord, how I hated him sometimes. He could be smug, but with the ability to make it look like he was grateful for my input. Unfortunately, I had no comeback for this so I remained quiet.

"Okay," Smythe went on, looking rather surprised at my silence. "We'll reconvene in my cabin after the search. As soon as those helicopters arrive, you can bet most of the passengers will be out on deck watching. So Mia and Chris, that's your chance to start talking to people."

"But now you guys can get some sleep if you wish," Dobbs suggested. "Phil and I are meeting with Garcia in a few minutes to start going through the footage."

"Do you need any help? It's an awful lot of footage," Chris offered.

"Thank you, but no. Too many people will make for more confusion," Smythe answered. "We'll see you both later." He stood with Dobbs and they marched off in the direction of the security office.

"*Too many people will make for more confusion,*" I mimicked in a tone loaded with sarcasm. "Who the fuck does he think he is!" I lashed out when I was sure Dobbs and Smythe were out of earshot.

Chris threw me a look of sympathy. "Don't worry, Mia. We have the better job. At least we get to talk to a whole bunch of people while Dobbs and Smythe will be sitting in a stuffy room, watching boring footage."

I sniffed but didn't answer.

"Besides," Chris added with a wicked look in his eyes, "you heard what Garcia said, they have approximately four hundred cameras, and guess what? They're all controlled by the ship's computer..." He let the comment hang in the air.

My head snapped to attention and a smile appeared on my face. "Chris, you wonderful boy! Next thing, you're going to tell me that you can hack into the security computer and get access to any footage we need."

He stated with confidence, "Yes, I know I can hack into the computer, but that isn't what I was going to say."

I gave him a perplexed look. "So what were you going to say?"

"I'm not a wonderful boy, Ferrari. I'm a wonderful young man." He winked at me and grinned.

I regarded him with the affection of a mother and laughed. I was proud of my clever and witty pseudo-son.

~~~

Smythe was correct. At around six in the morning, three rescue choppers approached the area where the ship waited and the decks filled with curious passengers.

Chris and I had just finished a bacon and egg sandwich each accompanied by a mug of strong coffee. We didn't go to sleep after Dobbs and Smythe's departure. Instead, we'd gone to Chris's cabin to spend some time looking through the footage Chris was able to access by hacking into the security computer.

We managed to find a clip of footage showing the murderer walking along the passageway on Deck 13 as he approached the exit door, which took him where the victim stood smoking. Unfortunately, all we could see was the back of the person. He wore dark clothing: black joggers, dark pants, and a black hoodie. His gait was a bit unsteady, as is usual when walking while the ship lurches in choppy waters.

I asked Chris to save the clip and we spent the rest of the time searching through more footage until just before six, when the buffet restaurant opened for breakfast. We didn't find anything on the CCTV footage; and when we went in search of the receptionist, we were informed he was not on duty because he knocked off early as he was rather shaken by what had happened. As a result, Chris and I went off for a quick meal before the helicopters arrived.

Now, it was crowded on all decks as Chris and I weaved our way through the throng of onlookers. We managed to grab a spot by the rail near the Deck Grill and watched while the choppers hovered, suspended in the air near the ship. Divers slid down on cable ropes and landed in the water, close to a couple of lifeboats that had been lowered from the ship. Here, the divers stored their equipment and had a platform on which to rest. The ship's crew manned the lifeboats and helped the divers onboard when they arrived.

Meanwhile, an announcement came over the PA system directing passengers to the ship's theatre for roll call. The passengers were grouped by deck and cabin number. While this happened, other passengers started to lose interest in the search and many of them commenced to drift into the restaurant for breakfast while some returned to sit out on deck with trays full of food and morning coffee.

Chris and I came away from the viewing rail. "This is a good opportunity for us to start mingling," I suggested. "I'll do the back of the restaurant and the decks on the stern of the ship. You start here and work this part of the deck up to the bow plus the front section of the restaurant. We'll meet at ten in The Mariners' Hub."

Chris nodded and we went our separate ways. I worked through the back of the restaurant quickly as everyone I talked to had seen nothing. So far, whoever I questioned simply told me they had been sleeping safely in their bed. It took me well over an hour to work through the restaurant. Then, I went to the back deck where some of the passengers sat eating their breakfast while enjoying the morning sun. I talked to a few people, with the same result, and noted by this time it was well past nine. I felt tired and in need of coffee.

"Mia, isn't it?" A voice called from behind me.

I turned and found Professor Tully having his breakfast at a table tucked away near the sheltered part of the deck, but still with a good view of the water and the search mission.

"Good morning, Professor." I smiled. "You have an excellent vantage point here, and you're away from the cool breeze, too."

"Care to join me?" He was eating alone.

"Sure, why not? Give me a couple of minutes while I run inside to get myself a coffee." I walked back into the restaurant and helped myself to a mug of coffee from one of the many dispensing machines, plus I grabbed a toasted ham and cheese sandwich from the buffet. The breakfast I'd consumed at six had by now gone down to my feet, and my tummy rumbled with hunger. I rejoined the professor within moments. "I'm starving," I uttered as I took a seat opposite him. "Have you been watching the search efforts?"

The professor was buttering a piece of toast very meticulously and I followed his actions closely as he began to cut it into precise squares of about one inch in size. Once this was done, he proceeded to add a dollop of strawberry jam to each little square. I thought of Agatha Christie's character, Poirot, who in the TV series did exactly the same. The only thing missing were the two, three-minute eggs of exact size, neatly placed in eggcups.

"It's like a tradition with me," the professor explained when he caught me gazing at his little routine. "My wife, Eden, did this for me every morning for thirty years; Lord bless her soul." He paused for a moment to gather his emotions and I noted a teary look in his faded blue eyes. "I'm sorry. I only lost her last year."

My heart ached for him. "No need to apologise. It's horrible when the one you love leaves you." I spoke from experience, even though mine had been a marriage break up and not a death. "Thirty years is a long time."

The professor nodded, once again overcome with emotion. I reached out and patted his arm. "Eden is a beautiful name."

This brought a smile to his face and he composed himself. "She was a beautiful girl," he responded, back in control. "Please eat up, young lady, before your sandwich gets cold."

I laughed, and he regarded me with surprise. "It's just that no one's called me *young lady* for a long time," I remarked. "These days it's *madam* or I'm simply invisible."

The professor frowned. "Invisible?"

I laughed again. "Yes. Didn't you know? A female over forty becomes invisible to others, especially one that's in her late forties." I felt a taste of bitterness in my mouth when I said this, thinking of my scumbag ex and the bimbo he'd dumped me for—younger than I, of course.

"Most modern men are stupid, my dear. They simply don't know women like the old timers. So I wouldn't let this bother you. To me, you look wonderful, and as far as I'm concerned, you're still a young lady." His tone held such gallantry when he spoke that I actually believed him.

"Well, thank you, Professor," I returned, almost blushing like a debutante.

There was something gentlemanly about the man that reminded me of the chivalry of men in the South during the American Civil War. The professor was like an elderly Rhett Butler in *Gone With The Wind*, one of my favourite movies. Of course, I reminded myself, Rhett was a bit of a wicked character, so perhaps I should compare the professor to Ashley Wilkes instead. There was no one I could use for comparison in Australian history; not with the convicts that had populated the land down under—and *never* in a gentlemanly way if what I read about this turbulent period in the life of my country was anything to go by.

While the professor ate his small squares of toast, I refocused on my purpose. "Professor, do you know anything about what happened with this passenger overboard situation?"

"Why do you ask?" he remarked before he popped another piece of toast in his mouth.

"Long story; but my friends and I are kind of helping out with trying to gather information about what happened. You see, I work for a company whose CEO is the business partner of the man who owns this cruise company. So it's kind of like a courtesy to give them a helping hand." I didn't want to divulge our real purpose or the fact we had a murder on our hands; therefore, I remained as vague as possible.

"Well, no. I don't know anything, my dear. I went to bed early last night and only heard what happened this morning when I made my way to breakfast."

"Yes." I sighed. "It seems everyone was asleep at the time." I said this more to myself than to him and quickly glanced at my watch. It was nearing ten, so I finished my sandwich and coffee. "Sorry, but I've got to go soon. I'm meeting my friends at ten."

"Is it that time already?" the professor exclaimed. "Well, my dear, you go. But feel free to call on me any time you want to chat. I'm travelling alone, as you can see, and I always welcome conversation." He smirked with a glint in his eye. "It's the only thing left to an old man."

I was sad for him, having recently lost his wife, and now travelling on his own, probably to distract himself from the grief. For some reason, I felt drawn to him and looked forward to keeping him company whenever I could. "I'll hold you to that, Professor," I replied and stood up in readiness to go. "How do I find you?"

"I'll be here most mornings. I like having my breakfast under the blue sky and away from the breeze. I'll also be here for afternoon tea, around four."

"It's a date then." I gave him a big smile. "I'll come in search of you soon and we can chat all you like."

He returned the smile and gazed at me with kindly eyes. "God bless you, my dear. I look forward to our next chat."

I gave him a little wave and made my way to The Mariners' Hub where I saw Chris sitting at a corner table. He nodded a greeting as I approached, but before I could return the gesture, Dobbs and Smythe appeared out of nowhere and reached the table before me.

Dobbs looked tired. Smythe, on the other hand, looked like he'd just been for a swim and had come out of the water all fresh and looking quite virile. An image of Tom Selleck in Magnum PI flashed into my mind and I instantly dismissed it. As a result, my good mood dissipated and I suddenly felt irritated.

"Good morning," I greeted everyone formally, though I managed to wink very quickly in Chris's direction.

"Mia!" Dobbs seemed happy to see me at least. Smythe hadn't even returned my greeting. "How are you? I hope you got some sleep."

"Er... yes, yes, I did." I wasn't going to tell them what Chris and I had been up to. This was our little secret.

I noticed Smythe's look of doubt at my statement but didn't care; nor did I turn toward him. The more I ignored him, the better it would be.

"Okay," Smythe began, dispensing with any niceties. "It's quiet enough to talk in here, so let's get on with it. We didn't find very much in the footage, though we did get a view of the killer going out to Deck 13."

Chris and I glanced at each other quickly. This must've been the same footage clip we had come across.

"Did you finish watching all the footage?" Chris asked.

"Not by a mile. We're going right back to it after we get some sleep. I only had time for a shower and breakfast this morning."

"And I'm beat," Dobbs announced. "After this, I'm off to get some serious shuteye. We can keep going later. Anything from you?" He looked at me, waiting for my report.

I shook my head. "No. Chris and I talked to as many people as we could, but no one I spoke to saw anything."

"Same here," Chris confirmed. "Everyone seemed to be asleep in their beds at the time of the incident. So it looks like we're back to nothing."

"Not quite," Smythe stated. "From the little footage we found, we know the killer's definitely a man. Even though he has his back to the camera, his build and gait are a dead giveaway."

"Well, we always knew it was a guy. The receptionist confirmed it, right?"

I turned to Chris and spoke before Smythe could respond. "What Smythe means is the caller, whom we also assume to be the killer, didn't disguise his voice to make it sound like a man. The footage confirms he's male, just as the receptionist that took the call reported."

Smythe's eyes held a gleam of admiration at my observation, but when he realised I caught his gaze, he quickly turned back to Chris.

"Any luck talking to the receptionist?"

"Not yet," Chris answered. "He went off duty early because he was upset about the incident. So we checked with Mark Evans and he told us the receptionist wouldn't be back on shift until tonight at eleven."

"Very well. We'll spend the rest of today going through the footage while you two keep talking to anyone you haven't talked to already."

I gave him an army salute. "Yes, sir!"

Dobbs shook his head at my attitude, but Smythe ignored my sarcasm. "We dock in Noumea tomorrow, so the captain will report the incident to the local police. Dobbs and I have offered to be present, albeit in an unofficial capacity."

I was about to protest at this when I saw Mark Evans approaching. He seemed to be looking right at me and smiling. I smiled back and didn't care who saw me. The guy was young and cute, just as I liked them. It seemed I wasn't so invisible after all.

"Good morning all," Mark said and shook his head when Dobbs went to pull up a chair for him. "No, I can't stay. I saw you as I was on my way to the Bridge and thought you should know."

"Know what?" I jumped in before any of the others could speak.

"The search has been called off. Unfortunately, they came up with nothing, as was to be expected under the circumstances. Very shortly, we'll be continuing our journey. We also finished the roll call exercise and we have a passenger unaccounted for."

All eyes turned to him with undivided attention as we held our breath.

"We're missing a Dr Bertrand van Horn. Early sixties, travelling on his own; but as part of the medical convention we have onboard."

"So how come no one noticed him missing until the roll call?" I remarked. "If he's been travelling with the convention, you'd think someone would've known he'd disappeared."

Mark replied, "I don't know the answer to that, but Officer Garcia had the lock of his cabin read, and it shows the doctor last using his key at around midnight."

"You mean to enter the cabin," Dobbs clarified.

Mark nodded. "That's right. He might have gone back out later; but if he did, he never returned."

"So this is our man overboard," Chris commented.

"We're fairly certain," Mark confirmed. "But we'll know for sure once we talk to all the convention members plus their coordinator, who is travelling with the group."

"Chris and I will be happy to do this for you," I volunteered. "You guys seem to be so busy with the footage and all." I glanced in Smythe's direction long enough to see the firm set of his jaw.

Mark smiled. "Thank you, Mia. Every bit helps."

"I take it we can also search his cabin." Then, I added, "If he's the missing person, of course."

Mark nodded. "I'll have a key cut for you. Come and see me later. I really must rush now." He said his goodbyes and walked away.

"Ferrari, who said you could go searching the cabin?" Smythe addressed me with his formal police voice.

"Who said I couldn't?" was my comeback. "You can't do everything, Smythe. You chose to search through the footage and left the people side of things to Chris and me," I pointed out smugly. "And this falls under the category of people. Therefore, I get to search the cabin."

Smythe went to respond, but Dobbs held up a placating hand. "This one's hers, Phil. You know she'll share any findings with us."

I felt vindicated and wanted to kiss Dobbs. About time he stuck up for me and put the high and mighty Smythe in his place.

CHAPTER 5

Enrico Lotti looked like a subject out of a Caravaggio painting, depicting Narcissus, the young man who sees his image reflected in water and falls in love with himself.

Lotti was a handsome young man in his early thirties with a hint of femininity about him and a wonderful athletic build. He had lustrous green eyes and a full, almost cherubic, mouth. "Kissable lips" was the first thing that popped into my mind as I regarded the tall, blond Enrico in all his glory.

I became momentarily lost in his Renaissance-like appearance when he met with Chris and me in the lounge area outside The Mariners' Hub. Enrico wore three-quarter black pantaloons with black suede boots; a white shirt with puffy sleeves unbuttoned halfway down his chest; and a brown leather vest that accentuated his athletic form by defining the slimness of his waist.

Chris nudged me with his elbow, making painful contact with my ribs, and I snapped out of my dreamy state immediately, almost yelping. I glared at my companion for a second; then, I turned to Enrico.

"Thank you for meeting with us, Enrico." I gave him my best smile. "The first officer said you're the person who might be able to help us. We're making an inquiry on behalf of the cruise company into the disappearance of Dr Bertrand van Horn. I'm Mia Ferrari and this is my colleague, Chris Rourke."

Enrico's beautiful eyes gazed at Chris with such interest that Chris went beet red while he cleared his throat and quickly shook Enrico's extended hand. Then, Enrico turned to me; and much to my surprise, he took hold of my hand and kissed the back of it.

"Piacere, Signorina," he uttered in a sexy baritone. "Ma lei parla Italiano?"

I had to force myself to remain focused and not melt over a young man who was very obviously gay—but oh, so very charming.

"I'm pleased to meet you, too, Enrico. And my Italian's rather rusty."
I felt rather than saw Chris rolling his eyes and doing everything to
try not to gag at the whole situation. He knew I was taken in by the
young man, gay or not.

"Va bene," Enrico uttered. "Very well, I mean." He smiled,
revealing brilliant white teeth. "Shall we take a seat?" He motioned
for us to follow him to one of the rectangular coffee tables in the
lounge area, which was flanked by two red velvet settees.

Chris made sure he sat next to me so the beautiful Enrico would
have to take a seat opposite us, on his own. A young waiter
materialised out of nowhere, holding an electronic order pad.

"Would you folks like to order?" he addressed us with an
American accent.

"I'll have a cappuccino, thanks," I said.

Chris nodded to the waiter. "The same for me."

"Espresso, please." Enrico ogled the waiter for a few moments;
then brought his attention back to us as the waiter scurried away with
a flush on his cheeks. "I can't believe someone would harm Bert. He
was such a lovely man," he declared with a sigh and eyes that
reflected the "tragedy of it all".

I tried to control my amusement at his melodramatic manner
and managed to stop my lips from twitching into a smirk. "So tell us
about your role with the medical convention."

Enrico sat back in the settee, crossing his legs and resting his
elbow over an arm placed across his chest, with his free hand waving
all over the place when it wasn't providing a resting place for his chin.
"We have around sixty doctors in total on this trip; some travelling
with their spouses. They meet once a year for a medical conference,
and we usually go on a cruise. I work for the events company that
organises this kind of thing and I've been looking after the doctors
for about five years now." He leaned forward for a moment as if
about to impart a secret. "They always ask for me, you know. They
tell me they can't do without my kind of services."

I couldn't help but smile at his more than confident manner but
managed to make it look as if I was truly impressed. "Sounds like a
great responsibility for you."

He sat back and his hand waved around his face. "Well, you
know how it is. I'm at their beck and call twenty-four seven, but I
provide the services they expect, and they love it."

I wanted to know what kind of "services" he provided but thought it prudent not to enquire further. Instead, Chris asked, "Are all the doctors Australian?"

Enrico regarded him as if he wanted to devour Chris, and I had to control myself once again lest I burst into laughter. "Oh, no, darling," Enrico exclaimed. "They come from all over the world—most of them from English-speaking countries, of course. So we're mainly talking Australia, America, Canada, and the UK. But we also have some South Africans and Indians."

"How come no one missed Dr van Horn last night?" I interjected before he went off on a tangent. One thing about Enrico, the guy loved to talk—mainly about himself.

Enrico shrugged. "I don't know. We had a dinner function until around eleven. Then, some people went to the nightclub, others to the casino, and the rest to sleep, I guess."

"Where did you go?"

Enrico leaned forward again and eyed me with delight. "Are you asking me for an alibi?" He seemed thrilled.

I shook my head. "Not exactly. I'm simply trying to get an idea of where everybody was at the time."

Enrico looked like he wanted to confide something, but wasn't sure whether to trust us. I gave him a few moments to see if he would keep talking. In the meantime, the coffees arrived, which was perfect timing.

The waiter placed our cups on the table and rushed off after I signed the bill to my room. I took my time stirring one sugar into my cup while Chris sat quietly, sipping his coffee. Enrico sighed, sat back, and rested his chin on his hand. Then, he sat forward again, as if to confide in us, but sat back once more and picked up his coffee cup.

I threw a quick sideways glance at Chris, and he spoke in the direction of Enrico. "It looks like you want to tell us something, Enrico."

Enrico leaned forward again, this time gazing straight into Chris's eyes with something like longing. "Well, I don't normally go around talking about my personal life to all and sundry, but you seem like someone I can trust."

Chris blushed at Enrico's lusty look, and I felt sorry for the guy. It wasn't enough that I'd used him as bait during my investigation of the drag queen murders, where one of the queens took a big liking to him. Now, I was practically throwing him to the wolves, knowing Enrico obviously had a crush on him. Poor Chris. Despite my making use of him to pump information out of Enrico, he managed to handle the situation without going homophobic on me.

"Of course you can trust me," Chris assured Enrico in a serious tone. "Anything you say to either one of us stays between us."

This was all Enrico needed to hear. He picked up his coffee cup again and finished his espresso before he turned to me. "In answer to your question, my dear Mia," he gushed, "I was engaged with a rather cute officer in my cabin... you know what I mean." He winked naughtily and grinned.

Chris buried his face in his cappuccino; probably trying to banish the image Enrico's confession must have conjured up in his mind. I wasn't as easily embarrassed. "So you weren't out and about the ship after midnight, I take it."

"Not a chance, darling. I was busy till dawn," Enrico answered, a sparkle in his eyes.

A choking sound from Chris told me it was time to end this line of questioning. "Very well. Thank you for your time, Enrico. If you can think of anything else, please give me a call. I'm in cabin 9269."

"I don't know what else I can tell you, but I'll definitely call you if I think of anything." Enrico stood to leave.

"Oh, before you go," I said. "Is it possible for you to provide us with a name list of the convention members? We'll need to speak to them all."

He nodded. "Of course, bella! I'll leave the list for you at Reception in the next hour or so. And now, I must go. Thank you for the coffee." He then turned to Chris and winked. "Arrivederci, caro mio."

I laughed when Enrico walked away. Chris turned to me with a hard look. "Listen, Ferrari, whatever he said, the answer is 'no'," he protested. "Man, I can't believe I always run into gay guys that flirt with me. You owe me big time!"

I regarded him with amusement. "Calm down. All he said was 'Bye bye, my dear'."

"I don't care what he said. I'm not going to talk to that guy anymore. He spooks me."

"Don't worry," I jested, "I'll protect you from him."

The look he gave me told me he doubted this very much.

~~~

We spent the rest of the day talking to several members of the medical convention according to the list Enrico provided for us. It was going to take some time to get through all of them, including their spouses.

"Dr van Horn was travelling by himself. He was a widower," one of the doctors informed us. "I don't know what he did after dinner last night. I went to catch the cabaret show with our group, but Dr van Horn wasn't with us."

Another doctor said, "Yes, I remember Bert in the casino with us, but he left just before midnight."

Chris and I finished talking with about half the convention members by around four in the afternoon. We'd missed out on lunch and after learning nothing new, Chris took off to get himself a burger at the Deck Grill while I made for the buffet restaurant, where I encountered Professor Tully enjoying afternoon tea at his usual table on the stern of the ship.

He saw me come out of the restaurant with coffee and a plate containing neatly cut finger sandwiches and a strawberry tart. He waved and motioned for me to join him.

"Good afternoon, Professor," I greeted him as I took a seat at his table. The professor was sipping on Earl Grey and had a couple of jam tarts on a plate waiting for him while he nibbled on the one in his hand.

"How are you, my dear?" His smile told me he was pleased to see me again. "And how is your inquiry going?"

I took a bite of one of the delicious finger sandwiches and swallowed before I answered. "No one seems to know what happened. We do, however, know it was a Dr van Horn who went overboard." I didn't see any harm in revealing the name of the victim as more than likely it would be all over the ship by now.

"Dr Bertrand van Horn?"

"Yes."

"I knew old Bert from my early days in practice," the professor explained. "Nice enough fellow. Poor man!" He shook his head.

"It's quite tragic," I commiserated, and finished my sandwich.

Then, I picked up another and uttered, "What can you tell me about him?"

The professor sipped some tea, looking thoughtful. "Nothing much, really. We were simply colleagues. You know, running into each other at functions from time to time. He was always pleasant."

"I didn't know you were a practising physician. Didn't you say you were a lecturer?"

"I was a doctor until my late forties. Then, the university offered me a lecturing role and I took it. More time to spend with my Eden, you see." His eyes took on a lost look, and I knew he was thinking of his loss.

"Tell me more about Eden," I urged. "If it's not too painful for you, that is."

The professor sighed. "Every day I live without her is painful, but I don't mind talking about her. I like to relive the good memories."

I waited quietly while he finished another tart.

"I met Eden when I was still in medical school," the professor began. "She was a dark-haired beauty—born in Argentina; land of the tango, you know."

"Sounds very exotic," I commented.

He laughed. "Yes, she was. She was a passionate girl, my beautiful Eden. I knew the moment I met her she'd be my soul mate for life."

The professor spoke with such conviction, I felt envious thinking of my own failed marriage and my unfulfilled wishes. "How did you meet her?"

"At a dance given by the medical faculty in the university. She attended with a girlfriend, who was studying medicine at the time. Eden studied languages, wanting to become a translator. It was a long courtship for us, and we married after I finished my internship and opened my own practice. We needed the start-up money back then. Later, Eden worked for a large import/export company as a translator. By this time, she didn't need to work though," the professor clarified. "But she liked to keep busy."

I wondered what it was like back in those days for a woman. Eden would have been at university in the late 60s or early 70s, assuming her age was similar to the professor's, which I still thought to be around mid-sixties to early seventies, just as I'd figured at our

43

first meeting. Although liberated even back then, most women chose to have children over a career. Then again, I didn't know if the professor had children.

The professor seemed to read my mind. "Eden couldn't have children so she settled for a career instead. As time went on, however, she tired of working for a large company and gave up her job to work for me, helping me run the practice."

"Well, despite the fact you weren't blessed with children, at least you were close and stayed together all those years. It's wonderful when love lasts for so long," I remarked, once again thinking of my failed marriage.

I caught a haunted look in the professor's eyes and thought he'd become upset reminiscing about his wife; but the look was fleeting and within moments, his faded eyes became cheery. "Yes. I was lucky in my marriage," he said, and then went on to finish his last jam tart.

I finished my coffee and sandwiches, and noted the time. "Forgive me, Professor, but I must go." I thought I'd catch up with Chris so we could go and pick up the key to Dr van Horn's cabin, which Mark had promised he would arrange for us. I wanted to search the cabin before we met up with Dobbs and Smythe for dinner. We also needed to talk with the receptionist when he came on duty this evening; although I wasn't sure what he could tell us aside from the fact he had received the phone call alerting him to the man overboard.

~~~

"You search the bathroom and I'll go through his luggage," I instructed Chris when we entered Dr van Horn's cabin wearing latex gloves so as not to damage evidence.

"What exactly are we looking for?"

"Anything that can tell us something about the victim," I answered and started to open the drawers of a bedside table. "We're obviously not going to learn much more about the killer unless Dobbs and Smythe come up with more footage. So we should try and find out as much as we can about the victim. This might reveal a motive for the murder."

"Gotcha." Chris opened the bathroom door and went in.

We searched quietly for approximately one hour, but found

nothing of great interest. From what we observed among the victim's belongings, we concluded Dr van Horn was an average dresser who purchased his clothing in the likes of Kmart rather than a more upmarket establishment. His toiletries told us the same thing—cheap brands of shampoo, toothpaste and aftershave. There were no medications at all to be seen and we assumed the good doctor was either extremely healthy or he simply kept them in the cabin safe.

Mark Evans had the housekeeping supervisor unlock the cabin safe for us; and this was where we looked last. I opened the small safe while Chris waited impatiently.

"C'mon, c'mon," he urged.

"What's the hurry?" I retorted. "Here. Get your teeth into this." I handed him a rectangular document wallet that held a passport and travel papers.

While Chris studied the contents of the wallet in more detail, I reached into the safe for the other contents—a laptop, a camera, a wallet, and a small leather-bound notebook. I took the contents with me and sat on one side of the doctor's bed while Chris sat on the other.

I noticed Chris's hungry eyes and handed the laptop to him. "You didn't think I'd try to break into it, did you?" I remarked with a grin. "Not when I have my IT expert right here."

Chris snatched the laptop from my hands. "Nothing irregular in his documents," he reported. "But the computer might reveal something different."

While Chris started on the laptop, I checked the digital camera to see whether there were any photos stored in its memory. There were none. Not even from before the trip. Perhaps, the good doctor had uploaded his shots to the laptop and deleted them from the camera memory. If Chris broke into the computer, we'd be able to check this out.

Next, was the wallet. A couple of credit cards, some cash, and a drivers license. I put away the wallet and picked up the notebook. It was small, around 3x5 inches, and it had A-Z tabbed pages. It was an address book. I thought it rather old-fashioned of the doctor to carry an address book. These days, most people entered all their contacts into a mobile phone. Interestingly, we hadn't found a phone amongst the victim's belongings, but he could have been carrying one when he was thrown overboard, and now it was fish food.

I flicked through the contacts in the notebook. They were mainly the names of colleagues, clinics, and hospitals. There seemed to be no personal contacts, unless some of these people were also friends. Every name in the book was a doctor of some sort. I sighed with frustration—so far, nothing out of the ordinary.

"How are you going there?" I noticed Chris had managed to break into the laptop.

"Easy," he replied with a self-satisfied smile. "The doctor's password was *doctor*, believe it or not."

"How original," I remarked. "See if you can find any photos or videos, and check his browsing history. I want to know what websites he visited."

"Don't worry. I'll be thorough with this baby."

While Chris went back to checking out the contents of the laptop, I gathered the items I'd checked in order to place them back in the safe. The little notebook fell to the floor when I put back the other items. I picked it up and gave it one last flick. It was then I noticed something on the back page. It seemed some kind of written inscription. I looked at it closely and read: NE PW NE1952.

"Chris, what do you make of this?" I took the notebook over to where he was sitting and let him read the inscription.

He shrugged. "Could be anything, of course. But from experience, I can tell you old people usually take to writing passwords so they won't forget them."

I grimaced. "Old? The guy was only sixty-one!"

Chris grinned. "Don't get touchy, Ferrari. You're nowhere near that age."

"Yeah, well, I'm only twelve years away from it," I frowned. "So are you going to call me 'old' when I get there?"

He smiled charmingly at me. "Ferrari, you'll never be old. You're too cool."

Although his words had a pacifying effect, I still shivered at the fact that time was running out for me. I was well into middle age. The thought depressed me and I had to shake myself out of my low mood to keep my focus. "You were saying about passwords?" I went back to the topic at hand.

"People who don't have a good memory," he amended, and I smirked at his effort to make me feel better, "usually write down passwords for things. See the letters 'PW'?" He pointed to the inscription. "I bet they stand for the word 'password'."

I regarded the inscription with interest. "So what you're saying is 'NE' could stand for whatever it is he's got the password for—meaning it could be a bank account, a website, anything. Then, 'PW' stands for password, and 'NE1952' is the actual password."

Chris nodded. "You got it."

"Hmm. It certainly makes sense. After all, if the guy was sixty-one, this is consistent with the number 1952—the year of his birth."

"Yes, but what does 'NE' stand for?"

I tapped the side of my face with the small notebook. "That, my friend, is the sixty-four million dollar question."

CHAPTER 6

We met Dobbs and Smythe for dinner at Horizons. Chris and I were first to arrive and requested a corner table so we could have more privacy in which to talk. When Dobbs and Smythe joined us a few minutes later, they looked absolutely exhausted.

"Damn!" Dobbs complained. "I think I'm seeing double."

I grinned. "Too much looking at CCTV footage, Dobbs. What you need is—"

"What I need," he interjected, "is a great big steak with all the trimmings and a glass or two of red wine. I'm so hungry, I could eat a cow."

"How did things go?" Chris addressed Smythe while we studied our menus.

"I think we pretty much covered all the footage, but no results other than what we uncovered at first." He sighed tiredly and turned back to the menu in his hand.

I threw him a quick look and noted the dullness in his eyes. I couldn't help but think it was his just deserts for trying to take charge of the investigation. Chris and I had ended up with the best part of the deal in the end; and although I had Chris breaking into the ship's computer to retrieve some of the footage, I soon lost interest in such a boring task. Smythe had been the one to suggest he and Dobbs watch the footage, and now I was glad of it.

"They have a nice chicken dish with wild rice and spring vegetables," I remarked, totally ignoring Smythe and looking at Dobbs instead. "I think I'll go for this one."

The waiter arrived just at that moment and took our order.

"I'm having The Works Burger," Chris said.

"I'll have the same as Dobbs," Smythe stated. "Rump steak, medium rare, with all the trimmings and extra fries."

The waiter noted down our order, including the beverages.

When he left us, Smythe continued talking, rubbing the back of his neck. "After sitting in that stuffy room, watching grainy footage all day, I need all the energy I can get."

Now I turned to him. "Is that a complaint I hear?"

He regarded me with what I perceived as suppressed irritation, which I didn't appreciate. "It's simply an observation, Ferrari."

Before I could open my mouth to tell him where he could shove his observation, Dobbs addressed me. "And how was your day?"

I knew he had diverted yet another outbreak between Smythe and me; and I was silently grateful. We were here to focus on a crime and not bicker over petty differences. "So far, we know the victim was last seen at the casino, but we still need to finish talking to the rest of the convention members. We also searched the doctor's cabin. This turned out to be a little more interesting."

I had their attention and told them about the notebook's inscription and the laptop. Chris further reported, "We think the letters 'NE' might refer to a website of some kind. We'll keep looking into it. As for the laptop—no photos, videos, and no documents of any kind—which is really strange."

"You mean like Word docs?" Smythe enquired.

"Yes. Most people have some documents stored in their computer, but this guy had nothing. Not even a browsing history or temp files."

"Browsing history, temp files?" Dobbs looked puzzled. He was obviously not a 'techie', but rather one of those 'old' people Chris had referred to earlier, I thought gloomily, remembering my own age.

Chris explained, "Browsing history is when someone surfs the net and the computer remembers what sites the person viewed. So next time they go to the same site, the computer will automatically supply the URL rather than having the person type it in all over again. The temp files are links that have been clicked on from a site that's been browsed. But the doctor's computer didn't come up with any remembered URLs, and I couldn't find any temp files either."

"Meaning?" Dobbs still looked perplexed.

I replied, "Meaning he erased them or changed the computer settings to erase them every time he shut down. You can do this so no one knows what you've been viewing."

"Which tells me the good doctor must've been hiding something," Chris observed.

49

"Do you really think so?" Smythe regarded him with renewed interest in his tired eyes.

The waiter arrived with our wine order and some sparkling mineral water, and we remained silent while he poured our drinks. We continued talking when he departed. "Put it this way," Chris told Smythe, "it's unusual for a person surfing the net to continuously erase their browsing history; meaning they have to type in the full URL again next time they want to visit a particular site. I think van Horn was doing this in order to protect himself in case someone else got access to his computer."

"Hmm." Dobbs gazed at Chris thoughtfully.

We then chitchatted until our food arrived, and we ate in silence like ravenous beasts. At that point, I didn't think anyone wanted to focus on the investigation. We were all too tired. Dobbs and Smythe managed to finish a whole bottle of red between them and we had to order a second one so Chris and I could have a glass each. I knew the other two would be sleeping like babies tonight, but Chris and I still had to talk to the receptionist on the night shift.

Tomorrow it would be an early start for all of us because we were docking in Noumea at 7.00am. I intended to question more convention members while Dobbs and Smythe accompanied the captain to report the incident to the local police.

~ ~ ~

As soon as we arrived the following morning, Dobbs and Smythe went off with the captain and Mark Evans after a hasty breakfast. Chris and I remained behind savouring the last of our coffees.

We were sitting out on deck near Professor Tully's favourite spot, but I couldn't see him anywhere and figured he'd opted for a late breakfast, or perhaps he had already gone ashore.

"So much for the receptionist," Chris remarked. "He couldn't even remember whether the voice was disguised or not."

"It doesn't matter. The phone call won't tell us anything." I drained my cup. "My suggestion is you keep working on van Horn's computer and while you're at it, do a background check on him."

Chris nodded in agreement. "What are you going to do in the meantime?"

"I'm going to talk to more of the convention members even though it's beginning to look like nobody saw anything. Still, you never know."

"So what time do you want to go ashore?"

I stood from the table in preparation to go. "Let's say around eleven. We're meeting with Dobbs and Smythe for lunch at noon, by the way."

"Okay." Chris finished his coffee and stood to follow me from the outdoor dining area. "I'll see you later at Mariners'."

When we reached the restaurant exit we went our separate ways, and I made for the Crossroads Lounge Bar on Deck 7. This was a large upmarket bar decked out with modern wicker chairs and sofas in cream-coloured cushioning plus square glass-topped coffee tables.

Crossroads was the location where passengers gathered to go ashore. Here, they were issued with a colour ticket for the tenders that would take them to land. Usually, the ship docked at the actual cruise terminal in a large port such as Noumea; but today it seemed there were another two ships in port, as the captain had informed the passengers earlier, so we ended up dropping anchor offshore and having to use tenders to get the passengers to land.

A couple of crew members sat at a trestle table busily issuing tickets while an officer called out the ticket colour whose holders would be next to board the tender going ashore. Meanwhile, passengers purchased drinks while they waited for their tickets to be called.

I noticed a few of the convention members sitting at one corner of the room consuming a myriad of drinks with multi-coloured cocktail umbrellas. A bit early to go on the grog, I thought; but these could simply be non-alcoholic drinks.

One of the women in the group saw me and waved. "Mia, isn't it?" She was a middle-aged woman that looked familiar. She smiled and motioned for me to approach the group.

There were about twenty people sitting around a couple of the coffee tables. "I'm sorry," I said. "I forgot your name."

"It's Mrs Joy Gerard," the lady replied. "You had some questions for my husband and me yesterday."

"That's right." I returned her smile and shook her hand. "You're with Dr Gerard, the orthopedic surgeon."

She nodded. "I'm glad you're here. I want to introduce you to

Mrs Martha Barry." She waved her hand toward a lady sitting next to her and turned to address her. "Martha, this is Mia... Mia..."

"Ferrari," I put in. "Mia Ferrari. Pleasure to meet you, Mrs Barry." We shook hands.

"Please, call me Martha," Mrs Barry invited. She was a fifty-something woman, tall and slender with ash blonde hair cut in an elegant bob. "Joy told me you're helping out with the investigation of Dr van Horn's death. Join us for a few minutes." She scooted over on the sofa and made room for me. I took a seat next to her, while Joy sat on her other side.

"We've been questioning the convention members in case any of them saw something," I explained above the noise of the group, who were talking and laughing among themselves. This wasn't the best place to speak with Martha, but if she had something to say, I certainly had the time to listen.

Martha placed a hand on my forearm, like she was about to confide in a friend, and spoke close to my ear. "My dear, I didn't see anything, but I wanted to tell you that Bert was a 'funny one', if you catch my drift."

I was all ears. "What do you mean by a 'funny one'?"

Martha grimaced and sniffed. "A bit of a sex pervert—into some of those porn sites, too, I believe."

I tried not to look surprised when I asked, "How do you know this?"

Martha took a look around the group to ensure no one was listening to us. Only Joy was part of our conversation, although she had kept silent up until now. Martha and Joy exchanged a quick look, and I saw Joy nodding as if to encourage her friend to keep talking.

"Well," Martha continued, "this is for your ears only, Mia. My husband is soon to become my ex-husband, you see. I recently discovered he's been cheating on me."

There was a look of hurt in her eyes when she said this, and I could relate to her immediately. Bloody men! "But what has this got to do with Dr van Horn?" I forced myself to focus on my line of questioning rather than think about cheating bastards.

"I'm not sure, but I think Bert and my husband belonged to some sort of cheaters' club." Her voice cracked a little and she took out a tissue from her handbag and sniffed into it. "I'm sorry, I don't mean to get emotional, but if truth be told I think Bert got what he deserved. Mind you, he wasn't married. But I blame him for encouraging other men that had wives."

I took a deep breath, trying to contain my growing excitement. This information could lead to the motive for the murder. "So what you're saying is van Horn was running this club?"

Martha shook her head. "I'm not sure about that. All I know is he and Jim, my husband, used to hang out together a lot."

I failed to see the connection. "But how do you know about this cheaters' club?"

Joy interceded, "Martha's a little shaken up at the moment, Mia. She only just found out about Jim on the cruise. You see, she overheard him talking to a colleague the other night."

I noticed Martha was wiping away at teary eyes so I addressed my question to Joy. "What exactly did she hear?"

"Jim was on the phone in their cabin just as Martha came out of the shower. He didn't see her and kept on going with the conversation."

Martha blew her nose. "I'll tell Mia, Joy," she uttered, looking more composed. Joy nodded, giving her a supportive smile, and Martha turned to me. "Jim was talking to Dr Cliff Downes. Cliff is a colleague and golf buddy of Jim's," she explained. "Anyway, as I was coming out of the shower I heard him say, 'Bert's death doesn't mean the end of the erotics' club, Cliff. Bert knew how to get those lovelies all lined up and ready to open their legs and mouths for us. So I'm sure someone else in the group will take over.'" Martha's voice trembled as she finished talking and she burst into tears.

Joy put an arm around her and handed her a wad of tissues. "As you can see," Joy said to me, "these bastard men belong to some kind of sex club. We've already informed all the wives onboard, but we're keeping it a secret for the time being. We don't want to alert any of the men until we find out more about this."

I nodded with understanding. "I'm so sorry, Martha. For what it's worth, my ex cheated on me, too. It seems to be a huge trend these days."

Martha gave me a watery smile. "Thank you, Mia. I don't know if this is helpful in your inquiry, but I thought you should know."

Martha had nothing else to say and I left the ladies just as their colour was called to board the tender. I looked around the room to see if there were any other convention members aside from the people in Martha and Joy's group, but I didn't recognise anyone. The best thing to do would be to wait until we were back out to sea before I talked to any of the others. Besides, I wanted to go in search of Chris so I could share with him what I'd just learned.

It was when I made my way to the lifts that I was intercepted by an officer who seemed to know my name. "Mia Ferrari," said a young Asian man.

I looked at his name badge. "Mike Yuen, Cruise Director," I read out aloud. "Nice to meet you."

We shook hands and walked away from Crossroads and out to the non-smoking side of the Promenade Deck. The passengers going onto the tenders were on the other side of the ship, making our side of the deck nice and quiet.

"Mark Evans told me to be on the lookout for you," Mike told me while we stood at the rail, looking out to the harbour. "He said you'll probably need my help in identifying more of the medical convention people."

I nodded gratefully. "Well, Enrico Lotti, the coordinator, did a great job of lining them up for me, but every little bit helps."

"I noticed you were speaking with Mrs Barry and her friend just now."

"Yes. I'd already had a chat with the Gerards; but Joy, Mrs Gerard, wanted me to meet Martha Barry."

"And you still have a few more convention members to talk to?"

"A few. But I decided to wait until we're on our way again. Right now, everyone's going ashore. Perhaps you can help me track down the rest of them this evening?"

"It'll be my pleasure," Mike responded with a smile. "In the meantime, what are your plans for the rest of the day?"

"I'll be going ashore soon with a friend."

"Well, I've been asked to invite your group to the captain's table tonight for dinner. Eight o'clock."

"That's wonderful, thank you," I remarked with pleasure. "Captain Wilkins seems a lovely man."

Mike frowned momentarily. "Yes, he is, considering."

"Considering what?"

"The poor man lost his wife a few years ago in an operation gone wrong, and now he's left with a young daughter to look after. Of course, she's away at boarding school seeing as her father travels so much."

"Oh! I'm so sorry to hear that." How tragic it must be to lose a loved one in a medical procedure simply because someone made a mistake. I wanted to ask more about what had happened to Mrs Wilkins, but Mike changed the subject.

"After the dinner, we have an excellent acrobatic show on the top deck."

The way he said this, with such longing in his eyes, made me remark, "Don't tell me you're an ex-acrobat."

Mike sighed despondently and nodded. "Am I that transparent?" He gave me a sad smile. "I used to be an acrobat, mainly working on cruise ships and Cirque du Soleil. But my career was unfortunately cut short. Then, through my contacts, I made a new career for myself as a cruise director."

"If you don't mind my asking, what happened?"

"I suffered a hip injury during one of my performances and had an operation as recommended by my doctor at the time. Unfortunately, this put an end to my career. Then, a short while later, I found out that I could've had physical therapy rather than an operation. If I'd done this, I would still be doing what I love most." For a moment, a shadow crossed his face. "These doctors are sometimes trigger-happy and think surgery's the answer to everything."

"But this is so sad," I commiserated with him. "I guess life throws these challenges at us and we have no option but to look on the bright side."

A smile came back to Mike's face, chasing away the earlier shadowy look. "You're right, of course. I love my job on the ship, and I get to meet many interesting people." He glanced at his watch. "But don't let me keep you. Noumea awaits you. I'll see you tonight with your friends, in any case." He bid me farewell and went on his way.

I stayed on deck a little longer, looking at the scenery around me as all the information I'd gathered in the last hour came crowding into my head. I needed time to sort through it all; but even before I disseminated any of what I had learned, I realised so far I'd come across three motives for the murder of Dr van Horn.

CHAPTER 7

"We have the cheaters' club plus two operations gone wrong—one killed the captain's wife; the other put an end to Mike Yuen's acrobatic career." I took a sip of my cappuccino and gazed across at Chris while we sat at The Mariners' Hub having coffee prior to going ashore.

"Wow!" he exclaimed in wonder. "You found all that out in the space of an hour?"

I shrugged. "You know how it is; people seem to open up to me."

"And you're modest, too." He grinned. "But seriously, this is a huge leap in the investigation."

I regarded him pensively. "I don't know. Right now, it's only supposition."

"True," Chris conceded. "But each of these people had a motive to get rid of Dr van Horn."

I put down my cup and speculated, "Well, yes and no. Don't forget van Horn wasn't a surgeon but merely a GP; and the captain and Mike Yuen's lives were turned upside down by a surgeon. So why take it out on van Horn? Plus we don't even know if it's the same surgeon who operated on the captain's wife and Mike Yuen; which means we could be looking at two surgeons. This still doesn't explain why van Horn was murdered."

Chris looked disappointed. "You're right, of course. The only one with a more solid motive, then, is Martha Barry."

"Yes. I guess van Horn was indirectly responsible for her husband's cheating. But I don't think she has a motive, either."

"What do you mean?" Chris exclaimed in surprise. "You just said—"

"I know what I said," I interrupted. "But don't you see? Martha only found out about her husband's philandering—*after* the death of van Horn."

56

Understanding dawned in his eyes. "Oh."

"Well, I'm fairly certain this is the case," I added for good measure. "Joy Gerard told me Martha found out when she overheard her husband talking on the phone to a Dr Cliff Downes. In the call, they discussed who would run the club now that van Horn's dead."

"In any case, Dobbs and Smythe are fairly certain the killer's a man; so it can't be Martha," Chris pointed out.

I nodded. "I tend to agree. The killer certainly walked like a guy rather than a female. Mind you, the CCTV footage's not very clear. But let's assume the killer's a man for now. How about you; did you find anything on the good doctor?"

"Nothing yet, except that he worked in a practice with four other doctors. He was a GP with an interest in sexual dysfunction."

I snickered. "I bet! Judging from what Martha said, the guy ran this cheaters' club where..." I stopped talking as a sudden thought flashed into my mind.

"What is it?" Chris leaned forward in his chair.

I held up a finger to indicate I needed a moment to formulate my thoughts. Chris sat back, waiting. After a few moments, I spoke. "This may be nothing, except a play of words, but when Martha was relating her story about overhearing her hubby on the phone, it seems he referred to the cheaters' club as 'the erotics' club'. At least, this is how she put it."

"Interesting word to use," Chris commented. "Maybe, it's a cheaters' club called 'the erotics' club'."

"Could very well be." I glanced at my watch. "Anyway, let's keep it in mind. Right now, we have to get on a tender if we're going to make it to lunch on time."

We stood and started walking toward Crossroads to get a colour ticket for the next tender going ashore. "I hope we're not lunching in some French place where we have to eat snails," Chris remarked, screwing his nose in distaste.

I smirked. "With Dobbs and Smythe you can be assured we'll get something like steak and fries, and never anything slimy. So don't worry."

"Yeah, but Noumea's French," Chris argued.

"And we're getting *French* fries," I quipped.

~~~

We ended up meeting for lunch in the brasserie at Le Meridien Hotel. The resort hotel was located on the touristy side of the island along with all the other big resorts. We took in the breathtaking view from Pointe Magnin, a small peninsula jutting into the clear blue waters of the Pacific. The hotel had been built on the tip of Pointe Magnin and the atmosphere was magic—white sandy beaches with sparkling blue waters flanking all sides of the triangular point-like peninsula, and framed by palm trees and a profusion of tropical greenery and exotic flowers.

When we arrived, we spotted Dobbs and Smythe seated at a table by one of the expansive windows with a multi-million dollar view. The men were already enjoying steak sandwiches on long baguettes accompanied by salad and fries. They'd ordered light beer to go with their meals.

I wore a look of amusement at the relief on Chris's face when he saw nothing slimy on their plates. We joined the men just as a waiter handed us our menus. "Couldn't wait, I see." I turned to Dobbs with a grin.

He looked up from his food long enough to explain, "Sorry, but we had nothing to eat since a very quick breakfast at around five this morning."

Smythe picked up the conversation while Dobbs kept eating like a man who had been starved for a month. "We disembarked extra early so we could talk to the local police before any of the passengers went ashore."

I noticed he looked rather refreshed considering he'd had to rise early. He wore white shorts and a floral-looking shirt that accentuated his tan. My heart fluttered for a moment and I despised myself for letting his good looks affect me. "Well, you both look more rested today," I uttered with a half smile and buried my face in the menu I was holding.

Chris went for a burger and fries. Surprise, surprise! I chose the Thai beef salad. French food was not to my liking so it was a relief the hotel offered an international menu. By the time our food arrived, Dobbs had finished his and was well into his dessert of crème brûlée. This was probably the only part of French cuisine Dobbs enjoyed—the fatty desserts.

"So how did you get on with the local cops?" Chris asked, popping a few fries in his mouth.

Smythe, who was only having an espresso, answered, "Just a formality. We gave them as much information as we could and then updated the police in Honolulu by phone. They'll be expecting us upon arrival."

"But we end our trip on the Big Island," I pointed out. "Rourke will be expecting us."

"It doesn't matter," Smythe replied. "The voyage ends in Honolulu for us. Dobbs and I are expected by the police."

I felt my hackles rise at his smugness. Who said he and Dobbs could go all the way through to Honolulu when Chris and I were just as much a part of this investigation?

Dobbs must've picked up on the building energy emanating from me because he looked up from his dessert and explained, "The captain asked us to liaise with the Honolulu police on this. We've already cleared it with Mr Rourke and Mr Teppler."

"But what about us?" I protested like a child. "How come we're not coming to Honolulu with you?" Was that a smirk on Smythe's face? I felt my temper about to erupt, but managed to control it lest I pick up his glass of beer and throw the contents in his face.

"Mr Rourke wants you both in Waikoloa," Dobbs reported and went back to his dessert.

I kept on eating silently, a frown on my face.

Dobbs gazed my way and added, "Mia, the boss wants you and Chris by his side. Besides, once we finish with the police we'll catch a flight across to join you. We'll only be gone two days at most. I plan a quick visit to Maggie and Rose while I'm there, and then we join you."

Maggie lived in Honolulu with her husband and baby Rose. Dobbs only got to see them once a year or so. Therefore, I couldn't berate the man. "Fair enough," I replied, my voice softening.

"So how did you guys go this morning?" Smythe remarked to break the tension in the air.

I updated them on my findings and theories about the motives.

"Well, you're way ahead of what we've been able to learn. Please keep us informed on further developments." This sounded like praise from Smythe and I took it at face value, giving him the benefit of the doubt.

Our lunch ended pleasantly enough and afterwards we took a stroll along one of the white sandy beaches before heading back to the ship. Once on the tender, I remembered our invitation to dinner. "By the way, we're all invited to dine with the captain this evening."

Dobbs looked pleased. "So we better wear our best bibs," he joked. "There's bound to be loads of nice food."

Chris chuckled. "Trust you to think of food, Dobbs."

Dobbs patted his tummy. "Murder makes me hungry, my friend."

It was in this jovial mood that we parted once onboard ship. Dobbs went to his cabin for a siesta and Chris announced he was going to run a few more searches on the victim. Smythe didn't say where he intended to go, but left us with a wave of the hand and headed toward the lifts. I was at a loose end and decided to go in search of Professor Tully for afternoon tea and a chat. First, though, I slipped into my cabin and changed from the white jeans and T-shirt I had been wearing, and into my swimmers. Over them, I threw on a gauzy forest green and gold see-through caftan that flowed around me like a dream and accentuated my figure to its best advantage. There was always the possibility I would run into Mark Evans, so I might as well look sexy while I was at it.

I headed for the Rockery first——a bar located on the stern of the ship on Deck 8 with two spa pools built into what looked like a rockery, hence the name. They also had the most comfortable deck chairs covered with soft canvas cushions. The back of the ship was usually quiet and rarely windy, so it was the best place to catch a nap in the sun. I thought I'd rest for a while before going in search of the professor.

When I came out the door leading to the back deck, I noticed the Rockery was full of people sunbathing in the early afternoon sun. My heart sank. But just then, I espied an empty deck chair and headed straight for it. Unfortunately, it wasn't until I reached it that I came face to face with Smythe, who lay on his back with sunglasses on and wet swimmers clinging to his powerful thighs as they dried in the sun.

I quickly did an about-turn, hoping to get away before he spotted me. Unfortunately, just as I was about to make my escape, his hand reached up to his face and he lifted his sunglasses to gaze my way.

"No need to leave on my account," he remarked with a smirk on his lips.

I wanted to hit him with something while I felt myself blush—and to top things off, I was in this flimsy garment that left nothing to the imagination, at least judging by the look Smythe gave me. I felt like a fool and had no option but to take the chair and pretend I was unfazed. So I spread out a pool towel I picked up from a neatly folded pile on a nearby bench for use by passengers and lay on the deck chair without taking off the caftan. Even though the blasted thing was filmy, it still gave me some cover. Of course, my reaction would have been a lot different had it been Mark Evans who saw me in the garment.

As if Smythe read my mind, he stated, "Mark was by earlier. He told me they managed to inform van Horn's next of kin back in Australia. A distant cousin, I think."

Damn! I had missed Mark. So there was no point in hanging around here with the devil. But I couldn't make a hasty exit just yet and give him the satisfaction of seeing me run from him like the wind. So I nodded. "Then, I guess we've done all we can for the time being." I felt his eyes on me and wished he'd put his sunnies back on. He did, just when I thought of it, but nonetheless he still looked at me as I lay there, stiff as a board. I made myself relax by thinking this man beside me—my archenemy—had not so long ago been involved in a love affair with my dear friend, Amanda Wilson.

Amanda had come to visit me from her home in the UK in order to get away from hubby problems. When she met Smythe, she fell for him straight away and the two ended up in a sexual liaison, much to my disapproval. And it seemed Smythe had more feelings for Amanda than the other way around, so Smythe's heart was broken when she decided to return to her husband. I took great satisfaction in this. It served him right for thinking he could pick up my friend with his charm.

"Heard from Amanda?" I put in suddenly. This should shake him a bit.

Smythe lay back on his deck chair and let out a sigh. He didn't answer, but I could tell I'd hit the mark. I felt wicked doing this, but my ploy had worked and he was no longer perving at me.

"Madam, can I get you anything?" I almost jumped out of my skin when a waiter appeared in my field of vision, breaking into my thoughts of retribution.

"Er... yes. I'll have a non-alcoholic cocktail. The one with pineapple juice."

"Very well." The waiter nodded and then addressed Smythe. "And for you, sir?"

Smythe ordered an alcoholic cocktail with coffee liqueur, chocolate, and other equally delicious ingredients. While he spoke with the waiter, I took the opportunity to admire his athletic build and long legs. I had to get out of here.

We hardly spoke as we waited for our drinks and merely exchanged a few comments on the weather and how pleasant it was to travel by ship rather than a stuffy airplane. Other than this, we said nothing. When the drinks arrived, I sipped mine at top speed so I could leave. I almost gave myself brain freeze in my haste to finish; but within a minute or two, I was done. I put down the empty glass and stood up.

Smythe regarded me with mild surprise and I felt compelled to explain, "I'm having afternoon tea with Professor Tully." I folded my towel and placed it under my arm.

"Who's Professor Tully?" Smythe's cocktail glass was still three quarters full.

"He's an elderly gentleman I met. The poor thing recently lost his wife and he's taking this cruise to grieve. Anyway, he likes chatting to me, and we sometimes meet for afternoon tea." Sheesh! Do I have to tell him all this? You'd think he was my father or something.

Smythe nodded slightly. "Well, I guess I'll see you at the captain's dinner this evening." His voice held a tone of amusement, and I turned away abruptly and left him without a word. Smug bastard!

CHAPTER 8

I was glad to get a seat next to Mark Evans at the captain's dinner; with the cruise director, Mike Yuen, on my other side. There were ten of us seated around the table—the captain, Jerry Garcia, Mark Evans, Mike Yuen, Dobbs, Chris, Smythe, Enrico Lotti, and strangely enough, Professor Tully. I was the only female present, but very much in my element.

We were in the ship's signature restaurant, Navigators; a fine dining establishment offering full silver service and a wonderful nouvelle cuisine menu with a touch of Italian. The surroundings were elegant, with muted lighting and the intimate atmosphere of a smaller dining room, which only held around sixty or so diners. The waiters seemed to glide silently around the room and the only sound that could be heard above the diners' voices was the gentle tinkling of a piano tucked away in a corner with the player sticking to slow contemporary tunes.

The officers at our table wore their whites while the rest of the men had a jacket over a smart casual shirt. I dressed in a sleeveless black sheath that hugged my figure and tapered its way to just below the knee. My only adornments were a pair of delicate drop-pearl earrings, a single strand of pearls around my neck, and a plain-band gold bracelet encircling my wrist. My short white-blonde hair framed a face with little make-up—just a touch of eyeliner and mascara accentuating my blue eyes and red lipstick adding the finishing touch to my mouth. I looked years younger than my age and by the glances I was getting, especially from Mark Evans, I knew I'd made the right choice in dressing simply, but with elegance.

While I chatted animatedly with Mark, I detected a bit of a scowl on Smythe's face, and I relished at the thought that he might be envious. For some time now, I'd been aware of the suppressed sexual tension between Smythe and myself, and I acknowledged we held a certain attraction for each other despite our mutual antipathy. Too bad he was an arsehole.

A waiter appeared out of nowhere to refill our wine glasses, just as our first course arrived, and I turned my attention back to Mark, who was regaling me with tales of his travels on different ships.

"So how long have you been working on this ship?" I asked when he finished telling me about a rather frightening storm at sea.

"Just on a year now," he replied while sipping some wine.

"Do they rotate you guys around?"

"Yes. Every couple of years we have the opportunity to work on another ship within the fleet. Of course, this isn't compulsory and one can stay on the same ship if they wish."

"But it's better to work on different ships and see the world, right?" I imagined doing the Pacific Islands long term would bore most people. There were only so many beaches and palm trees one could take after all. "If I worked on a cruise ship, I think I'd spend most of my time doing Europe."

Mark nodded in agreement. "Most of our officers and the crew go for Europe as a first option. It can get rather competitive at times. Mind you, the US is also a big attraction."

"True. What I'd really like to do one day is a trans-Atlantic crossing from Southampton to New York."

"And don't forget Alaska. The glaciers are breathtaking." Mike Yuen joined in on our conversation.

"Oh, yes," I remarked with enthusiasm. "That's another place I'd love to see."

When we finished with the first course, and the waiter started to clear our plates, I looked around the table and observed everyone engaged in conversation with the diners on either side of them. Chris was sitting between Dobbs and Smythe; Professor Tully had Jerry Garcia on one side and Enrico on the other. I turned to Mike. "Tell me, Mike, how does one get an invite to the captain's table?"

"Generally, the captain invites guests who've travelled with us a number of times." And before I could ask my next question, he went on, "In this case, however, we're having a special dinner. The captain wants to thank you all for your group's involvement in the investigation of Dr van Horn's death."

I nodded with understanding. "Okay. And I can see how Enrico Lotti fits in with us, as the victim was travelling as part of his group;

but what about Professor Tully? He's not part of that group."

"I know, but he's known to Enrico," Mike said. "And as we were one short to make up a table of ten, Enrico suggested the professor. I believe the old gent's grieving the loss of his wife."

I glanced across the table at the professor, who was in deep conversation with Enrico. "Yes. Professor Tully's travelling alone on this trip. He also told me he's a retired GP, so I assume he used to attend the type of conventions Enrico coordinates." Having said this, I couldn't see how this was possible. The professor had told me he'd retired years ago, and Enrico had said he'd been doing this job for about five years, so the two could not have met through a convention. I made a mental note to speak to Enrico later and find out how he knew the professor. I was so distracted with my thoughts that I missed whatever Mike was saying and only caught the tail end of it. "...taking into account his dislike for doctors."

"I'm sorry. I didn't quite catch what you just said."

"I was simply commenting on the fact that it was nice of Captain Wilkins to invite to dinner those here connected with the medical profession, taking into account his dislike for doctors."

My internal investigative antennae went up at this bit of information. "That's right. You mentioned the captain's wife died in an operation."

Mike stole a quick glance at the captain, who was engaged in conversation with Mark Evans, and then turned back to me. "Yes. I'm not sure what went wrong, but Mrs Wilkins had to have some kind of pelvic operation and the whole thing was botched. It seems the surgeon who performed the operation was under suspicion of taking drugs to stay awake—you know how they work such long hours and all. Anyway, the captain took him to court, but nothing was ever proven. Besides, the hospital stood behind the surgeon, plus they had the better lawyers. Cut a long story short, the captain lost the case. Since then, he won't go near a doctor if he can help it."

I grimaced. "That's horrible! And now he's left on his own to bring up a young daughter. But you know how these big corporations, including hospitals, stick together and protect their own. I mean, you have to be a multi-millionaire to fight them; and the legal system always seems to favour the bad guys. Very rarely do we get to hear about the underdog winning." At my bitter tone of voice, Mike gazed at me with curiosity. I quickly explained, "Don't mind me, I just hate lawyers." I frowned momentarily when I said this, thinking how I'd lost so much to my evil ex because I hadn't had enough money to fight him legally, which meant I'd had to call it quits. Bloody lawyers and their exuberant fees! What a waste of space they were.

Thankfully, our main course arrived and with it the captain called our attention by raising his wine glass and saying, "*Lady* and gentlemen." The men around the table smiled at the captain's reference to my being the only female present. "I'd like to propose a toast to wonderful company, great food, excellent wine, and hopefully an incident-free rest of the voyage."

"Hear, hear," someone said, and we all raised our glasses in a toast. Then, we went back to chatting with our dinner companions.

The entree had consisted of tasty and tender baby asparagus shoots with shaved parmesan cheese drizzled in extra virgin olive oil. There had been a choice of seafood and meat entrees as well, but I'd opted for the lighter vegetarian alternative. The main course presented us with a choice of pasta, meat, or fish. I chose the veal, which came wrapped in paper-thin slices of prosciutto, sprinkled in sage and accompanied with wild mushrooms. So far, the food had been delectable and I couldn't wait for dessert. I smiled in anticipation, thinking of Dobbs and his childlike enthusiasm for anything sweet.

Through the main meal, I chitchatted with Mark again, basking in his attention. The guy had to be at least fifteen years younger than I—but if he felt attracted to me, who was I to stop him?

By dessert time, the diners changed places around the table so we could talk to others in the party. I ended up sitting between Professor Tully and the wonderfully handsome Enrico Lotti. From the corner of my eye, I saw the look of relief coming from Chris, who was now chatting animatedly with the captain. I bet he was glad he hadn't landed next to the sensual Enrico. Meanwhile, Smythe conversed with Mike Yuen, and Dobbs teamed up with Jerry Garcia and Mark Evans.

I almost laughed when I briefly glanced at Dobbs while he tucked into his dessert of three slices of different-flavoured gelato, placed in a shell-shaped wafer structure that lay in an island of wild berry jus and dark chocolate shavings. Dobbs looked like a five-year-old, eyes wide with delight, just as I'd imagined him earlier. I chose

Zabaglione, which was served in a crystal goblet and topped with raspberries and blueberries encased in hot chocolate sauce.

"Professor, it's so lovely to see you again. I didn't know you hobnobbed with the likes of the officers," I said in jest.

"Ah, my dear!" The professor gave me a charming smile while he drank his espresso. "You look ravishing tonight. If only I were twenty years younger." He chuckled to himself.

Before I could respond to this compliment, Enrico took hold of my hand and planted a kiss on the back of it. "Bellissima!"

His smile weakened my knees and I didn't care that he was gay. I felt myself blush. "Boys, boys, you're embarrassing me! But I do thank you for your lovely compliments." I winked at them wickedly and they burst into laughter.

This attracted the attention of the other men and, while I noted Smythe's dry look, the rest simply smiled good naturedly, especially Mark Evans.

~~~

After dinner, I opted for a stroll along the Promenade Deck with the luscious Enrico. The professor begged off as he felt tired and wanted an early night. The officers went back to their duties and Chris, Dobbs and Smythe mentioned something about catching the acrobatic show on the top deck. Mike Yuen went along with them because he was playing MC for the show.

"I feel so sorry for the professor," I remarked while we strolled along the deck. I gazed at the white spray of the waves illuminated by the lights from the ship but beyond this point, there was only blackness except for the glittering of the stars on a moonless night. I shuddered at the thought of van Horn going overboard—if he was still alive when he hit the water, it must've been horrifying being left behind in the black watery void.

Enrico hooked his arm through mine in the Italian fashion. "Why do you feel sorry for him?"

"I mean, losing his wife of so many years; and now having to travel alone. It's really sad, don't you think?"

My companion sighed melodramatically. "Ahhh, che vita porca!"

I looked at him questioningly. "So you think it's a pig of a life? I have to agree with you."

He nodded. "Youth goes so quickly and we often waste it. And then, what is there left for us? If we're lucky, someone who loves us. But even this is taken away at some point."

Don't I know it! "This is why we must live in the present, Enrico, and make the most of what we have. So tell me, how do you know the professor?"

Another sigh from him. "I wish I could say it was under happier circumstances. But all the same, I'm glad we became friends."

I waited quietly for him to explain. By this time, we had reached the end of the deck, did an about-face, and resumed our stroll.

"I wasn't always an events coordinator. I was a doctor." Enrico stopped walking and went to stand by the viewing rail. I joined him, surprised at his disclosure. Enrico must've made a gorgeous doctor, I thought with amusement while I pictured a very long line of women, and gay young men, vying for his medical expertise. "You see," he continued as he looked out at the blackness of the ocean, "I worked for a large hospital when completing my internship, and I was doing very well. So much so, I was encouraged by one of my so-called mentors to apply for a position at the end of the internship. This would have been a great promotion for me and a good start to my medical career. But then..."

I remained silent and watched him struggle with his emotions. Enrico ran fingers through his hair as blond strands flew freely in the sea breeze and got into his eyes. He really was a beautiful looking young man.

"So sorry." Enrico turned teary eyes toward me. "I'm getting a bit emotional."

"Take your time." I patted his arm, trying to lend him some comfort.

He took a few moments to compose himself and then continued talking. "Well, it's like this: I'd just found out my partner was HIV positive. He was also a doctor in the same hospital; and it was a well-known fact that we were an item. To cut a long story short, the recruitment panel turned me down for the position. They also made it very difficult for Gianni to keep working there even though he wasn't symptomatic."

"But that's discrimination!" I argued.

"Tell that to someone who cares," he returned, bitterly. "Gianni had to leave his job because he couldn't cope with the snubs anymore. He decided to go back to Italy. I stayed on for a while, but then decided I wasn't going to get anywhere; and so I quit."

"Why didn't you go to Italy with Gianni?" I was astounded people could be so cruel and judgemental, even after all the awareness about HIV. Those with the virus could still lead a normal life if they were asymptomatic. After all, there should be no problems working any job if the person did not develop fully blown AIDS— even in health care. There would always be the question of safety, of course; but as long as measures were observed, I saw no reason as to why a doctor who did not develop the symptoms of the disease should be removed from his job.

"Gianni and I were not in the relationship for the long term. Besides, he missed his family, all of whom reside in Italy. I, on the other hand, have family in Australia."

"Okay, so you stayed on; but didn't get the job. What happened then?"

"Some colleagues supported my application at the time, including Professor Tully. Even though he was retired from practising as a doctor, he was well connected at the hospital plus many of the student doctors attended his physiology class at university. This is how I know him. Anyway, he stood by me all the way, but even he wasn't influential enough to overcome the prejudice in that place, especially from the likes of van Horn and the others."

My heart gave a jolt. "You mean van Horn was on the recruitment panel?"

He nodded. "A whole bunch of them were," Enrico answered. "Some of them are even on this ship, attending the convention."

"Who are they?" I could barely contain my excitement at this little bit of information.

Enrico looked thoughtful as if trying to remember all the names. "Let's see... There are Drs Barry, Weinstein, and Keyes, to name a few."

"And you're friendly with them now?"

Enrico shrugged. "That's life, isn't it? I need my job, and I want to keep the medical convention business because they bring high revenue to my company. Besides, they act as if nothing happened. And I suppose, in their eyes, nothing has. They think Gianni couldn't take the reality of his condition and that I quit because I needed a change. Their excuse for turning me down at the time was that I didn't have enough experience or some such rubbish."

"I'm so sorry for what happened."

"No need to be." Enrico smiled with resignation. "I'm happy in my work and well out of the 'clicky' hospital group. Ironically, I'm sad for van Horn's death. I dislike all these guys, but never enough to want to kill them." He regarded me with a serious look. "Interestingly, here's more than a coincidence for you—Captain Wilkins's wife was operated on by Dr Weinstein. And you probably know Mike Yuen lost his acrobatic career due to bad advice given to him by Dr Barry, who operated on him."

Before I could recover from my astonishment at this piece of news, Enrico glanced at his watch and informed me he had to meet someone. He bid me goodnight and disappeared while I remained on deck, gazing pensively at the dark waters on the black horizon.

"So there you are!"

I jumped with fright, my hand going to my throat. I seemed to be doing this a lot lately—jumping in fright; my nerves feeling jangled.

"Oh, I'm sorry," said Mark Evans, approaching me with a sexy smile. "I didn't mean to startle you. I was passing by, doing my rounds, and found you here looking very ravishing."

I recovered instantly and returned his smile. "Just thinking," I replied. "Did you get to see the acrobatic show?"

"No. I went on my rounds after dinner. Then, I found you all alone and couldn't resist coming over to make sure everything's okay." The gallantry in his voice was mixed with a flirty undertone.

I didn't allow his proximity to faze me. Mark stood so close, he invaded my personal space. But he smelled divine—a combination of fresh ocean breeze and a woodsy aftershave of some kind. I felt butterflies in my stomach. "And what is your conclusion; is everything okay with me?" I flirted right back, throwing him an impish look.

"It will be now." He moved quickly and before I knew it, his arms went around me and his mouth swooped down on mine in a kiss that became deep and passionate.

I felt my hormones go into overdrive as a hot wave of desire whooshed down to my pelvis. My arms went around his neck and my body melded with his while my mouth opened to meet his invading tongue.

The kiss grew deeper and I felt this as a prologue of greater things to come—going with Mark to his cabin to further explore each other. Sadly, it was not to be. Someone cleared their throat in the near distance and the spell was broken. I remained in the circle of Mark's arms as we both looked up toward the sound. Despite my dazed state, I made out the back of Smythe's body as he disappeared through the door that led back inside the ship.

~~~

I made my way to my cabin, pissed off at Smythe for having interrupted what could have been a night of hot passion. He should have kept quiet when he stumbled upon us, and simply gone right back to where he had come from.

When I entered my cabin, I peeled off my clothes and jumped in the shower to cool off. In hindsight, the thing with Mark was obviously not meant to be, and perhaps this was best. Getting involved with a ship's officer was not my idea of a relationship or even a liaison. Mark travelled constantly and his time on land was limited. Still, a night of pure sex would not have gone amiss. The last time I'd had sex had been months ago, and that was just a fling.

After the shower, I pulled on a short cotton nightshirt and went straight to bed where I immediately fell into a deep sleep. I had obviously been more tired than I'd thought, but woke up refreshed early the next morning when room service knocked on my door with my breakfast.

I was glad I'd had the foresight to order room service. This way, I was able to avoid Smythe after his interruption of Mark and me. I sat at the small coffee table next to the window in my cabin and enjoyed a strong cup of coffee accompanied by an assortment of Danishes and brioche. The sky outside was a clear blue and the ocean mirrored its colour in a darker hue.

We were en-route to Vila, Vanuatu, our next port of call. Arrival time would be 7.00am the following morning. Today, however, we were at sea, and this would be a good time to finish talking to the rest of the convention members.

Just as I thought this, there was a knock at my door and a voice called out, "Mia, it's me. Open up."

It was Chris, and he sounded serious. I threw on a summery

cotton robe before I let him in. His eyes were full of excitement and he was still in his pyjama bottoms.

"What the hell's going on?" I chided him. "It's not even seven yet. Can't I enjoy my breakfast in peace?"

Chris barged into my cabin and went straight for the coffee and Danishes. "I'm starved."

I shut the door and joined him. "Well, don't let me stop you!" I couldn't help the sarcasm in my voice. "There's enough food to feed ten armies on this ship, Chris; so why are you taking mine?"

"Because there's no time," he replied in between drinking coffee from my cup and shoving half a Danish into his mouth."

"Time for what?" I shot back with irritation.

"Time to eat properly," he answered. "I've just had a call from Dobbs. He's up on deck with the captain and another dead body."

CHAPTER 9

"Fishing twine?" I exclaimed in disbelief.

Dobbs nodded, holding out a length of fishing twine, about a foot long, for the others to see. "This is all I found. The rest must've blown away to sea."

Dobbs, Smythe, Chris, and I stood at the bottom of one of the external stairwells leading down from Deck 13 where the jogging track was located. Captain Wilkins, Jerry Garcia, and Mark Evans stood a few feet away from us, speaking with another officer. Meanwhile, we stared at Dr Jim Barry, Martha's cheating husband, whose body lay at the bottom of the stairwell, dressed in the shorts and training jacket he'd been wearing when he allegedly went for an early morning jog.

"Who found him?" I looked to Dobbs for an answer.

Smythe replied instead. "Dobbs found him on the way to his morning walk. Neck's broken. He rang me straight away and we found the fishing twine that tripped Barry tied to one side of the railing at the top of the stairs." Smythe's gaze kept darting from me to Chris and down to the victim. I hoped he wasn't thinking about last night's interruption when I'd been with Mark Evans; but I didn't think so, especially in view of the fact that we were now faced with a second murder.

The area around Dr Barry's body had been cordoned off with rope and canvas sheets that hanged from it like curtains in order to block the body from public view. At this time, however, there was no one around; plus the captain had closed off this side of the deck with "Do not enter—maintenance in progress" signage.

"Once we established this was no accident," Dobbs took up where Smythe left off, "we called the captain and he joined us immediately with Mark and the ship's doctor. The doc ID'd the victim since he knew Barry from years ago. He also confirmed Barry suffered a broken neck as a result of the fall. No defensive wounds, no signs of a struggle. The guy didn't even see it coming."

I looked up the stairwell and counted fifteen steps. Yes, a fall from the top definitely had the potential to kill someone.

"So what now?" This from Chris.

"Back to CCTV footage search," Dobbs replied with a sigh. "When I came out here, there was no one else about. I didn't know how long the victim had been dead, but the doc gave us an approximation of maybe one hour."

"What time did you find him?" I was thinking someone would have to break the news to Martha Barry; and this would probably fall on me because I knew her better than the others.

"It was around 6.15am."

"I take it no one went to see Mrs Barry yet?"

Dobbs shook his head. "No. We needed to secure the scene and close off access to any passengers who might wander this way."

Smythe cast a look at me. "Mia, can we count on you for this?"

"Sure. I already know Mrs Barry, so this is better coming from me. What are you guys going to do?"

"As I said, it's going to be CCTV duty for us," Dobbs answered. "That is, after we remove the body to the morgue."

"Jerry Garcia and his men will dust for prints around the railing, but I doubt they'll find anything," Smythe informed us. "Good thing Garcia's an ex-cop and always carries the essentials with him."

"Even a gun?" Chris asked.

"A few, I believe," Smythe said. "And it's just as well. I'm fairly certain this is the work of the same killer. And I have a feeling he's not finished yet."

I nodded in agreement at his chilling prediction. "We'll leave you guys to it. Chris and I will see Mrs Barry and hook up with you later."

The captain approached us with his companions just as we were about to leave. "Thank you for your help, Mia and Chris. I overheard you're going to see Mrs Barry."

"I was talking with her earlier, Captain. I'll report to you all after I break the news and talk to more of the convention people."

I grabbed hold of Chris's wrist in preparation to go, but not before I caught a glint of admiration in Mark Evans's eyes. I was therefore glad I'd taken the time to throw a flowing white cotton dress over me before coming out on deck.

~~~

"They have a morgue on the ship?" Chris remarked as we made our way down to the cabins.

"Yes. People do die of natural causes, you know. So they have to have one to keep the bodies until they reach port. What did you think?" I cocked an eyebrow at him. "They throw the bodies to the fish?"

He harrumphed. "Know it all!"

Martha Barry did not seem too devastated when I told her of her husband's demise, and I fleetingly wondered whether she'd tripped the cheating doctor to fall down the stairs rather than waste time on a divorce. My gut told me, no.

We'd had to knock on her door several times before she answered. When she finally opened it and saw us, she seemed genuinely surprised through her sleepy eyes; and after excusing ourselves, I'd asked her to telephone Joy Gerard to join us. I thought her friend should be present for support.

"I know I should be showing my grief in some way," Martha said as if reading my mind. "But in light of the shock at finding out Jim was cheating on me, I guess I'm still feeling angry."

Joy Gerard lay a hand on Martha's arm. "My dear, I'm sure the grief will come, irrespective of what he's done."

"We're very sorry for your loss," I put in on behalf of Chris and me.

Martha nodded a 'thank you' and regarded me with questioning eyes. "So you don't think this was an accident? I mean, who'd want to kill Jim?"

I'd told Martha about the fishing twine. She had a right to know someone had done away with her husband, and that his death wasn't an accident.

"Can you think of anybody who'd want to do this, Mrs Barry?" Chris took the opportunity to ask.

She paused in thought for a moment and then shook her head. "No. Not that I can think of. But then again, it seems I didn't know Jim very well after all." At this, the beginning of tears gathered in her eyes.

Joy handed her a box of tissues from the night table. The ladies were sitting on the edge of Martha's bed, while Chris and I simply stood, leaning against the cabin wall.

"If you don't mind, I have another question; and then we'll leave you be," I uttered.

Martha wiped her eyes with a tissue and nodded.

"What time did your husband go jogging this morning?"

"Around five," Martha replied. "Jim always goes... I mean, went... jogging at that time, even back home."

"Thank you, Martha." I gave her a sympathetic look. "And please don't worry about a thing. Captain Wilkins will be by later to chat with you. He'll make all the arrangements for your husband's body to return with you to Sydney."

"I appreciate it, Mia. I don't think I can cope with anything right now." She looked rather lost when she said this and my heart went out to her. Poor lady—finding her husband was a cheat, and now he'd been murdered by someone on the ship.

Joy took charge. "You leave her in my care, Mia. Martha will be fine. And if there's anything else I can help you with, be sure to call me."

Chris and I took our leave of the ladies and made our way to the buffet restaurant for breakfast. We sat outside, toward the back of the ship. The breeze was mild and the temperature was beginning to warm up. It was going to be a perfect day—except for the murder, of course.

"You realise we now have four suspects," I told Chris. "I want you to do an internet search on these people to see what you come up with. And while you're at it, check on Dr Barry. It's a shame we didn't ask Martha whether we could go through his belongings. Remind me to do this later. Who knows what we'll—"

Chris held up a hand in front of my face. "Wait, wait. Slow down, Mia."

"What is it?"

"You're going too fast, that's what." He took a sip of his coffee while I attacked my scrambled eggs on toast. "First of all, who are the four suspects?"

I swallowed what was in my mouth and took a sip of coffee before I replied. "Well, remember when van Horn was killed and I said we had three suspects? I thought Martha might have gotten rid of van Horn because he was the leader of this so-called cheaters' club."

Chris nodded. "Yes. And then we decided the timing was wrong because she'd only just found out about Barry cheating on her. We also decided the captain and Mike Yuen didn't have a strong enough motive, namely because van Horn wasn't a surgeon and, therefore, not instrumental in what happened to the captain's wife and Mike Yuen's career."

"Exactly. But now things have changed. There's Enrico Lotti for starters." At the look of confusion on Chris's face, I further explained. "I never had time to tell you since I didn't see you after dinner last night." Then, I told him about Enrico's story—his career as a doctor in a hospital where he was passed over for promotion due to his partner's HIV diagnosis; the doctors on the recruitment panel who'd turned him down, and who also happened to be on the ship; plus Enrico's quick way to reassure me he held no hard feelings despite everything that happened.

"Wow!" Chris exclaimed before I continued.

"Then, there's Mike Yuen. Guess who gave him the wrongful medical advice that led to an unnecessary operation."

"Barry!" Chris's eyes were the size of saucers.

"Enrico told me this while he was talking about his own problems. He also mentioned the captain's wife and her botched operation were performed by none other than Dr Weinstein."

"Wow!" Chris said again, this time looking thoughtful. "So there's a huge connection here—van Horn and Barry, both on the recruitment panel in Enrico's case; Barry cheating on his wife; Barry operating on Mike Yuen... hmm... And then there's Weinstein, operating on Mrs Wilkins."

"Shit!" I cried out rather loudly and attracted a few looks my way from some of the other passengers around us. I lowered my voice and said, "Weinstein's onboard this ship."

Chris grinned. "And I'm sure you're going to warn him."

"Bloody right, I am." I gulped down the rest of my coffee and stood up, already thinking ahead as to how I was going to bring up the subject of the murders in order to warn Weinstein that he could be next. But this would implicate the captain because he had a motive; and we had no proof at all as to who was behind the murders. I frowned at the conundrum.

"Don't go yet," Chris urged, breaking into my thoughts. "I'm still computing all of this."

I made a face at him. "Well, compute in a hurry, boyo. I've got things to do and so do you."

"Just think of this—two murders with possibly different motives, plus four suspects to boot."

I drummed my fingers on the table. "And your point is?"

"My point, Ms Ferrari, is this might not be the work of the same killer."

My eyes opened wide. "You're right. And if so, Smythe's wrong about this being the work of the same killer." I considered this for a moment; then said, "Okay. But what are the chances of having more than one killer onboard?"

"Hey, it's only a theory. We could be wrong, you know," Chris pointed out.

I threw him a confident look. "You might be wrong, Chris Rourke. I'm never wrong. So on this occasion, I'll have to reserve judgement until I know more."

He laughed. "I'll say this much for you, Ferrari; at least, you're confident no matter what."

"Shut up and pay attention." I mock-slapped him around the head. "I need to talk to Dr Cliff Downes before anything else."

"Who's he?"

"Barry's mate, remember? The one who's a member of the cheaters' club Martha alluded to. I mean, for all we know, most of these doctors could be in the same club, and Martha's lost it and decided to do them in for being cheating bastards. Only, I don't think she did it."

Chris sighed. "You're confusing me again. I say we discuss the whole thing with Dobbs and Smythe. Who knows, maybe they found something on the CCTV footage by now that'll give us more information."

"Yes, you're right." I frowned with frustration. The situation could go either way—we more than likely had a killer doing all the doctors or as Chris hypothesised, we had multiple killers. But this seemed improbable. Even so, we needed to consider every angle.

"What are you going to do about Weinstein?"

Chris's question brought me out of my reverie. "I don't think the killer will strike again so soon. I think he's satisfied for the time being. Let's discuss it with the others before we proceed to warn anybody. And we need to keep this between the four of us. After all, if Weinstein gets lopped off it'll look suspect on the captain. And if he's the killer, we don't want to alert him we're in the know."

Chris nodded. "This brings us back to the theory of multiple killers."

"I'm not so sure about that. Plus there's also another possibility—we could be absolutely wrong, and the killer is someone we haven't yet thought of." This had been playing at the back of my mind. I felt we had to find a common motive linking the killings to one murderer, especially if Smythe was right and the killer was not yet done.

A shiver ran down my spine and I pushed the gruesome thought away. I said to Chris, "You go and do your internet search and add Cliff Downes to the list. I'm going to find him and suss him out."

~~~

Dobbs called a lunchtime meeting so we could have a catch-up. We met at Horizons, the a-la-carte restaurant, at 1.30pm. We purposely agreed to meet late so the restaurant wouldn't be crowded and we could get more privacy.

We sat at a booth by the window and while we ate—all of us ravenous—we remained silent, occasionally glancing out at the ocean and the endless horizon beyond. Once we reached the dessert and coffee stage, however, we looked more energised and had full bellies.

"I don't know why I'm so hungry on this ship," Dobbs commented. "All I can think of is food."

I smirked. "It's the sea air, Dobbs; plus the fact that Eileen isn't here to stop you." Dobbs's wife would have kept him on the straight and narrow.

Dobbs made a face at me and stuffed his mouth with bread pudding. The rest of us had opted for coffee rather than dessert.

"We reviewed the CCTV footage after security removed the body," Smythe reported. "The only thing we caught was someone's leg. The angle of the camera was just so, that most of the stairwell was in a blind spot." His brow furrowed with frustration and I could relate to it.

"What did the leg look like?" I drained my coffee and signalled the waiter to bring me another.

"It seems to belong to the killer all right—black pants, black jogging shoes; just like the other night. Of course, we're not one hundred per cent sure."

Chris asked, "And that's all you have?"

Dobbs finished his dessert and sat back, looking replete. "Not all. We saw Barry while he jogged around the track. Then, he went off camera when he neared the stairwell. Unfortunately, we didn't see him trip and fall, but we're fairly sure he wasn't pushed. The fishing twine would've done the job of tripping him."

"So when did you see the leg?" I said.

"Earlier. It was around 4.00am and still dark. I don't know how the killer managed to evade the other cameras. All we saw was the empty track and then a leg appeared near the top of the stairwell. But the camera didn't show any more than this."

"It seems the guy knows his way around the ship and where the cameras are placed," I commented.

"He's obviously done his homework," Smythe remarked. "In any case, he was out there prior to the doctor taking his exercise. We can only surmise he came up the same stairwell from the deck below and tied the fishing twine near the top step. He then disappeared through a doorway near the stairwell on Deck 13. This is where the CCTV caught the image of his leg."

I sighed feeling tired and was glad when my cappuccino finally arrived. I needed another caffeine hit. The waiter asked if the others wanted more coffee, but no one had finished their first yet. "I take it there were no prints around the stairwell," I stated once the waiter walked off.

"No. It was a long shot, of course. The killer would've worn gloves." Smythe finished the rest of his coffee in one gulp and looked at both Chris and me. "How did you get on with breaking the bad news?"

I related what had happened at the interview with Mrs Barry plus the conclusions Chris and I reached regarding the suspects, their motives, and the possibility of multiple killers versus one killer, as Chris had suggested.

"While it's one thing to consider multiple killers," Smythe addressed Chris, "I'm fairly sure this is the work of one person."

Dobbs nodded. "I tend to agree."

"Yes, me too," I said. "However, it was a good point Chris brought up. It helped to illustrate we have different motives at present. There's the cheaters' club for Mrs Barry, a sabotaged career for Enrico, and two operations gone wrong—one for Mike Yuen and the other for the captain's wife."

"You're right," Chris agreed. "The chances of having a killer for each motive is too farfetched. But what you said later made sense."

"And what was that?" Smythe asked.

Chris answered before I could speak. "Mia suggested that for all we know, the person could be someone we haven't yet thought of. But if we could find a common thread among the victims we may be able to narrow the list of suspects."

Smythe threw me a thoughtful look and I quickly buried my face in my coffee, not wanting him to see me blush. "That's a good point," he conceded.

"I'm following the angle of the cheaters' club," I informed the group at large, keeping my gaze trained on Dobbs. "So far, we know van Horn and Barry belonged to the same club. It's the one thing they have in common."

"It's certainly worth looking into," Dobbs replied. "I mean, there's a strong possibility this could be the case for the others."

"Which brings me to the reason why I think we should actually warn Dr Cliff Downes," I put in. "I told you earlier about Mrs Barry informing me that her husband was talking on the phone to Downes about the cheaters' club as she was coming out of the shower. This is how she learned her hubby was cheating on her."

"So we think if the killer is after the doctors who belong to this club, then Downes could be next," Chris finished for me.

Dobbs and Smythe regarded me without speaking, each lost in their own thoughts. Finally, Dobbs nodded. "Well, I don't see any harm in warning the guy, do you?" He eyed Smythe.

Smythe agreed. "True. But bear in mind the doctor might deny everything because he doesn't want us to know he's a part of this club."

"Yes, I know," I said. "But I want to question him nonetheless. I couldn't find him this morning, so I'll go in search of him later. He may be able to shed some light into the club as well. After all, what we know about it so far is what Mrs Barry told us. There's also the question of whether we warn Weinstein about the killings. He's the one who operated on Mrs Wilkins."

Smythe looked dubious at this. "Let's just hold off a bit and pursue the cheaters' club angle."

"Meanwhile," Chris reported, "I found nothing of interest on the net, but I'll keep searching."

"Oh," I exclaimed, "before I forget; can we get permission to search through Barry's belongings?"

Smythe nodded. "If the captain's happy with it, why not? But what do you expect to find?"

I reminded them about the inscription Chris and I found in van Horn's address book. "It could be something trivial, but we think it might be some kind of website with the password; so it's worth checking into."

Chris took up the conversation, his eyes animated. "If we find something similar in Barry's belongings it could give me a clue as to where I should be looking next."

CHAPTER 10

I managed to make contact with Dr Downes and he suggested we meet in his cabin after dinner as he would be working on a paper he had to give the following evening at a special function. He could only give me a few minutes of his time.

During dinner with our group, I reported my progress. "He sounded quite busy, but a few minutes are better than nothing."

Chris nodded. "Let's hope he can at least point us in the right direction about the cheaters' club. I have a feeling they'll have a website."

"You think so?" Dobbs remarked and spooned soup into his mouth.

"It just seems strange that I couldn't find anything in van Horn's computer. It was clean as a whistle. Good thing we found the inscription in his little notebook."

Smythe said, "Yes, but that could be a password for online banking or something similar."

"True," I responded. "But if Downes can shed some light about the club, he may even give me the name of the website, if they have one."

"And how do you propose to bring up the subject?" Smythe regarded me with something like doubt in his eyes. "Do you think he's going to tell you freely about him being a cheater?"

I raised my chin, not liking his tone. "There are ways to get a person to talk, Smythe. I don't have to use the proverbial phonebook, you know."

Smythe was in the process of taking a sip of wine and he spluttered, almost choking on it. He glared at me as he wiped his chin with a serviette. "What's that supposed to mean, Ferrari? I'd watch my mouth if I were you."

Dobbs intervened. "Mia, not all cops resort to forcible

questioning. You've been watching too many police shows on TV."

I grinned. "It was only a bit of black humour. Sheesh! Take it easy, will you?" I directed this to Smythe.

He shook his head as if dismissing me. "You really know how to piss people off, don't you?"

"Yes, but at least it got you and Dobbs talking." I grinned.

Chris and Dobbs laughed. Smythe frowned and muttered something unintelligible. I ignored him and went on to finish my soup in silence. I loved baiting Smythe, and he fell for it every time.

After dinner, Dobbs and Smythe informed us that they were joining Jerry Garcia for another look at the CCTV footage just in case they'd missed something. Chris announced he was off to the bar for a drink. He hesitated when he said this with his eyes focused on the floor.

I smiled knowingly. "So who's the babe?" I teased.

His face went beet red and he called out as he walked off, "No one."

Dobbs, Smythe and I looked at each other in amusement. "That boy's hormones are playing havoc with him." Dobbs gave one of his belly laughs.

"Well, I'm glad I'm not a teenager anymore," I declared. "Hormones can make you do the most stupid of things." But then I thought back to the fling I'd had not so long ago. Of course, my raging hormones were being driven by perimenopause—yet another evil women suffered in this human condition we called "life". At least, men were spared this most horrendous passage on the way to old age. Good thing we were the stronger sex when it came to suffering though; for if men had to go through menstrual periods, childbirth and menopause, the human race would've become extinct thousands of years ago.

"I'm off to see Downes now, but before I go," I addressed Smythe, "did you get permission for Chris and I to go through Barry's things?"

He nodded. "The captain's quite happy for you to go ahead as long as you have Mrs Barry's consent."

"Well, that does it then. When Chris finishes flirting with his newfound *amour*, we'll go and see Martha."

The men left and I followed suit. Before I went to see Downes, however, I changed from my dinner dress and into black leggings and a white cotton blouse. I put on my red Nike sneakers and retouched my lipstick. I wasn't one for dressy affairs and always felt more comfortable in casual wear.

The doctor's cabin was located on the deck above mine, so I went up the stairs to Deck 10 and when I reached cabin 10111, I knocked on the door. Downes opened it almost immediately.

"You must be Mia Ferrari," he said and motioned for me to enter.

Downes was quite handsome in a dark, brooding sort of way. He reminded me of the actor Tyrone Power. He looked to be in his mid to late fifties, and had black hair peppered with grey and emerald-green eyes. For a man his age, his physique looked fit, and it was obvious he worked out. He wore jeans and a casual white shirt open at the collar. I couldn't help thinking why such a good looking man would need to be in a cheaters' club. But then, he was probably a bastard; just like all other good looking men I'd come across. I frowned at the thought and then pulled myself together. I wasn't here to judge the guy but to get information from him.

I shook his hand and his grip was firm. "Thank you for seeing me, Dr Downes." I decided to keep it formal.

"Please, call me Cliff," he said in a sexy voice that, while attractive, made me feel inexplicably uneasy.

"Cliff it is." I nodded.

He invited me to have a seat in one of the armchairs by a small coffee table, and he took the other. I blushed when I caught his eyes devouring me, and I became self-conscious. The leggings I wore hugged my figure from the waist down while the white flowing blouse made me look like a lady pirate, which at the same time complemented my breasts, courtesy of my Wonder Bra. I suddenly wished I'd worn something less revealing.

"So how may I help you?" The doctor's eyes appraised my breasts, making me feel even more edgy.

I couldn't believe I'd walked into this one. I should have asked to meet him in a public place. The guy reminded me of a wolf about to gobble down its prey. "Doctor, as I explained on the phone when I called you, I'm part of the investigation team looking into the two incidents involving Drs van Horn and Barry. I believe you were friends with Dr Barry and that you played golf together?"

He nodded. "Yes. Jim and I were golf buddies. It's a terrible thing that happened to him. I don't understand how he could have fallen down the stairs."

Outside of Martha Barry and Joy Gerard, who had both been sworn to secrecy, we had decided to pronounce Barry's death as accidental for the time being. The passengers didn't need to know the ins and outs of what had really happened. Besides, we wanted the killer to think we believed the incident had been an unfortunate accident. The killer would never know we found a section of the fishing twine.

"It is a tragedy," I commiserated. "But who knows about these things. Perhaps, Dr Barry was distracted and missed his step."

Downes nodded but remained silent while his eyes did most of the talking. And they told me he wasn't thinking about his friend's death right now.

I shifted in my seat, wanting to be gone from here. "Doctor... I mean... Cliff," I smiled uneasily. "I have something rather personal to ask you and I hope you'll be able to assist with this inquiry."

He shot me a look of curiosity. "What is it?"

"Well..." I wasn't sure how to broach the subject, and I remembered how I'd made fun of Smythe about having ways to make people talk. Downes, however, was creepy despite his good looks, and I didn't want to play games with him. The best approach, therefore, was to be direct. "We learned Dr Barry was in some sort of cheaters' club and we'd like to get more information on this if possible."

Downes's gaze suddenly sharpened and he exclaimed in a defensive tone, "And what's this got to do with me or with Dr Barry's accident, for that matter?"

I tried to reassure him without giving him any pertinent information about Barry's true cause of death. "Please, Cliff; I don't mean to be insensitive or judgemental in any way. I really wouldn't be asking this question if I didn't think it would be valuable in assisting us with the investigation. I do know for a fact that you and Dr Barry are members of this club."

Downes stood abruptly and I stood with him. He threw me a look of indignation when he responded, "How dare you! How dare you come in here asking inappropriate questions! I'm a married man, and I don't know anything about a cheaters' club. Whoever gave you this information is wrong!"

"Is your wife travelling with you?" I could see some of his clothes strewn around the cabin, but there was nothing feminine in the place.

Downes sighed with exasperation. "If you must know, my wife is with her sister right now. My sister-in-law's undergoing some medical tests and my wife wanted to be with her. So no, Ms Ferrari, my wife is not travelling with me. Not that it's any of your business."

I knew I wasn't going to get anything out of him, not judging by his reaction. "Very well, Doctor. I'm sorry to have upset you, but please know I'm only doing this because of the investigation. This is nothing personal."

Before I could take a step toward the door to get out of there immediately, which was what I wanted to do, Downes zeroed in on me like an eagle spotting prey and pulled me into his arms with a hand going directly to my breast. His mouth was inches away from mine as he uttered, "You know, I think when you heard about this so-called club, you were curious and wanted a piece of the action. And while there is no such club, I'm happy to oblige; if only to teach you a lesson."

His mouth came down hard on mine and he pushed me against the wall, trapping my body with his. I tried to push him off me, but he was too strong. Both his hands went straight to the waistband of my leggings and he tried to pull them down. When he couldn't, due to my squirming all over the place in an attempt to free myself, he simply slipped one hand inside the leggings. His fingers made their way into my panties and slipped between my legs. His other hand, meanwhile, wove its way inside my blouse and into my bra, his fingers finding one of my nipples and pinching it so hard, I yelped in pain despite his mouth still being attached to mine.

I managed to turn my face away from his and broke the assault on my mouth, but he kept me pinned to the wall. He pinched my nipple once again, sending waves of pain through my breast. Then, before I could do anything, his other hand came away from the leggings, and he unzipped his jeans. He pulled out his erect penis and I felt like gagging. He was going to rape me while I was pinned to the wall.

I closed my eyes and summoned up my strength through the anger I felt coursing through me at being violated in such a fashion. The bastard wasn't going to get away with this. I suddenly went limp and allowed him to lower my leggings and panties. He breathed hard and fumbled to try and find the opening between my legs with his cock.

I moaned as if excited and he glanced at me with triumph in his eyes. "I knew you'd want it," he whispered harshly in my ear and eased the pressure of his body against mine so he could position himself to enter me.

My arms were now free to move and I waited for my opportunity. Downes's jeans were bunched up around his ankles along with his undershorts, while one of his hands held his penis and the other rested on my hip, trying to position me for his entry. I cringed with repulsion when I felt the tip of his cock between my legs. Then, I struck.

My hand shot out from nowhere and grabbed hold of his dick so hard that Downes yelled in pain, a look of shock in his eyes. I pulled on his member with all my strength and he went down screaming, at the same time trying to get my hand off his organ.

When he fell to the floor writhing in pain, I pulled up my panties and leggings and I kicked him in the balls for good measure. The good doctor wasn't going anywhere for a while. I stood over him briefly and looked at him with contempt. "You fucking, hypocritical bastard!" I yelled. "Count yourself lucky I don't cut your prick off with a knife."

Downes didn't have the energy to respond. He simply stayed down; now lying in a fetal position and groaning. I kicked him in the ribs and made him scream again before I got out of the cabin, slamming the door shut behind me.

I then ran down the passageway and headed for the lifts. And when I turned into the lift foyer, I collided with Mark Evans. He took one look at my dishevelled appearance and placed his hands on my shoulders to steady me.

"Mia, are you all right?" He gazed at me with concern. "What happened?"

"Oh, Mark..." This was all I managed to say before I collapsed against him. My legs went weak and I was sure I was going to fall. Mark picked me up in his arms as if I weighed nothing and when the lift arrived, he entered with me still in his arms. I hung onto him, still processing the shock of what had just happened, and kept my eyes closed.

A few moments later, I felt myself being deposited on a bed with Mark leaning over me, softly checking parts of my body in case I was injured. I opened my eyes and realised I was not in my cabin but his.

"I'm calling the doctor," Mark said when he couldn't find anything wrong.

My hand shot out before he could turn away and I grabbed hold of his wrist. "No. No. I'm okay, really. Just give me a moment to catch my breath and I'll tell you what happened."

He looked relieved. "Let me get you a drink. It'll help to calm you. How about cognac?"

I nodded and he came back with a small glass filled halfway with the golden liquid. I swallowed the contents down in one gulp, feeling the fiery drink make its way to my stomach and warming me up. Mark took a seat on the bed, eyeing me closely. "Can I get you anything else?"

I shook my head and sat up, leaning back against some pillows. "No, I'll be fine. Thank you. I just need a moment." I ran my fingers through my hair.

"Your lipstick's smeared all over your face," Mark said. "I'll get you a damp towel."

He disappeared into the bathroom and returned momentarily with a face towel and shaving mirror. I took the mirror and looked at my face. It was a mess—red lipstick smeared all around my mouth and mascara running down my cheeks, making me look like a sad clown. I wiped away at the make-up until I removed all traces of it. Then, I handed back the items to a waiting Mark and asked for another cognac.

When he gave me another glass, I sipped the liquid slowly. "Dr Cliff Downes just tried to rape me."

The look on Mark's face was one of horror. "My God! Did he hurt you? I should call the doctor plus security. I'll have the bastard thrown in the brig!"

I placed a hand on his arm to reassure him. "I'm fine. Honestly. He didn't hurt anything vital. I'm a little bruised because he pushed me against the wall, but I'm okay. He's the one who's going to need help, though." I then related what I did to the guy and saw the growing amusement in Mark's eyes.

"He deserved it."

I agreed. "Let's just say he won't be using his pecker for a long time."

"Still, Mia, you took a big risk; and he did try to rape you. The captain has the power of arrest, you know. We can throw him in the brig until we reach Hawaii and then hand him over to the police."

"No, Mark. I think he's been punished enough. Besides, it'll be his word against mine. Plus he could try to press charges against me for kicking him in the balls. I'm sure he's going to be more bruised than I am; and he won't forget this for a long time to come."

Mark smiled and caressed the side of my face. "Very well. Whatever you say." His eyes regarded me with admiration. "I see we're all going to have to watch out for you."

I became momentarily lost in his gaze and knew if he made a pass at me I would respond, but now was not the appropriate time. "I... er... It's late. I'd better get going. Thank you for helping out." I went to stand up and he assisted by taking hold of my hands and pulling me gently to my feet.

"I'm walking you to your cabin," he offered.

We made our way to my cabin and I glanced at my watch when we stopped outside the door. "It's quite late. I'm sorry I took up so much of your time."

"Don't be silly," he assured me. "I'm doing the graveyard shift tonight in any case."

"Well, thank you once again, and good night."

I went to turn to open the door, but not before he took hold of my face between his hands and kissed my lips softly. "Sleep well," he muttered against my mouth, and then he was gone.

I stood outside the door for a moment, watching him walk away. It was when I turned to go inside that I noticed Smythe frowning at me from his open doorway.

Chapter 11

"So this is what you get up to when you're supposed to be investigating a crime!" Smythe pushed my cabin door open just as I was about to close it. He stood in the small foyer of the room, glaring at me.

I sighed tiredly. This was the last thing I needed after the episode with Downes. My body cried out for sleep, and the one thing I didn't want to do was lock horns with my archenemy. "Can't this wait till tomorrow? I'm beat." I heard the exhaustion in my voice.

Smythe didn't seem to notice my fatigued countenance or the look of my face; now bare of make-up, which I imagined didn't make my appearance exactly enticing at present. "Of course you're beat!" he barked at me. "Don't you ever give up getting involved with younger men? Need I remind you what happened last time?"

He was referring to my fling of months ago, during the gay mardi gras murder investigation. I wasn't proud of my mistakes when it came to the men with whom I became involved, but it was another thing when someone like Smythe reminded me of it. It was then I felt my ire come to the fore.

"First of all, Smythe, it's not what you think!" I spat out with barely suppressed rage. "And second, it's none of your damn business." I then added with a cocked eyebrow, "Unless, of course, it bothers you to see me with another man." At this, I turned away from him and made my way to the vanity mirror where I proceeded to check my appearance and brush my rather messy hair.

Smythe didn't speak for a few moments, stunned at my outburst. Finally, he found his voice. "Ferrari, you flatter yourself if you think I'm jealous, but we have to—"

I dropped my brush on the vanity top and rounded on him. "*You* said jealous, not me. But then, considering Amanda dumped you to go back to her husband, I'm not surprised you'd turn to anybody on the rebound, even me."

This time, I hit the mark. Smythe stood there, arms hanging by his side, speechless and with a look of hurt in his eyes. I felt the stirrings of conscience nag at me and thought I'd gone too far. Smythe had truly fallen for my friend and he'd been heartbroken when she left.

I was about to apologise to him—a first for me—when he abruptly turned away and walked out the door, slamming it shut behind him.

~~~

Early the next morning, we docked at Port Vila. I telephoned Chris in his cabin and roused him from sleep.

"Hello..." answered a sleepy voice.

"Rise and shine, Chris, my boy!" My tone was chirpy. "I thought we'd do breakfast in Port Vila seeing as Dobbs and Smythe will be tied up with the authorities."

"Wh... what time is it?" Chris still sounded half-asleep.

"Seven," I replied. "So get up and get ready. I'll knock on your door at eight."

Now, he sounded awake. "Hey, what's the hurry all of a sudden? I got to bed at three this morning."

I made light of his protest. "Not my fault if you go chasing after your ladylove so late."

"She's not my *ladylove*!"

I chose to ignore his defensive tone. "Whatever. I want off this ship before we run into Smythe," I informed him. Then, I added with distaste in my voice, "I've already had my fair share of run-ins with him in the early hours. And trust me, it wasn't fun."

Chris laughed. "I knew it! The tension between the two of you at dinner last night told me something was going to blow up sooner or later. So do tell."

"I'll tell you over breakfast. See you soon." Before he had a chance to respond, I hung up and went to get myself ready for the day ahead.

By around nine, Chris and I were seated at one of Vila's many cafés, located in the town centre, breakfasting on ham and mushroom omelettes and washed down with strong coffee. It was still early for shoppers; however, there were people walking purposely to their places of work. It was a weekday, and it was business as usual in the city. Leisure time was reserved for those of us on holiday or for the spouses of rich expats, who started to appear here and there to meet for coffee prior to engaging in a shopping spree in the modern stores, including the many duty free shops.

It was a perfect day out with temperatures in the high twenties—thankfully, not too hot for this time of year. The cyclone season was approaching and soon the temperatures would average at around 30C with loads of humidity and rain, which made it uncomfortable for sightseeing.

While we ate, I told Chris about the rape attempt by Dr Downes. Chris was shocked and suggested the same thing as Mark Evans.

"How can you let him get away with it?" he exclaimed incredulously. "He should be locked up! I'm just glad he didn't hurt you, otherwise—"

"You know I can take care of myself," I interjected and took a sip of my coffee. "Besides, I don't want him locked up. What if he's the killer? We need to catch him in the act."

Chris finished his food before replying, "Good point, although I don't see a motive for him."

"Well, he could be the next victim," I further suggested.

"That's more like it," Chris concurred.

"We'll have to ask Dobbs and Smythe to keep an eye on him when we sail this evening. If he's the killer's next choice..." I let the sentence hang in the air.

"We're still not one hundred percent sure we're looking at one killer, although it's beginning to seem that way," Chris remarked. "In any case, someone's going to have to warn the guy."

"And it isn't going to be me," I stated firmly. "For once, I won't be sorry if the killer whacks him—not after what he tried to do to me."

Chris nodded and changed the subject. "Let's not talk murder for a while. Just try and have some relaxation time." He sat back, arms behind his head while he enjoyed the sunshine.

"Very well," I agreed readily. I certainly needed some rest and relaxation. Besides, I didn't want to explain about my run-in with Smythe. "So tell me about your new lady," I remarked in order to distract him from asking me anything personal.

He sat up straight, a faint blush touching his cheeks. "She's not *my new lady*. In fact, she's not mine at all."

"I can see you're attracted to her, though," I persisted.

He shrugged his shoulders and said nonchalantly, "She's simply a pretty girl I had a drink with."

I could tell he didn't want to talk about the mysterious girl, so I let it slide. "Why don't we rent a jeep to drive around the island?" I suggested, thinking it might be fun. Dobbs and Smythe would have finished reporting Dr Barry's murder by now and I didn't want to run into them if they decided to go sightseeing around the city. It would have been different if Dobbs had been by himself. Since Smythe came along on this voyage, I'd seen little of my friend. Yet another black mark against Smythe.

"Hello there!" A familiar voice called out just then, bringing me out of my reverie about Smythe.

I looked up at the approaching figure of Professor Tully, making his way over to us slowly as he leaned on his walking stick for support. "Hi, Professor!" I called back with a smile. "Please, come and join us for coffee."

When the professor reached us, he took a seat at our table and I introduced him to Chris.

"You're the young fellow who goes to Sydney University," the professor remarked when he shook hands with Chris. "Mia told me about you."

"Yes. She also mentioned you lecture at uni. You look familiar, but then I probably saw you around the place," Chris replied.

We ordered another round of coffees and some watermelon juice to cool off our palates.

"I'm in physiology, young man; so our paths are not likely to cross. Still, you may have seen me in the library. I frequent it often."

"And how are you enjoying your trip so far, Professor?" I asked, noticing he looked relaxed despite his difficulty walking. I figured the man probably suffered from arthritis.

"So far it's been excellent, except for the two unfortunate deaths we've had onboard."

"Oh, so you heard about Dr Barry," Chris remarked.

"Yes. I knew him. In fact, I know most of the older doctors with the convention group. I came across them on and off during my days of running my practice. Of course, I don't know any of the younger men. My, how time flies." His face reflected a pensive countenance, and I wondered whether he was thinking of his dead wife.

"Well, let's not dwell on bad things on a day like today," I jumped in before this turned into another talk of gloom and doom. Frankly, I'd had enough for one day and simply wanted to have some fun. "Professor, Chris and I were about to rent a jeep to drive around the island. Would you care to join us?" I expected the professor would welcome the company.

He seemed delighted at the idea. "If you young people don't mind an old fogey like me, I'd be pleased to come along."

Chris smirked. "Young people? I mean, c'mon, Professor! Mia's hardly a young person now, is she? But you're more than welcome to join..." His voice trailed off when he took in the thunderous look I threw at him. He cleared his throat and added, "What I meant to say was, although very good looking, Mia isn't a teenager like me. She's not old or anything..." He broke off again.

I laughed with the professor joining in. "Never mind, Chris," I reassured him. "Whatever you say, it's too late now. But don't worry, I know what you meant."

Chris sighed with relief and nodded toward the waiter. "Oh, good! Here comes the coffee."

~~~

We were back onboard ship by 4.00pm. The professor thanked us for a fabulous day and announced he was going to his cabin for a rest. Chris and I looked on as he hobbled away.

"Poor guy," Chris remarked. "I hope the jeep didn't rattle his bones too much. The suspension was a bit rough, don't you think?"

I nodded. "Well, at least I let him sit in front where it was more comfortable. Stuck in the back wasn't any fun for me, you know."

"Hey, I wasn't the one who invited him. So don't blame me," he protested.

"Don't get upset. I didn't mind him joining us. The poor thing lost his wife recently, and I hated to see him wandering around on his own."

Chris patted my shoulder. "Then, you did a good thing by asking him along."

"Anyway, I'm off to have a nap, seeing as I'm an old woman," I said pointedly.

Chris made a face. "You know I didn't mean it that way. I was only trying to say you're not as young as I am."

I waved a hand in front of his face in a dismissive gesture. "No matter what you say, it's too late to fix it now, kiddo. So let's leave it at that and I'll see you at dinner. I need to bring Dobbs and Smythe up to date with what Downes did, and we also have to check through Barry's belongings. I'll call Martha from my cabin and see if we can do it before we eat."

We made our way to our respective cabins and I was thankful we didn't bump into Smythe. I knew I'd have to see him this evening over dinner, but not looking messy and stinking hot, like I felt right now.

~~~

Martha Barry was more than cooperative and when Chris and I arrived at her cabin just before dinner, she had all of her husband's clothing and personal effects spread out on the bed.

"I thought this would make it easier for you to search," she said after greeting and inviting us in.

"That's great, Martha, thank you," I replied. "I really appreciate it, especially under the circumstances."

Martha regarded us with a spirited look. "Of course I'm grieved about Jim, but somehow I can't help thinking he got what he deserved for being a cheater."

I commiserated with her. "I can relate to a cheating husband. But you'll still find yourself grieving for the trust he betrayed."

Martha nodded. "Of course, you're right, Mia. I find myself going from grief to relief that I'm single again; and then back to grief. It's an awful way to be, but I'm sure in time I'll feel better."

I patted her arm in reassurance. "That's a definite. It takes time, but you'll come out much stronger in the end." I then referred to Chris. "You remember my young friend, Chris. He's helping with the investigation."

Martha smiled at him. "Yes. I may have been in shock last time, but I never forget a handsome young face," she addressed Chris with a sparkle in her eyes.

Chris blushed. "It's a pleasure to see you again, Mrs Barry."

"No need to be so formal, young man. Call me Martha."

He smiled. "Martha it is, then."

Martha returned his warm smile and went back to business. "If you're going to be a while, Mia, I'll go up to have a pre-dinner cocktail with Joy. Just slam the door shut when you leave."

"Will do. And we promise not to make a mess," I assured her. "But before you go, do you mind if we look inside the safe? There might be a document or something that could give us a clue."

Martha went straight to the safe, opened it, and took out all the contents. She then deposited them on the coffee table. "As you can see, it's mainly our passports and travellers cheques. But you're welcome to go through Jim's wallet."

Both Chris and I looked through the passports, the cheques, and a few receipts for purchases made on the trip. As we checked the items, I handed them back to Martha and she put them back in the safe. I then took out all the contents from Barry's wallet—credit cards, drivers' license, a few more receipts, some cash, and what looked like a few TAB betting slips.

"Your husband bet on horses?" I asked.

"Not in a big way," Martha answered. "But Jim liked to have the odd flutter now and then. Those are a couple of winning bets he never had a chance to cash in as we were coming on the cruise. He figured he'd cash them upon our return."

I looked at the names of the horses: "Adrenaline Rush" and "Neurotic Boy". Something inside me stirred. "Did any of Jim's friends have an interest in horses, as in betting or shares in ownership?"

Martha shook her head. "I don't really know. But they did like to bet from time to time."

"Do you know anything about these horses?" I persisted with my hunch, still holding onto the betting slips.

"No..." she said thoughtfully. "At least..."

"At least, what?" I felt a growing excitement, but didn't know why. I noticed Chris threw me a questioning look.

Martha looked pensive for a few moments before she spoke, "Well, this may not mean anything, but Bertie, I mean Dr van Horn, used to bet on horses whose names related to anything with medical or physiological terminology. My husband and his friends started to do the same thing. It became a bit of a game with them."

"Can you remember some of the other names they bet on?"

"Hmm. I never paid much attention. But some of the names were funny and rather clever. Let me see now..." She became pensive again, and I waited with barely concealed patience. "I remember Jim mentioning some of the names because he won on those particular bets at the time. In addition to the ones in his wallet, I remember Footloose, Deep Throat, Sally Pox, Abreast of Everything... and I think, Erotic Heart. They're the only ones I know of."

I kept my tone neutral even though I felt like shouting for joy. I was sure I'd just uncovered a clue. "Thank you, Martha. That's really helpful." I put all the items back into Barry's wallet and handed it to her.

"If you don't need me anymore," she said, taking the wallet from me, "I'll put this away and go to meet Joy while you finish up here."

I nodded and we said our goodbyes. As soon as Martha left, Chris turned to me. "What was that all about?"

I needed time to work things out in my mind before I told him, so I said instead, "Just give me a moment. First, let's look through his belongings."

Chris sighed impatiently and turned to the bed to start going through Barry's things. We checked his clothing, shoes, toiletries, and other ad-hoc items Martha had left out for us. We also looked around in drawers, cupboards, and the bathroom, in case Martha had missed something.

An hour later, we went back to my cabin and sat having a sparkling water from the mini-bar fridge while we rested before getting ready for dinner.

"Okay, Ms Ferrari, care to share what's in that devious mind of yours?" Chris said. "It's almost dinnertime and I'm starving."

I didn't want to keep the poor guy in suspense any longer so I finished my water and told him, "I have one of my feelings. Now, I realise this could mean zilch, but I'm pretty sure there's something to it."

Chris rolled his eyes. "Is there a point somewhere on the horizon?"

"Patience is a virtue," I teased him.

"And teasing someone like this could lead to murder," he returned with mock affront.

"Temper, temper!" I smiled, but immediately turned to business.

"Okay, here it is. When I first spoke with Martha, she told me about Barry's cheating and mentioned the cheaters' club. On one occasion, however, she referred to it as the 'erotics' club. So when I saw the name of the horse, *Neurotic Boy*, I got to thinking about the possible website van Horn had the password for. The initials were *NE*, remember?"

Chris nodded, now starting to look excited.

"This is why I asked Martha about the horses. I mean, it's a long shot, but when she started to rattle off those names, one of them was *Erotic Heart*. And then I thought, 'erotic' or 'erotics' plus 'neurotic'. You know, NE! So what if these initials stand for Neurotic Erotics?"

The look in Chris's eyes mirrored my own.

CHAPTER 12

I found myself seated next to the luscious Enrico Lotti at dinner, with Mike Yuen on my other side. Chris and I had been late in joining the others at the buffet restaurant and all the tables were occupied. When we arrived, we saw Dobbs toward the back of the dining room at a table with Smythe, Mark Evans, Enrico and Mike. Dobbs spotted us and waved, pointing to the two chairs they'd been saving.

"Thought you guys got left behind in Vila," Dobbs remarked cheerfully as he tackled a plate mounted with food of all sorts.

Chris and I set down our food trays on the table and I made sure to take the chair in between Enrico and Mike so Chris would sit between Mark and Dobbs. I noted the disappointment in Mark's gaze when I didn't sit next to him, but I didn't want to give Smythe anything else to criticise about me.

"No, nothing like that," I answered. "We had a few things to do before dinner."

Now was obviously not the time to tell Dobbs and Smythe about Downes's assault, but from the way they were looking at me I had a feeling Mark Evans had mentioned something. Of course, no one brought up the subject while there were others present, so we ate and chitchatted companionably. Every now and then, I caught a glance from either Dobbs or Smythe that told me something was definitely afoot.

I intended on enjoying my dinner, especially after the hot little clue I'd uncovered; although this had as yet to be confirmed. And judging from Chris's animated countenance, I knew he couldn't wait to get to his computer and start his search for the suspect website.

"How are things going with the convention?" I asked Enrico while the others engaged in a conversation about Vila and its attractions.

Enrico had finished his meal and was sipping on an espresso. He lifted the demitasse delicately to his lips with one pinky up in the air.

Then, he took a sip, which he savoured for a few moments, before finally placing the small cup back on its saucer. His green eyes turned to me, passion written in them. "With all the excitement on this trip so far, I think the doctors are getting rather nervous. But how exhilarating this is—no one knows who's going to be the next victim."

I frowned with concern at his comment and remembered we hadn't yet warned Weinstein. "What makes you think there's going to be a next victim?"

He waved a hand in the air to emphasise the drama of it all and his eyes grew larger as he moved closer to me and whispered in my ear, "Come on, Mia. You know there's a pattern here. Somebody's knocking off the doctors."

I threw him a wary look. "Is that what they all think? Aside from the man overboard, we haven't yet released any details about Dr Barry's incident." I didn't want to say any more as Enrico was still on my list of suspects, but I wondered how he knew that Barry had been murdered, especially since we asked Martha and Joy not to talk about it to anyone.

"Mamma mia!" Enrico threw his hands up in the air in grand Italian fashion. "Any fool can see what's happening here. You can't keep a secret for long, you know. People talk."

I speculated Martha or Joy could have let slip to someone that Barry had been murdered rather than killed in an accident. Or perhaps Enrico obtained the information from a crewmember. After all, he seemed to be sexually involved with one or more of them. As far as other passengers outside the convention group were concerned, however, the whole thing had been an accident; and we hoped to keep it that way. "Well, whatever the case may be, there's no evidence there'll be a next victim," I told him rather abruptly, putting an end to the conversation.

Enrico pouted and turned his attention back to his coffee. I could tell he was disappointed because he wasn't able to get any information from me to further fuel the gossip circulating among the convention members. I finished the rest of my dinner in silence and waited for our group to break up. The officers left to go back to their various duties as soon as they were done. Enrico followed suit after consuming another espresso while he threw sulky glances my way. When he finally departed, this left Dobbs, Smythe, Chris, and I to talk in peace.

"We know about Downes, Mia," Dobbs spoke as soon as the others left. "I say, throw his sorry ass in the brig!"

I smiled at his concern and shook my head. "Mark's obviously filled you in on what happened."

Dobbs nodded. "Of course. You didn't think he was just going to let it go, did you? He said you didn't want to report it."

My gaze slid over to Smythe. I could tell by the contrite look in his eyes that he felt bad about our argument of the previous evening. He'd thought I was having a fling with Mark Evans.

"I'm okay. Honestly," I answered, addressing Dobbs. "There was no harm done. Besides, I fixed the guy by kicking him in the balls. So I don't think he's going to be shagging anybody any time soon. I'd say he'll be too busy seeking medical advice for his sore privates."

Chris smirked at my comment, but Dobbs frowned. Smythe's look was hard to read.

"I told Mark I didn't want the guy charged," I continued. "I think we should keep an eye on him in case he's our killer. He certainly seemed to have the temperament for it; although I can't fathom what motive he'd have for knocking off his colleagues."

"In any case, we're going to pay the doctor a little visit," Smythe finally spoke up. "We'll let him know how lucky he is you didn't have him up for attempted rape. We'll also make it clear that if he comes anywhere near you again one of us will break his face."

The ferocity in Smythe's tone surprised me. "Police brutality, Smythe. I never thought I'd see it firsthand. Very arousing." I grinned and winked, taking refuge in humour. I didn't want him to think I was touched by his concern.

Dobbs threw me a serious look. "Ferrari, you do beat all, girl. I can't wait until we get to Hawaii so we can keep you away from these people. You could be in danger for sticking your nose where it's not wanted."

I glared at him, my good humour disappearing in a puff of smoke. "Hey! While I appreciate your concern, we're here to run an investigation. Besides, I'm not the only one in danger. Any one of you could be targetted. So lay off!"

"Yes, but you're a girl," Chris piped in. "And..." And the rest of his words withered away when he saw the look in my eyes.

"I can take care of myself, Chris. Now, let's change the subject and tell Dobbs and Smythe what we found."

Chris didn't need further encouragement and proceeded to fill in the other two on our theory about the "neurotic erotics" website, if indeed it existed.

Smythe regarded us with admiration in his eyes. "That was a good observation. You've done well."

Chris said, "It was Mia's theory, really."

"Yes," I interjected, "but I couldn't do without you and your computer skills. So let's just say we make a good team."

Chris blushed at my praise, but made a speedy recovery as he practically jumped up from his chair. "And on that note, I'm off to run a search."

"I'll come by later for a catch-up," I called out at his retreating form.

"That boy's a bright one," Dobbs commented. "He's going to make his father proud."

Smythe nodded. "I must admit I've been tough on Chris when Mia embroiled him in my past investigations, but the information he came up with proved to be invaluable."

I shot Smythe a look of derision. "*Embroiled?* Say what the real truth is, Smythe. How about 'Chris and I had to solve the case for the police'—and for this, you're grateful?"

Smythe regarded me tensely. "And how about: I saved your life not so long ago? I hope you're grateful for that at least!"

Dobbs made a "T" shape with his hands when he saw the look of affront on my face. "Time out, you two! How many times do I have to remind you that we're working together on this one? Wait until we get back home to wring each other's necks." He chuckled to himself and stood up. "I'm off to get some dessert. Your arguing makes me hungry."

When Dobbs moved out of earshot, I remarked with defiance in my voice, "If you're such a great cop, why haven't you come up with any clues yet? At least, Chris and I are making some headway."

Smythe's usual blue-green gaze seemed to turn a few shades darker. "You've got a real smart mouth, Ferrari. I'd keep it shut if I were you."

I stood up. "Well, it's a good thing you're not me, then. And by the way, you guys had better warn Weinstein, in case the killer should be in the mood to strike again." I gave him a dismissive look and walked off, leaving him alone with his thoughts, which I was fairly sure consisted of an image of him choking the life out of me for being a wisearse.

~~~

I made my way to the Promenade Deck to get some fresh air. After my little spat with Smythe, I couldn't focus and needed to cool off before I dropped in on Chris to check if he was making any progress on his search.

The deck was empty when I stepped out. At this time, most guests were either at dinner or gone on to see a show, so I had the whole deck to myself. The breeze cooled and soothed me, and the moon cast a magic aura by reflecting its silvery light onto the ocean. This was a night for romance and not one for thinking of archenemies. Against my will, however, my thoughts returned to Smythe. The man simply got under my skin. So much so, that I always felt like lashing out at him whenever I was in his company. What upset me even more was my reaction to his physical presence. The irony of this was that Smythe wasn't a younger man, like one of the bad boys I usually went for. He was only a few years junior to me, but nowhere near the "toy boy" category.

"I thought I'd find you here."

I turned toward the voice. Speaking of toy boys, here was Mark Evans, walking toward me. "It's a beautiful evening," I remarked as my heart skipped a beat. "I thought I'd come out for some peace and quiet."

Mark stood next to me, elbows on the balustrade of the viewing rail, gazing at the moon in the horizon. "Very beautiful indeed," he agreed. "I tried to get your attention at dinner, but it seemed you were having a heated discussion with Mr Lotti."

"Enrico likes hot gossip and was sniffing around. I put him in his place and he didn't like it."

A smile touched Mark's lips. "You seem to be doing a lot of that lately, Ms Ferrari. First, you kick Dr Downes into submission and now, you silence Mr Lotti with a few words." Suddenly, he laughed. "Good thing you didn't take a knife to the passionate Enrico!"

I conjured up an image of me, threatening the dramatic Enrico with a knife, and he holding his arms back in shock and begging for mercy. With his Renaissance looks, it was easy to picture this scene out of a Caravaggio painting. "I would never take a knife to Enrico. He's too good looking," I teased. "Besides, I don't see him as a killer. He's just a handsome guy looking for spicy gossip."

Mark turned, placed his arms around my waist, and drew me to him. "Then, thank God for me the very handsome Enrico is gay."

Before I could reply, his mouth found mine and we kissed deeply. My arms wrapped themselves around his neck and I brought my body closer to his. When we came up for air, Mark nuzzled my neck and whispered, "Come back to my cabin."

Oh, the temptation! Just the feel of this man's muscular body against mine was enough to compel me to throw caution to the wind and let him make love to me. All I had to do was say yes or simply nod. But something held me back despite my growing desire; and Smythe's image flashed into my mind to spoil the moment.

I gently disengaged myself from Mark. "I'm sorry, Mark, but it wouldn't work out," I explained while he regarded me with hurt in his eyes. "If this were a year ago, I wouldn't have thought twice about it."

"Then why—" he started to say.

I shrugged. "I can't explain it. I can only say after a long-term marriage gone wrong plus a crazy fling, I need time out." I shook my head, trying to find the right words. "The thing is I'm still confused. And much as I would love to go with you to your cabin, I don't think it's the right thing to do."

Mark looked disappointed but nodded with understanding. "I think I know where you're coming from, Mia. I'll let you be now. But if you change your mind, you know where to find me." He planted a gentle kiss on my lips and walked away, leaving me to my thoughts.

I must be growing soft with old age; I berated myself as I headed back inside the ship and made my way to Chris's cabin.

~~~

"Nothing yet," Chris reported when he opened the door at my knock, and then headed back to his computer. "Help yourself to coffee. I ordered some from room service."

I grabbed a cup and poured the liquid into it, savouring the aroma of the freshly ground beans. "How can that be?" I queried and took a seat on the bed next to Chris, looking at the screen of his laptop.

"I don't know," he answered. "I ran a search on 'neurotic erotics' and nothing came up. Then, I tried a few derivations, such as 'neurotic exotics', which turned out to be some sort of rock band. Nothing for 'nervous erotics' or 'nervous exotics'. Finally, I searched the words in different order, like 'erotic neurotics', 'exotic neurotics', and so on. Nothing there either."

I sensed his frustration. "We've only been speculating about the name of the site, you know," I pointed out. "It may not be a website after all."

Chris said with defeat in his voice, "That inscription could just be something really innocent, like the initials of van Horn's bank plus the password. God, it could be anything!" He sighed and slammed his laptop shut. "I need another coffee."

"It's getting late," I told him, glancing at my watch. "Let's start afresh tomorrow. We've got plenty of time now."

"What do you mean?" He turned to me, coffee cup in hand.

"We have four days at sea before we reach our next port of call at Pago Pago."

"True. Nothing much to do until then," he observed.

A knowing smile lit my face. "Except flirt with your girlfriend and search for whatever 'NE' means in between."

"Hey, I told you it was only a drink! Why do you have to read so much into it?"

Chris's defensive tone surprised me. "I'm sorry; I was only teasing. It's none of my business what you do."

He drank more coffee and waited for a few moments before he replied with a frown, "I'm the one who's sorry. I shouldn't be jumping down your throat. I really liked Julia, but she's not interested. I think she used me to make her ex-boyfriend jealous. He happens to be on the ship, too, by the way."

His confession, plus the look of vulnerability on his face, touched my heart. "Oh, Chris, I didn't know I hit a raw nerve. This girl doesn't know what a treasure you are; and so good looking, too!" I comforted him. "Why, if I were twenty years younger, I'd go for you myself."

This brought a smile to his face, but he corrected me. "Thirty,

Ms Ferrari. Try thirty years younger."

It was now my turn to frown.

~~~

I found it difficult to sleep even though it was past midnight. What with the offer to visit Mark's cabin plus the coffee I'd consumed with Chris, I paced my room for a long time before my nerves finally settled into some semblance of peace.

Both my body and mind were exhausted after the day's activities and the excitement of coming across a clue that I thought was the first real breakthrough to solving the murders. Then, there was the lingering reaction of shock after the attack by Downes; my run-in with Smythe; putting a stop to Enrico's attempt at pumping me for juicy gossip; and finally, the passion when Mark kissed me.

I now lay in bed, allowing myself to be lulled to sleep by the gentle rocking of the ship while I let all thoughts float past me. But before I knew it, I was enveloped in a sensation of arousal with Mark making love to me, and my body responding with excitement. Gone were all my inhibitions and feelings of confusion about having a fling. I had Italian blood running through my veins after all; and Mark was an attractive young man with a virility that stirred my senses.

We were in my bed with him kissing me wildly, our bodies perspiring with the sensual rhythm of our movements—the heat of our exchange drove me toward an explosive climax. I moaned with desire.

Just as I felt myself being enveloped in bliss, however, I was abruptly dropped onto a hard surface. The shock of this forced my eyes open. My mind cleared instantly; and I groaned with pain as I realised I'd fallen off the bed, the erotic dream still lingering in the nether regions of my memory. Loud knocking at my door soon dispelled everything else.

"Mia, Mia! Open the door!" Chris called loudly from outside and followed with more knocking.

I stumbled to my feet and made my way to the door, flinging it open; a tirade of abusive words ready to tumble from my lips. But when I saw the look on Chris's face, I uttered gravely, "Don't tell me. We have another murder."

CHAPTER 13

"This is getting to be a habit," I complained sleepily while I followed Chris to the Promenade Deck.

After Chris had alerted me to the murder, I jumped into a pair of jeans and pulled a windbreaker over a T-shirt. Within less than five minutes, we were on our way to the scene.

"Who called you?" I practically had to jog to keep up with Chris's stride.

"The captain alerted Dobbs, and he and Smythe went straight to the deck as soon as Dobbs knocked on my door. He said he tried your door, but you didn't answer."

"I must've been out like a light. What time was this?"

"Only about fifteen minutes ago."

"What time is it now? I'm not wearing a watch."

"Neither am I," Chris answered without breaking his stride. "But Dobbs knocked on my door at around 3.00am or so."

"Well, then it must be at least quarter past by now." I sounded somewhat puffed out. "Hey, slow down, will you? My legs aren't as long as yours."

Chris simply smirked. By this time, we had reached the lifts and stepped into the first one that arrived. Chris punched the number seven button and within seconds we exited onto Deck 7. I then followed him outside.

"I was here only a few hours ago, taking in the sea air," I remarked, thinking of the kiss I had shared with Mark.

Chris seemed to read my mind and gave me a saucy look. "Is that what you call it?"

My eyes threw daggers at him. "Oh, shut up!"

We made our way toward the stern of the ship where a group of men stood around something on the ground. When we reached them, I saw the "something" was a body lying face down with blood pooled around his head.

"Mia, Chris," Dobbs greeted us with a grave look on his face.

"This is Dr Hamish Weinstein. He was killed with a blow to the back of the head, possibly with a putting golf club. The killer seems to have cracked open the victim's head, which explains all the blood."

"How do you know who he is; where's the murder weapon; and who found him?" I addressed Dobbs, but the captain answered instead.

"Dr Weinstein was my late wife's surgeon." He looked distressed; but as far as I was concerned, he was still on my list of suspects. After all, Dr Weinstein had allegedly botched up the operation that killed Mrs Wilkins. Therefore, the captain had a strong motive.

"We caught the whole thing on CCTV this time," Smythe reported. "The killer flung the murder weapon into the ocean once he was done with it. It looked like a golf putter."

"We already viewed the footage and can confirm a putter was taken from the ship's putting green," Jerry Garcia added. "The body was found on a routine CCTV check carried out by one of the security guys at around 2.30am. Unfortunately, the killer wore a balaclava so we still can't ID him."

"All we know is he's still onboard," Mark Evans interjected. "He didn't get off in Port Vila, as we feared he might, and it looks like he still has more unfinished business."

I suddenly thought of Enrico Lotti and what he'd said about the convention members discussing who would be next. It made me wonder whether Enrico was trying to tell me something, or perhaps he was the killer. "You know, it would've been better if the killer had disappeared in Vila after all," I remarked. "We now have four days at sea before we reach Pago Pago, and you can bet everybody on the ship's going to wonder who's next—especially if our friend Enrico has anything to do with it."

"What do you mean?" Dobbs asked.

"He was already yapping that the convention members were speculating as to who would be next." I then added when I noticed Dobbs's querying look, "He told me all about it at dinner last night while he was fishing for gossip. I didn't comment, of course; and this seemed to piss him off. In any case, you can rest assured before long the whole ship's going to know we have a loose killer on our hands."

"Can't we throw Enrico in the brig?" Chris suggested.

Mark Evans said, "What, for gossiping?"

"Well, at least someone should have a talk with him and tell him to keep his mouth shut," Chris replied.

"Chris is right," the captain stated with a frown. "Things could get out of hand among the passengers if Mr Lotti starts talking."

"Dobbs and I will have a little chat with him to warn him off," Smythe offered and looked at Jerry Garcia. "With your permission, of course."

Garcia nodded. "No problem, Phil. But I'll come with you guys so I can threaten him with the brig. I want him to understand that creating panic on the ship can only be harmful. And if he's going to indulge in gossip to flame the fires, I'll personally lock him up and throw away the key."

Before Dobbs and Smythe could respond to Garcia's comment, I drew them aside. "Didn't you guys warn Weinstein he might be next?"

Smythe said, "We tried to have a quiet word with him after dinner, but he was either too drunk to care or he didn't believe us."

Dobbs added, "The guy was really in his cups, Mia. We even tried to broach this cheaters' website thing you're looking into and he ignored us."

"Most unfortunate," I replied, taking one last look at the victim. He should have listened to the warning. As for giving us information about the cheaters' site, it was now too late. "So what's happening with the body?" I asked, addressing the rest of the group.

"The doctor's on his way to take the victim straight to the morgue," the captain said and then turned to Dobbs. "We'll need to get through to the Honolulu police on this one, Guy. The murder was committed in international waters and, though we'll also talk to the police in Pago Pago, we should keep Honolulu up to date."

Dobbs agreed. "Don't worry, Captain. If we can get through via telephone, I'll make the report to my colleague over there."

"We should be able to pick up a satellite signal to make the call," Mark Evans answered for the captain.

"Okay." The captain turned to Smythe and Garcia. "If you can both stick around until the body's removed, Mark and I will go with Guy to make the call."

"And Chris and I will keep working on our end of the investigation," I chimed in, not to be outdone by the men.

We agreed to reconvene on the Bridge for a working lunch, at the suggestion of the captain, and then went on our way. Chris and I made for his cabin.

"We need to revise everything again, Chris. So far, every victim's connected to one or another person on this ship in terms of motive, but we still don't seem to have a common thread among the victims."

"I know," Chris replied, deep in thought. "I'm sure there's something linking all the victims to this 'NE' website."

"*If* it turns out to be a website." I sighed with frustration. "We haven't found it yet."

We completed the rest of our way to Chris's cabin in pensive silence.

~~~

It was close to five in the morning when Chris and I took a break from trying to guess what "NE" stood for. We sat at the small desk in his cabin, his laptop resting between us, and sipped on our third cup of coffee.

"If I don't eat something soon, I'm going to be sick," I complained, patting my stomach. "All this coffee's playing havoc with my tummy."

Chris put down his cup and picked up the phone. "I'll get room service. We need sustenance if we're going to keep going with this. Burger okay with you?"

I nodded tiredly. "I never thought I'd have a burger at this ungodly hour, but yes. And make sure they add plenty of fries to go with it."

Chris ordered the burgers, asking for extra fries, plus a couple of bottles of Pellegrino. We were both coffeed out by now.

"Okay," he said after he replaced the phone receiver. "As soon as we eat, we can return to our search."

I cast him a concerned look. "What if it means nothing? We could be barking up the wrong tree, you know. The 'NE' could very well turn out to be the initials for a bank or some other site that has nothing to do with the cheaters' club."

"True," Chris conceded. "Although, I doubt it."

"But we agreed to the possibility that NE could be van Horn's bank or something like it. So how come you changed your opinion?"

"Well, for starters, we don't have any banks in Australia with the initials 'NE'. At least, not that I know of."

"It could be some obscure credit union," I suggested. "Like the Newcastle Credit Union."

"Then, that would make the initials NCU," Chris returned.

"Probably." I tried to keep the disappointment out of my voice.

"Don't beat yourself over the head with this, Mia. We'll find it. I know we will," Chris said encouragingly.

"You're right, of course. Don't mind me, I'm tired and need to sleep."

"Then go and have a lie down after we eat. I can keep going by myself."

I eyed him with determination. "No way, Chris Rourke. I want to be here when we crack this thing."

Chris grinned. "You're one determined chick, you know that?"

I nodded. "Older chick, to you," I quipped.

He laughed. "You're not going to let me forget what I said earlier, are you?"

"About my not being twenty but thirty years older than you?"

He gave me a sheepish look for an answer.

"Well," I continued, "I may not be twenty years older than you, but I'm certainly not thirty. Not yet, anyway."

Chris did not answer. I had a feeling he valued his life too much. We therefore remained quiet, resting our eyes, until the food arrived. Once we started to eat, we became more animated.

"I was thinking," I said between bites of the scrumptious burger, "about the horses with the names that referred to something medical."

"And?" Chris shoved a bunch of fries in his mouth.

"And we have two options—either the website has something to do with horse betting, and this might be the common denominator with our victims. Or, some of the horse names Martha mentioned might have been used in a combination other than simply 'N' and 'E' to make up the name of the cheaters' club site. What I mean is that there may be more names involved than just those starting with the initials N and E."

Chris spluttered, almost choking on his food. "Good God! Why didn't we think of this before?"

I shrugged and kept eating.

"We don't know whether the latest victim was into betting,

although I'm sure I can find out easily enough," Chris said thoughtfully. "If this is the case, what we're looking for may well turn out to be some kind of online betting site."

"But if it's a cheaters' site instead, a combination of a few of the horses' names," I stated, "including 'Neurotic Boy' and 'Erotic Heart' could help us come up with the actual name of the site. I know you already tried several versions of 'neurotic erotics', but perhaps van Horn purposely left out something from the inscription in case someone went snooping through his things. Just a wild guess."

A look of excitement flashed in Chris's eyes as he put down his burger, wiped his hands with a paper napkin, and grabbed the laptop. "Okay. Let's look at 'neurotic boy and erotic heart' and combine them with some of the other horses' names." His fingers flew over the keyboard of his computer while I finished my burger and made a start on the fries.

I ate in silence for a few moments while I watched the expressions change on Chris's face. In the space of approximately ten minutes, they went from inspiration and hopeful excitement to frustration, and finally, vast disappointment.

"Nothing's coming up, I'm afraid," he reported, stopping the search. "There could be hundreds of combinations if we consider all the horses' names."

I sighed. "I think we should sleep on it. Perhaps, when we've had some rest, we'll be able to think more clearly."

"I guess so." As if on cue, Chris yawned. "I must say, I'm exhausted."

"Let's touch base in the early afternoon sometime. I'm skipping the lunch on the Bridge. I'm sure Dobbs will fill us in if something important comes up." I stood and stretched. "I'll give you a call later."

~~~

I awoke feeling refreshed, and after a cool shower I was ready to face the afternoon. It was almost four and I was positively starving. I called Chris from my cabin phone.

"Wh... what is it?" said a sleepy voice.

"You obviously missed the lunch with the boys on the Bridge and are in need of more sleep," I replied with amusement. "I keep forgetting how young people don't have much energy after all."

This got the reaction I was looking for. "Hey, watch it, Ferrari," he warned, sounding insulted.

I laughed. "It's good to see 'old folks' like me are good for something. I'll call you later." I hung up the phone just as he groaned in annoyance.

Afternoon tea with Professor Tully would be just the thing, I thought as I dressed in jeans and a white and red striped T-shirt. I hadn't seen the professor for a while and wondered how he was getting along.

I found him at his usual table enjoying lemon tea and mini strawberry tarts. I grabbed an assortment of pastries and a coffee from the buffet before joining him.

"My dear!" the professor greeted me with delight in his eyes. "How lovely to see you again. And I see you're rather hungry this afternoon." He motioned with his hand toward the plate I carried, which was almost overflowing with sweets.

"Good afternoon, Professor." I gave him a cheery smile. "I actually missed out on lunch. Late night, you see; and then I had to catch up with my beauty sleep."

He nodded while he sipped his tea. "Well, as always, you look young and full of vitality."

I put a hand over my heart. "Aw, you really know how to make a girl feel wonderful. Whatever happened to the gallantry of days gone by, I wonder?"

A slight frown marred the professor's face. "Dead and buried, unfortunately," he answered in a rather serious tone but did not elaborate.

I wondered whether an unpleasant memory had surfaced in his mind, but before I could follow up on this, he changed the subject altogether. "It seems there's a serial killer on the loose."

Now, it was my turn to frown. "Don't tell me Enrico's been going around spreading rumours." I thought by now Dobbs or Smythe would've warned him to keep his mouth shut.

The professor popped a strawberry tart in his mouth and waited until he swallowed it before he replied, "No idea where the rumour came from, but people are talking, Mia. The convention members are getting worried. I heard about Dr Weinstein, by the way. Tragic!"

I knew that sooner or later news of Weinstein's death would

have leaked out, but I hadn't expected for it to be so quickly. Perhaps, the body had been spotted as it was being transported to the morgue this morning. "Yes, it is tragic," I responded. It was no use denying the event had taken place. "As for a serial killer, however, I doubt it."

"How so? Three doctors have been murdered now."

"I'm not sure how the details are getting out and about, Professor; but irrespective, I don't believe we have a serial killer." He searched my eyes, and I further explained, "Generally, serial killers have the same MO. They kill in the same way, and some of them even take trophies. But in this instance, the victims are being killed in different ways."

"You mean because the first victim went overboard and the second looked like he tripped down the stairs?" The professor looked thoughtful.

"Yes." I didn't want to add any other details about the murders because there was no telling how much more the talk among the convention members would escalate. "Look, I'd rather we change the subject if you don't mind. Needless to say, the killings are being investigated."

I noticed the professor looked slightly put out, and I hoped I didn't give offence. But it wasn't my place to release any new information. I sipped my cooling coffee and remained silent, waiting for the professor to speak. He gave me a smile and said, "Of course, my dear. Please forgive an old man. I guess at my age, any kind of excitement is better than none."

I suddenly felt remorseful. "I'm the one who's sorry, Professor. I didn't mean to be abrupt. It's just that the captain doesn't want us to discuss the details of the investigation. As you can see, word gets around very quickly, and this can complicate matters."

He gave a little laugh and nodded. "I totally understand. So let's change the subject and put unpleasant thoughts behind us."

We went on to chat about the professor's days in practice and how he missed having Eden, his wife, helping him out.

"Is this why you gave up your practice?" I asked, marvelling that love could last a lifetime for some people.

There was a faraway look in the professor's eyes. "Not exactly. I was already teaching part-time at university for years, but I maintained the practice a little longer, until I could wind it down. I didn't want to abandon my long-term patients, you see. By the time Eden passed on, I was lecturing exclusively; but I miss coming home to her."

I gave him a kind look. "I guess after so many years of being together, you must feel desolate."

He turned a watery glance my way. "Yes, that's right. But what do you do after a lifetime of memories is taken away with the death of a loved one?"

I didn't have an answer for this, so I finished the coffee and pastries without responding. Both the professor and I gazed out to sea, wrapped in our own thoughts of loss.

CHAPTER 14

"**F**errari!" Dobbs called while I was walking along Deck 12 on the way to my cabin after I'd finished afternoon tea with Professor Tully. "Where the heck were you and Chris at lunch? We waited for you," he admonished as he caught up with me. We walked together past the Deck Grill and swimming pools, on our way to the inside foyer and lifts.

"Where's your shadow, Dobbs?" I couldn't help the sarcasm in my voice.

Dobbs rolled his eyes and sighed with frustration. "Okay," he declared, putting a hand on my shoulder. "I'm sick of this! I've had it; and it's about time I told you something I've been meaning to tell you for years."

It was only my surprise at his comment that kept me from pushing his hand off my shoulder while he steered me in the direction of a small internet café located near the door leading to the lifts.

"Feel like a coffee?" He didn't wait for an answer. "Go and grab a table. I'll join you in a moment."

The café was only a corner nook holding a few tables, mostly with computer monitors for those wishing to use the net. I headed to a small table at one corner of the room that did not have a monitor on it, but which provided us with a view of the ocean from a large window.

Dobbs returned with two cappuccinos and handed me one before he took a seat opposite me. "What; no protest for being railroaded from whatever you were up to?"

This brought a smile to my lips. "Don't be a smartarse."

He laughed deeply, his belly shaking. "That's rich coming from you, Ferrari. The attitude is probably rubbing off on me because I hang around you too much."

I shrugged nonchalantly. "No one's forcing you."

But Dobbs saw right through me, as he always did. "Hey, I know you're upset because I haven't had time to hang out with you and Chris, and because Smythe's along on this trip and you hate his guts." I went to reply, but he shushed me and kept talking. "I can't help the fact that my time's been absorbed helping out with this investigation, but I've come to the decision to give you one bit of information I should've given you a long time ago—only your father didn't want me to."

Of all the things I expected to hear from Dobbs, this was the last one—something to do with my father, who had now been dead for over ten years, and somehow involving Smythe. "What's my father got to do with any of this, Dobbs?" Even after so long, talking about Dad pierced my heart with a burning pain I could barely stand. Dad had gone quite young, riddled with bone cancer. He'd never reached sixty, like his best friend in the force who now sat opposite me.

"Mia..." Dobbs hesitated for a few seconds as if he didn't know how he was going to put this to me. I felt sudden concern.

"What's wrong, Dobbs? You're worrying me." I was on tenterhooks. My intuition told me whatever he was about to share with me would change something in my life that up until now had played a big part.

Dobbs sipped his coffee while mine remained untouched. I drummed my fingers impatiently on the tabletop, waiting for him to continue. He put his cup back down on its saucer and looked straight into my eyes. "Okay, here it goes. Your application to the police force was not rejected because of anything Smythe did. It was a bit more complicated than that."

It took me a few moments to recover my power of speech at this bit of news, but when I could speak, I exclaimed, "What are you saying? Of course Smythe was the one who convinced them not to take me on. My father told me so!" Anger started to bubble away inside me.

Dobbs shook his head. "Rosario—Ross—didn't want you to know the truth. He thought you'd think badly of him."

My eyes flashed as I banged my fist on the table, attracting curious looks from a couple of patrons in the café. I took a moment to compose myself and lowered my voice on purpose, even though all I wanted to do was to scream. "You're confusing me, Dobbs! You better tell me straight out what in blazes is going on."

Dobbs drained his cup. My coffee still remained untouched. He eyed it, and I shoved it across the table toward him. He took a sip from it, frowned because it was lukewarm by now, and put the cup back down. "You knew Ross was passed over for promotion and Smythe got the job instead. Since that time, they never saw eye to eye on anything; and they had a number of run-ins after this."

I nodded. "Yes, I knew that. Dad told me he hated working for a younger man, and that Smythe was an arsehole."

"Well, what you don't know is that around this time Ross found out about his illness. He didn't want to tell you yet and made me swear I wouldn't say anything. But he changed, Mia. He was angry at life and very bitter. Of course, I don't blame him for feeling this way; but he took it out on Smythe. I guess he felt Smythe robbed him of the chance for promotion and that he now had little time left to do anything else in the force. So to cut a long story short, Ross received a few disciplinary letters because of his antagonism toward Smythe."

I was stunned and remained silent as Dobbs proceeded to reveal more of the story.

"When you went in for your interview, the recruitment panel made a bad decision. They were against you because they believed you'd end up being just like your dad. In those days, things were quite subjective when it came to recruitment, especially where it concerned women." Dobbs paused as if gathering his thoughts, and then continued, "They turned you down, Mia—and contrary to what you believe it was Smythe who actually tried to convince them to change their minds. He knew about Ross's illness and understood why your old man was having so many problems. But like me, he also respected your dad's wish to maintain silence over his health issues. In the end, though, Smythe could only push so much against the panel's decision, and they ended up overruling him."

I placed my elbows on the table, my head between my hands, and my eyes gazing straight into Dobbs's. "So you're telling me because of Dad's declining health, his work performance suffered. As a result, he had run-ins with Smythe. On top of this, because of those run-ins, he received disciplinary warnings and the recruitment panel was biased toward my joining the force because they thought I would have the same attitude as Dad. Smythe, who knew about the illness but couldn't divulge the true reason for Dad's attitude, tried to persuade the panel to give me a chance, but they rejected me all the same. Right?"

Dobbs nodded, a grave look in his eyes. "I admit the department treated your father badly, but Ross didn't want to escalate the situation. He knew his time was short and he made me promise to stay silent."

"But why? I would never have condemned him. It wasn't his fault the bloody cops turned me down!"

"I know. But he didn't see it that way."

I sighed with exasperation. "And if Smythe knew all this time, why did he let me go on believing I missed out on a police career because of him?" I knew the answer even before Dobbs told me, but I didn't want to feel beholden to Smythe.

"He had too much respect for Ross," Dobbs echoed my thoughts. "He didn't want to cause you pain, either. He knew your dad was ill and that he hadn't told you as yet. So he played the part of the baddie. And I guess afterwards it was all too late to do something about it."

I felt close to tears for my dad, for Dobbs, and even for Smythe. They'd all kept this a secret to try to protect me from knowing about how my father felt. As a result, I'd gone on believing Smythe was the one who had influenced the recruitment panel against me, hence the reason I hated his guts. Now, I felt mortified.

"This happened so long ago," I uttered in a hoarse whisper. "Why didn't Daddy tell me he found out he was ill at the time? Why did he want to keep it a secret for longer than necessary?"

Dobbs reached across the table to rest a hand upon mine. "For what it's worth, he was told there was a small chance that they could do something about treatment. So he didn't want to worry you unnecessarily. Then, when the doctors tried everything and couldn't help him, he was forced to tell you. But he couldn't bring himself to explain the panel's decision about you. He knew it was due to his own attitude toward Smythe, and that this was the strongest factor influencing them against your application."

I freed my hand and ran shaky fingers through my hair. "I need time to digest all this, Dobbs." I smiled weakly. "Thank you for telling me. But why now?"

"Because I'm fed up seeing you and Smythe going at it all the time. I thought you'd get over your antipathy eventually, but you didn't. So I had to tell you." Suddenly, he grinned. "It's amazing what the ocean air can do for one's conscience, huh?"

He stood, patted me on the shoulder, and went on his way.

~~~

I didn't want to deal with what I had just learned. Therefore, I went straight to my cabin and telephoned Chris.

"I was just about to call you," he said when he picked up. "Where were you?"

"Caught up with Dobbs."

"Any news?"

"Actually, we didn't talk about the investigation. We chitchatted, that's all," I said, not wanting to reveal the subject of our discussion. "Look, it's getting close to dinnertime." I glanced at my watch and saw it was almost five. "What say you we stay in, order room service, and keep working on finding this elusive website? I really don't feel like socialising tonight."

"Works for me," Chris replied. "I couldn't be bothered getting all cleaned up for dinner."

"So you'd rather stink up the cabin?" I jested.

"No, silly! I meant getting dressed up. I'm comfortable in a T-shirt and shorts right now, but I assure you they're clean."

"Okay. I'll come over at six. How's that?"

"Perfect," he said. "But tonight, we're ordering pizza."

"Nothing could please me more. See you soon." I rang off and headed for the shower. I needed to wind down, and the hot water would help relax my tense muscles.

After a long shower, I dried off and slipped into khaki shorts and a white T-shirt. Then, I made my way to Chris's cabin and we ordered two pizzas, a ham and pineapple for me, and a pepperoni for Chris.

We sat at his desk while Chris powered up the laptop. "I thought we'd run a search using all the horse names at once instead of trying combinations of them."

I nodded. "Excellent idea."

Chris tried this, but still didn't come up with anything except for a number of porn sites with some very explicit videos and photos that picked up namely on the words 'deep throat' and 'erotic'. For a while, Chris seemed glued to the screen of his laptop; and I began to feel rather uncomfortable.

"Um... shouldn't we try something different? I don't think this is where you'll find any clues."

Chris managed to peel his eyes off the screen. "What are you talking about? Any of these sites could belong to the cheaters' club."

"But there are no names, no blogs, and no comments. So we won't be able to find any worthwhile information, except for a whole lot of filth." I didn't mean to sound prudish, but this was how it came out.

Chris smiled. "You disappoint me, Ferrari. I thought you liked hot sex."

I glared at him. "What? Where the hell did you get that impression?"

"Well...er... You know... The younger men and such..." A shade of red started to creep up his face.

I slapped the back of his head. "Hey! Just because I sometimes like younger men doesn't mean I'm into porn. Now, start a new search or I'm leaving. I didn't come here to watch porn movies, Chris Rourke!" I stood with the intention of walking out.

Chris shut down the site he'd been leering over and threw me a penitent look. "Sorry. I kind of lost my head."

"You'll lose more than that if you keep watching such crap!"

"And what's that supposed to mean, Ferrari?" He challenged me.

I warned him in a serious tone, "You'll become a sex pervert that plays with himself."

Chris exploded into laughter and couldn't talk for a while. Thankfully, the pizzas arrived at that moment and this broke the tension between us. I answered the door and signed for the pizzas; then deposited them on the coffee table.

"Let's eat, shall we?" I said in my normal tone, grabbing a couple of small plates from the mini-bar and some paper napkins.

Chris joined me and took a seat on one of the stuffed armchairs that were placed on either side of the table. I sat on the other one, and we started to eat.

"Any Coke?" Chris was himself again.

I got up and took two cans out of the small fridge.

"Thanks," Chris said as I handed him one.

We ate without talking for a few minutes. Then, Chris said, "I'm sorry, Mia. I guess it's a guy thing. Anyway, I promise I won't turn into a sex pervert and play with myself." He couldn't help the smile on his lips as he spoke.

I grinned. "I'm sorry, too. I shouldn't have overreacted. You'd think working in a hotel that's located in the red light district I would have seen it all. I really don't know what came over me." But I did know. It was the unsettling information I had learned from Dobbs. Suddenly, I was overcome by grief for my dad again; but this time, nursing a new hurt because he hadn't felt he could confide in me about what had happened with the recruitment panel. I also felt mortified for how I'd behaved toward Smythe all these years.

"Mia?" Chris waved a hand in front of my face. "You okay?"

I managed a smile. "Yes, of course. It must be all these murders on my mind."

"Well, let's get back to it. We can eat while we work."

We did this, and time flew. By eleven, we were spent. We'd tried all we could think of, but nothing of interest came up.

Chris rang room service for fresh coffee as we had already consumed a whole jug of it earlier. While he did this, I played around on the laptop, entering different search words in Google. On impulse, I added the word "horse". I came up with a mix of results, most of them to do with horse breeding, racing, and betting. Then, something jumped out at me. It was an article about horses that had won the Melbourne Cup over time. I clicked on the link and it took me to a list of the actual horses that had won the famous race in the last thirty years. I scanned the list of names, not really knowing what I was looking for. At least, none of the horses Martha had told us about had run this particular race. Then, I saw it.

"What is it?" Chris noticed the look of incredulity in my eyes.

I turned to him, trying to quell my growing excitement. "This is really farfetched, of course, but you may call it one of my hunches. Look at the name of this horse." I pointed on the screen to a particular horse, which had raced in the early '90s.

"Superimpose," Chris read out the name. "Yeah, so?"

"So think of the meaning of the name—when you superimpose one thing over another, you see something different. This could be a drawing over another drawing or a string of words over another. The way you look at it changes its meaning."

Chris looked confused. "Okay, but I don't see what this has to do with 'NE' or the names of the horses we've been searching."

"That's right. It has nothing to do with it." My eyes sparkled, and I couldn't wait to try out my theory.

"Man, what drugs are you on? Because I'd like to take some, too."

I cocked an eyebrow at his smart comment. "Focus on this: the inscription we found in van Horn's book was NE PW NE1952."

Chris nodded. "Yes, and?"

"And we've been looking for a site that has at least two words— one beginning with the letter N and the other with the letter E. We also tried the inscription itself as a URL earlier on with no results." This was the first thing we'd tried after we discovered the inscription in van Horn's notebook, all the while knowing it couldn't possibly be that easy. "What would you say if we 'superimposed' the order of the characters in the inscription?"

I looked on in silence as realisation dawned on Chris's face. "My God! Why didn't we think of this before?"

"Because we focused too much on the order in which the line was written. But if you superimpose the inscription over itself, or rotate it back to front, you'd get 2591EN WP EN."

Chris shoved me out of the way and planted himself in front of the laptop. He typed in the URL: www.2591EN.com.au, and a sign-in page came up only asking for the password. He entered EN. An error message came up, telling us password was incorrect. Chris tried again with WP and was unsuccessful. He then tried WPEN; and when this didn't work, he entered ENWP. Again, no success.

"Try 'eroticneurotic'," I suggested.

He did this, and suddenly a new page came up prompting us to enter the username. We held our breath. "We're almost there! The site seems to have accepted the password, but what is the username? What does 'WP' stand for, I wonder?" Chris ran frustrated fingers through his hair.

"Well, if you look at it logically, it should stand for the word 'password', but the other way around—first word last, last word first," I answered.

"Aw, c'mon, Mia. That doesn't make sense," he argued. "Besides, we already guessed the password. It's the username we need now."

"But it worked with the actual password, didn't it? It was the reverse order of 'neurotic erotic'. So we must presume van Horn also reversed the order of the words for 'PW', which is hopefully the username. Therefore, 'WP' should stand for 'wordpass'."

Chris looked skeptical but followed my advice, entering the word I suggested in the username prompt. As soon as he hit 'enter' the page changed to a dark purple colour and a button reading 'Click to enter' appeared at the bottom of the screen.

"Yes!" Chris exclaimed excitedly as he clicked on the button to enter the site.

The page changed to a deep midnight blue; and with delighted looks on our faces, Chris and I read the words that flashed before us in large white letters: "Welcome to the Neurotic Erotics Club".

CHAPTER 15

Chris and I spent a long time in front of the laptop, our eyes glued to the screen while we scrolled through the website. The purpose of the site was "To unite members of the medical community and their spouses or partners in order to explore the delights of illicit liaisons and other sexual practices."

"It's a forum," I remarked, looking at the summary page that was full of discussion threads.

"And it has chat rooms as well." Chris pointed to an icon at the bottom of the screen where members could enter into public or private chats.

I glanced through some of the thread topics: spouse swapping; threesomes; men with men; women with women; fetishes; S&M; interracial; oral sex; anal sex; hardcore; illicit liaisons; and the list went on.

"Good God!" I exclaimed, my eyes still on the screen. "Where do we begin?" The task of finding a common thread for the victims was going to be immense if we had to explore the whole site and all its threads—not to mention the members would have avatars hiding their true identities.

"Since Martha mentioned a cheaters' club, I would start with 'illicit liaisons'," Chris suggested. "But before this, let's look at who the administrator is." With a few strokes of the keyboard, Chris went into another screen that told us the administrator was Neurotic Boy.

"Great! So how the hell do we confirm Neurotic Boy is really van Horn?" I sighed with frustration, still taking in all the information we would have to wade through. And this was only a hunch. We could very well be barking up the wrong tree.

"Seeing as Martha was the one who overheard the conversation about van Horn running the cheaters' club, we have to assume Neurotic Boy is van Horn," Chris's voice cut into my thoughts.

"True; but we also know Neurotic Boy is the name of a horse, which Barry bet on. So who's to say Barry is not the administrator?"

"Let's not worry about this just yet. I'll need a bit of time to trace the site back to the real identity of the owner," Chris pointed out. "For the time being, let's have a look at some of the entries and see if something jumps out at us."

I agreed and we spent the next two hours reading a huge amount of threads within the topic of illicit liaisons. By around 1.00am, my eyes started to close. "I think we're going to have to stop soon, Chris. We read so many threads, my head's spinning. Plus we didn't even find anything that sounds familiar."

Chris ignored my comment. "Look at this one." He went on to read from one of the threads. The comment was from someone who called themselves *Multiswitch*. "I had the wildest experience recently, and we did it in my husband's surgery. Of course, it was after hours. He went off with a few of his friends to shoot some golf balls— boring!—while I shot some *golf balls* of my own—much more exciting! Two of my husband's colleagues and I had a threesome in his office. One man had me sit in front of him with my legs spread open while the other one putted golf balls my way to see if he could shoot a *hole in one*... if you know what I mean (blush, blush). Needless to say, one ball found its way in with a little bit of help from the guy who held me. Oooh! Now I know what it's like with those exotic Thai dancers who shoot ping-pong balls out of their... you-know-what. LOL. Golf balls feel much firmer. Mmmm." When Chris stopped reading, he looked my way.

"Charming," my tone was full of disgust. "Some people are really sick!"

"Hey, whatever happened to 'live and let live'?" Chris smirked.

"Whatever turns them on, Chris. I don't care what they do, but to write about it and be so glib. It's heartless, I tell you. This bloody tart's cheating on her husband with not one, but two men, and she's got the nerve to share it for all the world to see. What the hell is the matter with these people?" I hated cheaters. There was no excuse whatsoever to cheat on someone. If a person wasn't happy in their marriage or wanted to have sexual relations with others, they should at least have the balls—no pun intended—to put an end to their current relationship before cheating with someone else. Only cowards, like my ex, cheated behind their spouse's back. Why?

Because they had no cojones!

"Wow! Talk about hell hath no fury like a woman scorned," Chris remarked, still smirking.

I turned on him and exclaimed in an impassioned tone, "What do you know about the pain of betrayal and dealing with people whom you thought you could trust?" I stopped and drew a deep breath to calm myself. Chris looked surprised at my outburst. "I'm sorry. Put it down to my Italian blood. But I feel strongly about some things."

"I'll say! But, Mia, you forget my mum cheated on my dad. So I do know a little about betrayal."

"Touché." I thought back to Chris's mother, Elena, and how she'd spent most of her married life to David cheating with other men and barely caring about her own son. I was more of a mother to Chris than Elena had ever been. I sighed, this time with exhaustion. "Look, I'm going to get some sleep. If you want to keep working, try to find the identity of the site administrator and while you're at it, see if you can identify this *Multiswitch* person. She mentions a golf putter, and this could mean something. We can continue going through more threads tomorrow."

Chris nodded. "Okay. I'll catch you sometime in the morning."

I bade him goodnight and left. Then, just as I was about to unlock the door to my cabin, another door opened on the opposite side of the passageway and Smythe's head popped out. "I thought I heard your voice," he said. "We missed you at dinner."

I was about to deliver one of my smart comments, accusing him of spying on me, when I suddenly remembered my talk with Dobbs. I stopped myself just in time and gave him a smile instead. It was time to face the music.

"Chris and I made a bit of a breakthrough," I explained. "So we ended up having room service in his cabin."

Smythe shot me a look of surprise. He had probably been expecting a tirade from me instead of civility. "Oh."

"I was just heading for bed but if you have a few moments, I can bring you up to date with what we found."

The look of surprise hadn't left his face when he replied, "Just give me five and I'll change and join you." He closed his door softly.

I went into my cabin and left the door ajar so he wouldn't have to knock when he came over. It was obvious Smythe was confused by my friendly manner. I felt a smile on my lips, which felt quite dry after eating pizza. I quickly brushed my teeth in the bathroom and made myself more presentable. I looked tired, but with a little powder and lipstick I soon restored some semblance of order to my ravaged looks.

"Mia?" Smythe called out before he walked in.

He'd called me Mia instead of Ferrari. I was ready to go easy on him after what I'd learned, but calling him Phil would be a huge leap for me just now. "Come on in," I said as I came out of the bathroom. "Do you want some coffee?"

"No, but thanks," he replied and took a seat when I motioned him toward one of the plush chairs by the coffee table. "So what did you find?"

I took a seat on the adjacent chair and told him about the Neurotic Erotics' site. "As you know, Chris and I believe there's a common link among the victims," I explained. "So we stuck with the search. Of course, it's going to take some time to come up with something, if anything. There are so many threads, you see." I went on to tell him about some of what we found but left out the comment about the golf balls. Just the thought of what the woman wrote was enough to make me blush to the roots of my hair. Plus talking "sex" with Smythe was not something I was ready to do.

"It sounds like you guys are making great strides," he commented. "Meanwhile, we can't find anything worthwhile. We must've watched the CCTV footage a thousand times, and all we keep coming up with is that the killer is definitely the same perpetrator. You know; same gait, same height, build, and so on. But beyond this, we have nothing. No prints, no murder weapon, and no witnesses." He sighed, looking as tired as I felt.

"Well, whoever's killing these doctors must have one huge grudge. We still have a number of suspects, of course, but we've yet to connect the victims who've been targetted. This is why the cheaters' club might provide us with a reason for motive."

Smythe regarded me thoughtfully. "You mean the victims could all be members and supposedly cheating on their spouses?"

"Yes. We already established this when Martha Barry overheard her husband talking with Cliff Downes. According to Martha, van Horn, Downes, and her husband belonged to the club."

"Okay, but it doesn't make sense," Smythe remarked. "Let's

assume Martha killed her own husband, why would she kill the other two? Besides, we established the killer is a male."

"Yes, I know. And you're right, it doesn't make sense that Martha would go after the others when only her husband was her concern as far as the cheating went." I scratched my head absently as if this would help me discover the answer to the mystery. "We may be looking in the wrong place, of course, but if there's some kind of clue on the site that can help with the investigation, Chris and I will do our best to find it."

Smythe glanced at his watch. "It's getting late and we're both tired. Why don't we get together with Chris and Dobbs over a late breakfast and continue this discussion?"

We stood. "Good idea," I concurred. Then, as he started to walk toward the door, I said, "Wait. There's something else I need to tell you."

He stopped and looked questioningly at me. He didn't speak but waited patiently while I gathered my thoughts.

"Well... it's like this... I mean..." I didn't know how to say it.

"What is it?" he asked softly, taking a step closer to me. "Are you okay? Did Downes try something on you again? Because if he did, I'll—"

"No, nothing like that," I reassured him. Then, I blurted out, "Dobbs told me what really happened when my application to the force was rejected. He said it was because of my dad and nothing to do with you. He wanted to set the record straight seeing as all this time I've been under the misapprehension that you were responsible. Now, I know it was never you. And so, I wanted to say I'm sorry. I just wish someone had told me sooner."

An indiscernible emotion crossed Smythe's face. "Ross was a good man, Mia. Despite the fact that we had our differences, I respected him too much to say anything to you while he was alive. Then, after he passed, you seemed to have made up your mind about me. Plus Dobbs told me your dad didn't want you to know what had really happened—you know, that a few of the panel members were biased because of those disciplinary instances on Ross's record. Anyway, I didn't think it was my place to tell you otherwise."

"Yeah, but all this time you let me go on, hating your guts," I argued. "Generally, I'm not such a bitch, you know."

He smiled then. "Well, how about we call a truce now? And

perhaps we can be friends."

The idea sounded foreign to me, but Smythe was right. There was nothing stopping us from being friends—or at least, civil to each other. "Only on two conditions," I said with a smirk on my lips. He raised a querying brow. "One, I don't have to call you, Phil; and two, I can still appear to be a bitch. After all, I have a reputation to maintain."

Smythe laughed and nodded. "You're on, Ferrari. And now, I bid you goodnight." With this, he exited the cabin and closed the door behind him.

I felt relief at having set things straight between us. But my thoughts were in turmoil about our future friendship. I instantly recalled how safe I had felt when I lay in his arms not so long ago—when he'd saved my life—and how my body tingled when he gazed at me with those blue-green eyes. I knew I was on shaky ground.

~~~

I slept fitfully, my sleep haunted by dreams of my father and his bombshell secret; plus Smythe and our future friendship. I tossed and turned, torn between the pain of grief for my dad and sexual desire for someone I'd tried my best to hate. In fragments of my dreams, I argued with my father at the unfairness of what he'd created by keeping his secret. Then, the dream changed to my lying in Smythe's arms while unconscious, and my father's voice telling me from somewhere in heaven that "he'd keep me safe", meaning Smythe.

Later, I was in Mark's arms, kissing him passionately; but when I looked at his face it wasn't Mark's, but Smythe's face that I saw. Then, the dream changed to a woman who looked like me, sitting naked on a carpeted floor and resting against Smythe's body, which was also naked. Mark Evans stood a few feet away from us, dressed in his undershorts and about to hit a golf ball my way. Before he could do so, however, Smythe's body covered mine and we sank back down on the floor while I opened myself up for his delicious invasion.

Thankfully, I jerked awake; my skin feeling clammy despite the air-conditioning in the cabin. I looked at the bedside clock—it was gone past eight. I had expected to sleep in until at least nine, but with the troubling thoughts going around in my mind, plus the disturbing dreams, I decided to get up and shower.

I expected to meet the others for a late breakfast around ten, so I took the time to compose myself. Meanwhile, I also berated Chris in my thoughts for reading out the woman's comment about the golf balls.

CHAPTER 16

We ended up meeting for a very late breakfast in Horizons. It had just gone eleven so it was more like brunch. While we ate, Chris gave us a rundown on how we'd discovered the site, mainly for Dobbs's benefit as I'd already related most of this to Smythe when we met in my cabin. Like me, Chris had the good sense to leave out the bit about the golf balls.

"Anyway," Chris remarked, "after Mia left, I kept working, trying to identify the administrator of the site. Unfortunately, the satellite signal must've been weak because the connection kept dropping. So after a number of attempts, I gave up. I'll get back to it after we eat."

"So where are we up to with all of this right now?" Dobbs asked.

I answered for Chris. "We're going to see whether the victims participated in any of the threads. This would establish a common denominator."

Smythe observed, "That's going to take a lot of work, especially since you told me there are so many threads in the forum."

I gave him a shy smile. I wasn't yet used to a "nice" Smythe. "Exactly. So Chris and I will be very busy beavers."

"At least the sexy comments will keep us awake," Chris dared to put in.

I kicked him under the table and he did his best not to cry out in pain as my foot made contact with his shin. "Don't worry." I looked from Dobbs to Smythe. "I'll make sure Chris doesn't read any X-rated material."

"Hey!" Chris protested. "I'm not a child, you know." He then leaned forward and started to tell Smythe about the golf ball comment.

I couldn't stop him so I drew Dobbs's attention away from the conversation and told him, "I ran into Smythe early this morning, when I left Chris."

Dobbs's look of mirth told me he was enjoying the situation. "Yes, he told me you were rather cooperative for a change," he replied, and added when he saw the look of thunder in my eyes. "No, I'm not teasing you, Ferrari. Smythe was really pleased that you guys cleared the air. He said he looks forward to working with you."

I shot him a suspicious look. "If this is his way of trying to butter me up—"

"He really meant it, girl. So get that look off your face." He then threw me a warm smile. "And I'm glad I did the right thing by telling you. I think we all make a pretty good team; and now we can truly work together without my having to smooth the path between the two of you."

"Hmm." I decided to hold judgement on that one. I turned to Chris instead, who had just finished telling Smythe the spicy tale of the golf ball lady. "Can we get back to business here?" I said rather firmly.

Chris gazed back at us with an official air. "As I've said before, as soon as we're done with breakfast I'm off to see whether I can get a signal so I can keep working."

"What about you two?" I addressed Dobbs and Smythe.

"Phil and I have a meeting with Jerry Garcia," Dobbs answered. "Despite our warning to your fancy boy, Enrico, not to gossip, it seems the convention members are talking about nothing else and things are getting out of hand."

I rolled my eyes. "He's not my fancy boy, Dobbs."

"Well, whatever the case, Garcia suggested we have a group discussion with the convention members to tell them to stop speculating and gossiping. The last thing we want is panic to spread through the whole ship."

Smythe added, "We're also going to give them some security tips so they can stay safe."

"You mean not to wander alone, especially late at night or early in the morning?" I remarked, not at all hopeful this would work.

He nodded. "Yes, among other things. Until we catch this killer, we need to ensure we can keep him from striking again."

"Well, we have another two days at sea before we reach Pago Pago. I hope the murderer's not planning another kill even as we speak," I stated. "It's obvious the most dangerous time is when we're at sea." I frowned with concern, and it seemed the others echoed my sentiments because we ate in silence until we finished our meals.

"I'm off." Chris was the first to speak. "Mia, let's catch up in the afternoon so we can keep working through the threads."

I nodded and Chris left the table. "I'm going to talk to Martha Barry again. She may be able to remember something more." I stood to leave.

"Shall we meet for dinner?" Smythe suggested. "We can have another catch-up then."

Dobbs nodded. "I'm in."

"Yeah, why not?" I said. "Let's go to the buffet restaurant so we can seat outside. It's lovely sitting at the back of the ship away from the breeze and gazing at the night sky." I didn't know why I suggested this. Smythe was going to think I was in a romantic mood. But it was too late; it was already out there and I couldn't take it back.

"Good idea," Dobbs replied. "Say around eight?"

"Done." I hurried away, feeling Smythe's eyes on my back.

~ ~ ~

"Mia, so glad you suggested we meet up," Martha greeted me when I joined her and Joy Gerard at The Mariners' Hub. "Only yesterday, Joy and I were saying we haven't seen you for a while."

I took a seat opposite them and ordered a fruit cocktail from the waiter who glided over to me. The ladies were enjoying iced coffees.

"I've been keeping busy with all that's been going on," I explained. "Then, I learned Enrico's been going around talking about the killings, and the word is convention members are now taking bets as to who is going to be next."

Joy sniffed. "That Enrico is nothing but trouble, I tell you. I think it's a good thing he never stayed on working at the hospital."

I gazed at Joy with interest. "You know all about that?"

"Of course!" She harrumphed as if disgusted with Enrico. "I believe he's told everyone on this ship, including all the crew. Well, what can you expect from someone who's bed hopping his way through all the gay males onboard?"

Martha laughed. "Oh, Joy! You have such a way of putting things. What the young man does is his business."

Joy glared at Martha. "All the same, when he goes around telling tales of woe about his hard-done-by life he makes everybody feel uncomfortable. Besides, he could be the killer playing a game of cat and mouse with us all."

Joy's comment reminded me not to discard Enrico as a suspect in the investigation; but then, we also had Mike Yuen and the captain. Martha seemed an unlikely suspect by now plus my gut told me she was not the killer type. "Ladies, let's not talk about Enrico anymore; but at the same time, let's not give him more ammunition he can use to cause panic among the group."

"You're right, Mia," Martha concurred. "It's just that many of the members in our group are truly panicking. After all, the victims have all been doctors so far."

She didn't look too upset when she said this considering her own loss, so I ventured to ask, "This is what I wanted to see you about, Martha. Aside from what you told me so far, is there anything, no matter how small, you think may be of help?"

Martha looked from me to Joy and back to me again. "Not that I can think of at the moment. I already told you about overhearing the phone conversation with Cliff Downes. And then you found the horse racing betting slips. I gave you the names of the horses I remembered; and that's pretty much it."

I sighed with disappointment. It really didn't look like Martha was going to be able to offer any more help so I changed my line of questioning. "Regarding Cliff Downes, what do you know about him?" Perhaps, Martha could shed some light into the despicable Dr Downes.

Martha shrugged. "Not much. He played the odd game of golf with Jim. We didn't really socialise with him outside the hospital." She paused and thought for a while. "I know he's considered a bit of a looker by the ladies, and he's always seen with a different woman."

"And you're positive he's in this cheaters' club?"

She nodded. "As far as I know. I mean, Jim was talking to him about this on the phone conversation I overheard. So I'd say yes."

"But he's married, right?"

"Who knows with him," Joy interjected. "It seems his marriage is already on the rocks, hence his wife's absence. Whatever he told you, Mia, is probably a lie. He's tried to crack onto practically every woman here on the ship."

This was news to me. "Oh?"

Joy didn't need encouragement to keep talking. "And he doesn't seem to discriminate between younger and older women. He tries it with all of them—he even tried it on me!" She sniffed at the idea.

"Really? And did you tell your husband?"

"No. I didn't want to have any trouble, but I did tell Cliff to take a hike or I'd kick his balls in."

I laughed, remembering how I'd actually carried out what Joy had threatened him with.

Joy threw me a knowing look. "I see he tried it on you, too."

"Yes, he did," I told her, trusting her to keep it to herself. "But he didn't get very far."

"It seems he's been keeping a low profile of late though. Someone saw him limping only the other day," Joy said with humour in her voice. "Could it be you almost castrated the man? If so, you deserve a medal, my dear."

We had a good laugh at this. Then, my drink arrived and I turned back to Martha. "About the horses, can you remember any more names other than the ones you gave me?"

Martha looked thoughtful for a few moments and shook her head. "No. I'm so sorry, Mia. I would love to be able to help you, but the names I remember are the ones I already gave you. And the only reason I remember them is because Jim won quite a bit of money on those horses. There was...one horse..." She paused, as if trying to remember. I held my breath, not wanting to break her concentration. "Well," she said finally, "this may not be anything of value, but there was this one horse that seemed to be a favourite with Jim. He was always talking about it and said he'd won on this horse more than on any other."

"And the horse's name is?" I prompted.

"Erotic Heart," she replied, a curious look in her eyes. "The only thing that confused me was instead of saying he'd won on the horse, Jim actually used the word 'scored'. I'm not sure if this is horse racing lingo or not, but there you have it."

I sat, transfixed, my heartbeat suddenly accelerating to a rapid tempo. I wanted to kiss Martha. Without knowing, she'd provided me with a clue, and I couldn't wait to go and see Chris to share the information with him.

~~~

"I think I got it, Chris!" I was so excited when I entered his cabin that Chris had to take me by the arms, guide me to one of the stuffed chairs, and push me into it.

"Calm down and tell me all about it," he ordered as he took the other chair.

"I think the common denominator among the victims is a woman—a woman with whom all the victims had an illicit affair. And she goes by the name of Erotic Heart, just like the horse."

Chris regarded me with wide eyes. "How did you come to this conclusion?"

I told him about my conversation with Martha and Barry's favourite horse. "And here's the clincher," I remarked, my eyes shining with elation. "Barry told his wife he 'scored' on this horse more than once! Martha was confused and thought he meant he'd won on the horse, but I think he had an affair with whoever Erotic Heart is."

"Shit!" Chris rubbed his temples, trying to take in the implication of the situation. "So what you're saying is the members of the cheaters' club took on names like the horses they used to bet on. At the same time, Erotic Heart is probably the wife of one of the doctors or she could be single—we don't know this yet—but she had affairs with each victim?"

I nodded. "It's exactly what I'm saying. And if I'm right, I think Erotic Heart is married."

"Why do you say that?"

"Because, my young friend, the killer is a male. And I think these are crimes of passion. We're not dealing with a serial killer, only a multiple killer. The kills are not very organised, are they? The MOs are all different. So my take on it is that the killer is Erotic Heart's spouse and he's found out about the affairs and is now killing off her lovers one by one."

Chris sat, looking stunned. I smiled with satisfaction as everything seemed to make sense all of a sudden. When Chris recovered, he shook his head in wonder and said, "Man, it looks like we're dealing with a male version of a bunny boiler!"

I nodded. "I'm afraid so. Which means we need to identify who this woman is pronto! If we find her identity, we'll be able to get to the killer."

"But what if the killer disposed of her, too?"

"That's a chance we have to take. We've had no female victims to date. So the killer either took her out and dumped her body back home somewhere, in order to come on this cruise to wreak his revenge, or she's travelling with him even as we speak, but she's none the wiser as to what hubby's up to."

CHAPTER 17

"**W**ell, this is going to make our job slightly easier," Chris stated. "At least, we have the common denominator. So rather than read through thousands of forum threads, all we have to do is search for all the posts made by Erotic Heart."

"Is the internet connection back on?" I asked, sipping on coffee we'd ordered from room service.

"It sure is." Chris poured himself a cup of coffee and stirred in a teaspoon of sugar. "By the way, I've been able to confirm van Horn as the administrator of the site."

"How did you do that?" I pulled up a chair next to his at the small desk so we could both be in front of the laptop screen.

"Too long a story and very technical for you, Ferrari. Needless to say, it's definitely van Horn. He used a different name on the actual site, but I traced a number of IP addresses coinciding with some of his posts back to his ISP." He saw the confusion in my eyes, and explained, "Basically, each internet service provider, or ISP, uses a whole bunch of IP numbers, or addresses, for their users. These numbers identify the actual service provider, among other things. They also tell us when the user posted to a site or used the internet. This creates a log of dates and times when the user is on the net, and..." he paused and shook his head when he saw the glaze over my eyes. "Never mind, just take it from me; I confirmed van Horn as the administrator and owner of the site despite the fact that he used Neurotic Boy as his avatar and his internet account is under the name of Burt Horner."

"Then, how did you connect him with van Horn?" I was still confused.

"Because he used a real credit card to pay for his internet service, and this is how I knew the account belonged to him."

I was impressed. "Well done. We'll leave aside the fact that you're doing something illegal by hacking; but well done all the same."

Chris smiled his thanks and turned to the laptop, bringing up the Neurotic Erotics Club site. "By the way, Multiswitch, whose real name is Wanda Kerr, made a one-off post on the forum. I don't think she's the common denominator, not if we're right about Erotic Heart."

I agreed, and Chris then searched for the name Erotic Heart. Suddenly, the page changed to a summary of comments posted by the user under different threads. I looked at the bottom of the screen and saw there were twenty-seven more pages of comments. It seemed Erotic Heart was a very busy lady.

"Man, this chick's into everything!" Chris exclaimed while we did a quick look-through of the threads she had posted under.

"I think we're on the right track with her," I replied when my eyes scanned all the categories—illicit liaisons, threesomes, fetishes, anal, S&M, and a whole lot more.

Chris clicked on a few random summary pages. "There's so much she posted. So where to from here?"

"I guess we read through some of the comments to see if she mentions anybody in particular, especially if any of the other horse names come up in her posts."

Chris nodded and clicked back to page one on the summary of posts. The first comment was under the illicit liaisons thread; it was dated 5 August 2012.

"Today is my seven year anniversary on this site. I wanted to say I'm so happy I found you guys. Before this, I used to have to make do with internet dating and in my younger years, it was all done by posting ads in a newspaper. I've enjoyed every steamy minute of my sexual encounters and can't wait for more."

Following this post, there were a few replies of congratulations, but none of them were from names we recognised. "She looks like she's been at it for a long time," I commented as Chris clicked on another post. This one came from the threesomes thread and it was dated 8 January 2007, one of her early posts.

"They say there's a first time for everything, and this was a big first for me. I had the hottest sex in years with one sexy stud taking me from the front and one from the back at the same time. Let's just say I was the meat in the sandwich." The post was followed by a smiley icon with its tongue hanging out

of its mouth. Again, we looked to the replies, but did not recognise any of the names. SexManiac said: *"You were worth it, darling. I loved your tight butt."* Erotic Heart came back with: *"And I loved your big, hard cock."* MysteryMan posted: *"Enjoyed sticking it to ya, love!"* To which Erotic Heart replied: *"And you're finger lickin' good. Mmmm."*

"This is disgusting!" I protested. Despite this, I felt wet between my legs and knew I had to get out of the room lest Chris see me blush. When he didn't reply, I turned to him and noticed his own flushed face going right to the very roots of his hairline. One look down at his shorts told me the reason why. "Okay, that's it!" I declared firmly. "We can't do this together."

Chris remained silent, probably absolutely mortified at his erection. I took pity on him. "I tell you what. Let's take turns doing this. I read through the comments on certain pages and you look at others. We'll keep tabs on which pages we've searched and look for anyone posting with one of the horse names."

Chris simply nodded and handed me his laptop. He said in a low tone, "You stay here and continue. I'm going out for a walk." He slammed out of the cabin before I had a chance to reply.

I went back to the comments, feeling a lot more at ease without Chris looking over my shoulder, and worked my way through ten pages. It took me around two hours to do this, but I didn't stop to read the details of the posts that were sometimes so explicit they brought colour to my face and wild images to my mind. Instead, I simply looked at the usernames of those who commented on Erotic Heart's posts. I had been going at this for about an hour and a half with my eyes feeling dry and tired, when I finally spotted one. At last, a name I recognised! Footloose.

This gave me renewed energy and within another half hour, I came across Neurotic Boy and Adrenaline Rush. I was now on a high, but before I could continue, Chris returned.

He looked more relaxed than when he had left. "Sorry about before," he apologised when he entered the cabin. "I—"

I gave him a reassuring smile. "No need to explain, Chris. It happens to the best of us. Now, get yourself over here. You're going to be a busy boy tonight, hacking whatever it is you hack into."

All other thoughts forgotten, Chris took a seat on the chair next to me and I explained what I'd been doing. "It was taking too long to read the comments themselves, though they are more than spicy; so I simply started going through the posts and scanning for names that might jump out at me. So far, aside from Neurotic Boy, which I knew we'd find sooner or later, I found Footloose and Adrenaline Rush."

Chris looked happy all of a sudden. "That's excellent work! Thanks, Mia."

I stood and stretched. Time for a rest—and later a shower to cool myself off. "Try to find out who these people are. We'll update the others at dinner. And tomorrow, I'll look through some more of the posts and see if I can come up with anyone else. We need to identify if the victims match the names I found on the forum. We also have to find out who Erotic Heart is—and if we have time, try to come up with any other names we can link to the medical convention list. I mean, for all we know, half of them could be part of the cheaters' club. And if any of them had something to do with Erotic Heart, we could have a huge body count on our hands."

Chris nodded, already at work.

"I'll give you a call before eight. We're meeting Dobbs and Smythe at the buffet restaurant." I left the cabin and went to mine, where I fell into a deep sleep the moment my head hit the pillow.

I slept for a couple of hours and awoke feeling refreshed. My neck was a little stiff after sitting for so long in front of Chris's laptop, but a hot shower would soon take care of this.

Whilst the rejuvenating stream of steamy water cascaded over my body, I thought about all I'd been able to unearth from the cheaters' forum. I was pleased with the results and with any luck Chris would come across further information.

My mind kept busy as I got out of the shower and started to get ready for dinner. I tried to imagine Erotic Heart. For some reason, I saw her as a blonde siren with beguiling green eyes and red pouty lips—a woman whose passions ruled her completely. Although I hadn't spent too much time reading the details of her posts, I'd gleaned enough to know she was a truly erotic creature with a voracious appetite for sex and experimentation.

I was no prude myself, but some of the stuff Erotic Heart was into shocked me to the core. Not so much because she seemed to enjoy it, but because she allowed her body to be used by the men she went with. She allowed pain and humiliation in her sexual adventures with S&M; she took part in not just threesomes but sexual parties of four, and even five, where she was the only female. Men used her body in the most depraved of ways, and yet she seemed to be proud of it, enough to post about her exploits in the forum.

I shook my head when I saw my reflection in the mirror. I was a passionate woman who enjoyed lusty sex, and I had a penchant for younger men. In addition, I wasn't averse to trying certain things, but certainly none of what Erotic Heart was into. I respected myself, and my body, too much to allow anyone to use me in that manner.

This made me wonder what went on in the woman's head. My intuition told me she was obviously very unhappy in her marriage. I recalled she'd mentioned this in one of her posts; something about her steady marriage and how her husband was more or less the "missionary position" type. So I could relate to why she wanted to experiment, but to go so far!

The other thing I wondered about was her age. In the post, she talked about her seven-year anniversary on the forum. She also mentioned that prior to this she'd used internet dating and newspaper ads. I tried to remember when internet dating first became popular. This must've been around the late 90s. So the time span between now and back then would have to be around fifteen or so years. Plus she didn't mention how long she was answering newspaper ads. Therefore, depending on how old she was when she started doing this, she could have been cheating on her husband for more than fifteen years!

I thought back to the days of newspaper ads, plus actual matchmaking agencies, and this brought me to my early twenties, which meant Erotic Heart could be of a similar age to me or older. She'd mentioned in a post that she mainly stayed in her marriage for the financial security.

Again, I shook my head and then dropped my line of thinking. I only hoped Chris would surprise us all with the identity of Erotic Heart.

~~~

"What do you mean you can't find out who she is?" I exclaimed with frustration.

Chris, Dobbs, Smythe and I were sitting at one of the outdoor tables on the stern of the ship, just outside the buffet restaurant. The night air was bracing, but not too cold to eat out. Even so, most diners sat inside and we pretty much had the whole deck to ourselves.

When we'd met at the restaurant, Chris and I gave them a rundown of what we found. Smythe seemed to enjoy some of the details I gave on Erotic Heart's adventures, even though I glossed over them quickly. I detected a smile that told me he was picturing the woman in all the acts I described, though I kept them as circumspect as possible. Dobbs, on the other hand, looked vaguely interested, but seemed more interested in his food. I found this humorous and this made it easier for me to relate my findings.

Once I reported my side of it, Chris took over. "After Mia left, I was able to identify Footloose and Adrenaline Rush."

I leaned forward, waiting in anticipation for him to go on.

"We already know Neurotic Boy was van Horn," he said. "As for Erotic Heart, I can't find out who she is."

This was the point at which I'd exclaimed, "What do you mean you can't find out who she is?" I leaned back in my chair, wondering why this was so. We just had to find out her identity. Right now, she was our only lead to the killer.

"Ferrari," Dobbs said in between bites of roast chicken. "Let Chris finish first."

I remained silent, feeling like a five-year-old who'd been admonished by her father. From the corner of my eye, I noted Smythe giving me a look of sympathy. I blushed, thankful it was dark out and he wouldn't be able to see the colour creeping up my face. A sexy image flashed into my mind of Smythe and I engaged in a passionate sexual act that suddenly had me quaking in my shoes.

"... So what do you think?" Chris's voice suddenly pierced its way into my mind, thankfully dispersing what Smythe was about to do to me.

I almost jumped out of my chair. "Huh?"

"Ferrari!" This from Dobbs, again. "Pay attention, girl. Good God, I don't know where your head is tonight."

If only he knew. "Sorry, Chris." I turned to him. "I was just thinking of something to do with the case. What do I think about what?"

Chris threw me a querying look but didn't berate me. Instead, he replied, "I just explained how I found two of the victims' identities through the ISP. I guess you tuned out of all the technical talk."

I grabbed onto this like a lifeline. "Yes. Exactly right. I didn't even understand it the first time round. I guess my mind wandered. But you were saying?" I could kiss the boy.

"Well, I traced the accounts for Footloose and Adrenaline Rush. Footloose is Dr Barry and Dr Weinstein is Adrenaline Rush."

"Good work, Chris," Smythe remarked. "Ever thought of joining the force?" He sounded quite impressed with Chris's efforts.

Chris looked pleased. "Not a chance, Smythe. IT's my life."

"Yes, but the police also needs IT experts."

I turned to Smythe and laughed. "Don't encourage him, Smythe. If Chris went into the police force, plus worked with me on the side, we'd be the Batman and Robin of the NSW Police and you guys wouldn't have anything left to do."

My comment was made good naturedly and I felt pleased when Smythe joined in the laughter around the table while gazing my way with his attractive eyes.

I thought I was going to blush again, so I said, "Chris, what about Erotic Heart?"

Chris looked perplexed. "Well, this is the thing. Remember how we went through the summary of her posts?"

I nodded. "How could I forget?"

"Did you notice how her most recent post was August 2012?"

I stopped with the fork midway to my mouth, looking stunned. I put the fork back down. "Shit! Why didn't I see this?"

"Probably too busy lapping up all the sex details," Smythe teased.

I screwed my nose at him and thought how pleasant it was to have friendly banter without us being at loggerheads all the time. I espied Dobbs's satisfied smile as his glance encompassed us both. But now it was back to business and I turned to Chris. "I kind of did notice the last post was in 2012, but it didn't really register that the summary was in chronological order."

"You're right. It wasn't. And at first, I thought the same as you. She was in so many threads that some posts would've been more recent than others," Chris explained. "But when I went looking for some of her IP addresses, so I could crosscheck them with the log from her ISP, I couldn't get anything after August 2012."

Dobbs held up a hand. "Whoa. Now I'm lost. What do you mean by some of her IP addresses?"

Chris said, "When a person posts, they don't always get allocated the same IP address. The IP addresses are kind of "leased" out to the customer when they're on the net posting something or simply surfing around. But if they don't use the service for a period of time, the IP's leased to another customer. You see," he added when he saw the frown of confusion on Dobbs's face, "each internet service provider has a series of IP addresses allocated to them, which they rotate among their customers. So if today you post to a blog, you'll get one IP address from your service, but if you don't post or use the net for a while, someone else will get to use that same IP and the system simply generates another one for you when you go back online."

Understanding dawned on Dobbs's face. "So the IP isn't fixed to anyone customer. It's like 'lent out', right?"

Chris nodded. "Yes. As long as the IP belongs to the same internet service provider, you could have a whole bunch of different numbers over any given period of time. You know, like a usage log."

I then jumped in. "Which means Chris has to gather a few IPs and match them with the times the person logged in and posted to the forum. Basically, he has to cross-reference the activity of the forum members and match those same exact details with the ISP logs. This way, he can pinpoint who the user is. You see, he carries out a search to find the same sequence in the ISP logs in order to confirm it's the same user and hopefully, he can find out their real identity by getting into their accounts data."

Chris threw me an impressive smile. "You *were* listening after all, Ferrari!"

Smythe shook his head in disbelief. "I don't know how you do it, Chris. It's mindboggling. And I have no idea what you're talking about."

"Chris is brilliant, Smythe. This is why we're generally way ahead of you cops." I winked playfully. "Well, it's just that we move faster because we don't need search warrants and all that red tape stuff. But back to Erotic Heart," I prompted Chris.

"She didn't post for just over a year," Chris replied. "This could mean she changed her internet provider, although I still couldn't find any other posts after this date. So it's more probable that she decided to change her identity altogether."

"You mean she could be using another name?" I remarked.

Smythe shrugged. "Nothing illegal about that."

Chris concurred. "Exactly. So I'll need more time to search for her."

"We have two more days at sea before we reach Pago Pago," I reminded him. "Let's hope we can get to whoever this woman is before then. The last thing we want is another murder."

As if on cue, when we started on our coffees, Mark Evans made an appearance. He barely spared me a smile as he approached our table with a serious look on his face. My heart sank and I knew something was terribly wrong.

"I'm glad I found you together," Mark said instead of greeting us. "The captain sent me to fetch you."

We all stood at once. "What is it?" Smythe spoke for us.

"One of our turndown service attendants just found the body of Dr Cliff Downes."

"Where is it?" I asked.

"Lying naked in his bed with his throat cut."

"He bled to death?" This from Dobbs.

Mark nodded. "It's not a pretty sight. The ship's doctor is currently gathering more info about cause of death to confirm how and when it happened. But he thinks the killer cut both the jugular veins and carotid arteries. So it was very quick."

Mark looked visibly upset, but Smythe, Dobbs and I were old pros. I said, "Lead on, Mark. Although terrible, this can't possibly top a dismembered body in a bathtub. Trust me."

Mark looked rather dumbfounded as he started to walk and we followed. Only my group knew that I had been referring to one of my finds during the grisly gay mardi gras murders.

.

CHAPTER 18

The body of the victim was covered by a towel around the pelvic area so we wouldn't have to see him in all his naked glory, although I didn't see why Downes deserved such dignity after the way he had attacked me. Aside from this, he lay face up, his throat cut from side to side, with the bed linen around him saturated in his blood. His mouth was open in a chilling grin while his eyes were frozen as if gazing into a void of terror. He had probably seen his killer coming directly at him.

Aside from our group, only the ship's doctor and Jerry Garcia were present at the scene. "The captain just left to make a call ahead to the authorities in Pago Pago," Garcia informed us as he nodded a greeting and momentarily stopped taking photographs of the victim. His face looked grim. "This brings back memories of my days in homicide. One of the reasons I quit the force."

Dobbs nodded with understanding. He could obviously relate. Smythe, in the meantime, had a quiet word with the doctor and then went on to examine the scene while he took notes. I turned to Chris to ensure he was okay. He'd probably never seen anything so horrible, but he seemed to be handling it. We stood back from the scene so as not to get in anyone's way or contaminate any evidence.

From my vantage point, I noticed something shiny sticking out from under the bed. "Smythe," I called and pointed with my chin toward the object.

Smythe got closer to take a look but didn't yet touch it. "Doc, did you see this?"

The ship's doctor moved to where Smythe was crouched and shook his head. "No."

"May I?" Smythe asked and helped himself to a pair of latex gloves from a box, which someone had had the foresight to bring along.

"Go right ahead." The doctor went back to examining the body.

"What have you got, Phil?" Garcia came to stand next to Chris and me, followed by Dobbs. The cabin was too small for all of us to wander about, plus the atmosphere felt oppressive.

Smythe drew out the instrument. "A scalpel," the doctor exclaimed when he saw what Smythe held by the tip of his gloved fingers.

"You'll have to check if any such equipment is missing from the ship's medical centre, Doc," Smythe suggested. "Meanwhile, we'll run this for prints. Garcia?"

Garcia grabbed a plastic bag from the evidence kit he had with him and bagged the item.

"What if someone brought it onboard?" I suggested. "After all, we have a whole bunch of doctors running around."

Garcia nodded. "We always run the luggage through x-ray, of course, but it could've been easily missed or mistaken for something else. This item can look like a nail file or some sort of hair clipping instrument. So yes, one of the convention people could have brought it onboard."

The cabin was getting really stuffy with all of us in it, and I noticed Chris had started to go a bit green around the gills. "Why don't we leave you gentlemen to work the scene for now? Chris and I are in the way here." Then, I turned to a surprised-looking Smythe. "Let's all meet up later for a catch-up." He nodded with the hint of a grateful smile.

I took hold of Chris's arm, in case he should faint, and turned to go. Dobbs stepped out into the passageway with us. "That's a good thing you did, Ferrari," he said with pride in his eyes.

"What's that?"

"Staying out of the way willingly," he returned with a smirk. "And no sparks flying, either! You and Smythe have come a long way."

I grinned. "Don't push your luck, Dobbs. Just be thankful Chris needs a breath of fresh air."

Chris was too immersed in his own thoughts to comment and Dobbs went back inside the cabin with a smile on his face. I led my companion away from the scene.

~~~

We regrouped with Dobbs, Smythe and Garcia a couple of hours later at The Mariners' Hub. It was almost midnight, but the staff kept the café open just for us. Rather than coffee this time, we ordered alcoholic drinks. I figured this was one night when we all needed a stiff drink.

"You're right about the scalpel, Mia," Garcia began while we sipped on our drinks. "Doc Jones checked the medical centre time and again, and not one piece of equipment was missing."

"Was he able to establish time of death?"

"He said somewhere between five and seven this evening, judging by body temperature and the onset of rigor mortis."

"I noticed the aircon in the cabin was quite cold when we first arrived at the scene," I commented. "I guess the killer wanted to throw us off the time of death as much as possible."

"But why do this? We still don't know who he is," Chris stated, sipping quickly on a multi-coloured cocktail.

I shrugged. "I think he enjoys playing around with us. But one thing is for sure."

"What's that?" Smythe asked. He was drinking straight whisky.

"The guy's either a doctor or he has medical training of some kind." I fleetingly thought of Enrico.

"You're right, of course," Chris piped in. "Using a scalpel takes some skill."

"Not only this," Dobbs put in while sipping on a coffee liqueur and cream concoction. "Doc Jones definitely confirmed the killer sliced right through both the jugular veins plus the carotid. The guy died within a minute."

"That would explain the blood splashing all over the place, and it points to the killer having the medical knowledge of knowing exactly where to cut to get to all the arteries at once," I stated. "But why was Downes naked?"

"Taking a nap when the killer happened upon him?" Garcia suggested.

"Was there any sign of sexual interference?" I still had Enrico in the forefront of my mind. Perhaps, the good doctor had been bi-sexual and he'd enjoyed his last afternoon delight before being dispatched to the great beyond.

"Doc said he doesn't think so, but we'll know more when we get to Hawaii and get the experts to take a look." Garcia knocked back his tequila shot in one gulp. "Aside from this, there were no fingerprints I could find on the scalpel. But again, we don't have the latest technology onboard; so this'll have to wait, too."

I turned to Smythe. "Any CCTV outside the cabin?"

He shook his head. "Some. But believe it or not, this guy must know exactly where all the cameras are positioned because we didn't catch anything."

We all sighed at the same time, feeling stumped. Then, Garcia stood. "The captain's waiting for my full report, so I have to go." He turned to Dobbs and Smythe. "Tomorrow, my department will run the safety information seminar with the convention group. I'd appreciate it if both of you attend. I think the group will feel more reassured knowing we have some police presence."

Smythe sounded cynical when he remarked, "Yeah, right, after four murders."

Garcia shrugged. "At least we can give them a few ideas on how to keep their wits about them."

Dobbs nodded. "True. Safety in numbers; that sort of thing."

"Well, I bid you all good night," Garcia said, "and thank you for your hard work. It's a good thing you people happened to be on this trip. I can just imagine how much more work we'd have on our hands if we were alone. Our department's not equipped to handle this type of thing." He gave us a parting smile and went on his way.

"Why is the killer getting bolder?" I played with my drink of rum and Coke.

Dobbs finished his drink and gazed my way. "You're right. At first, there was all this skulking around, but now the guy's walking straight into people's cabins."

"Which means he knew his victim," I jumped in just as Smythe was about to make an observation that was probably the same as mine.

Smythe nodded, confirming my supposition. "Not only this, but unless Downes slept in the nude, I have to wonder whether there's an element of sexual humiliation in there somewhere. Providing, that is, the victim was not engaged in any sexual acts pre-mortem."

I felt a jolt of excitement at his statement. "You're right! Remember I talked about Erotic Heart's S&M activities? She was into humiliation. This would add to the theory that the killer is Erotic Heart's partner and he's seeking vengeance in kind. Perhaps, Erotic

Heart and Downes were into S&M together, hence the reason the killer wanted the victim to go in a humiliating way."

Chris interjected, "I would hardly call slitting someone's throat while they're naked humiliating; it's more like terrifying."

"True," I replied. "But perhaps the killer made him undress first and perform some kind of humiliating act, like begging for his life or something."

"Then, why not cut his balls off instead?" Chris suggested with frustration. "That's humiliating enough."

It was obvious the events of the evening had affected him more deeply than they had the rest of us. I became concerned. After all, Chris had recently turned twenty and he'd probably never seen a dead body. "Chris, I think you should get some rest. I'm going to have some homework for you to do in the morning."

This seemed to perk him up. Anything to do with IT, he could handle. "What is it you want me to do?"

"I want you to identify which threads the victims were most active in, and see if you can find a link between them and Erotic Heart. At the moment, we have all the victims, except for Downes, posting on the forum. But we need proof they actually engaged in sexual activity with Erotic Heart. Not only this, I'm sure Downes is in the S&M forum somewhere, but you'll need to come up with his username and link him to Erotic Heart."

Chris looked a lot more animated as he stood. "I'm off to work on this right now. There's no way I can sleep after seeing that guy's blood all over the place. I'll see you in the morning."

When Chris left, I remarked, "This is my fault. I should watch out for Chris more closely, but he's so clever and mature that I sometimes forget he's so young."

Dobbs patted my arm in reassurance. "Mia, you're doing your best. And don't worry about the boy; he can handle it."

"Yeah, well, let's hope his father doesn't chew off my head for exposing him to all this."

Smythe remarked, "Mia, don't forget it was Mr Rourke who suggested we investigate in the first place."

"Yes, but he meant us, the adults—not his son. David has no idea Chris helps me with investigations," I confessed.

Dobbs remained silent and Smythe frowned momentarily. "Well, don't worry your head about it just now. I'll deal with Rourke when the time comes."

I was surprised at his comment but felt warmed by it, or perhaps it was the alcohol I'd consumed.

Dobbs stifled a yawn and glanced at his watch. "It's almost 1.00am. I say we all get some shuteye. Nothing more we can do tonight."

We left the café and started making our way toward the lifts. "I need a walk first," I said to the others. "I can't go to sleep with my thoughts in such a jumble."

Dobbs yawned again, and this time he couldn't suppress it. "You go, Mia. I'm done for." By this time, we reached the lifts and one of them stopped on our floor, its doors swishing open. "Phil, you coming?"

"I think I'll walk with Mia. Remember, safety in numbers."

I tried not to smile when I caught a wink from Dobbs before the doors slid shut. Smythe led the way to the Promenade Deck that was deserted when we went out and leaned at the rail, looking out to sea. No moon was present, but the stars in the indigo sky provided us with a twinkling dome of light.

"Not too cold for you?" Smythe asked, glancing at the sleeveless white cotton dress I wore.

I warmed up under his gaze and felt like a heater had just been switched on. "Um... no, no," I assured him. "The breeze is surprisingly mild tonight. Not a nice night for murder, is it?" I decided to keep our conversation on a professional level.

"Is it ever?" His eyes skimmed the horizon that was practically invisible as you couldn't see where the ocean met the sky in the moonless night.

I shrugged. "I guess not. You know, it's just spooky this killer is getting so bold. I mean, going to the victim's cabin is a huge leap from pushing someone overboard in the dark."

Smythe nodded. "I know. But oftentimes this kind of killer wants to be caught, albeit at a subconscious level. Remember, he probably called in the first kill himself. I guess he felt a certain power in doing so."

"You mean so the world can validate his acts?"

"Something like that. I'm no forensic psychologist, but I've dealt with enough cases in my career. First, they're really careful, but in later kills they seem to get less guarded, sometimes even sloppy."

I frowned. "But we're not dealing with a serial killer. It's just multiple homicides—a crime of passion."

"Sometimes there's a fine line between them," Smythe replied, his jaw firm. "Whatever they are, I hate these guys. They're the scourge of society."

I thought back to the last case I'd worked where Smythe saved my life. I shivered involuntarily and almost jumped when I felt his hands on my shoulders.

"You are cold after all," he said. "Let's go back inside."

"No, it's okay. I was just thinking about... well... the last case. I never did thank you properly for looking after me." I did nothing to shake his hands off my shoulders, nor did he take them off.

He turned me to face him squarely. "Mia..."

The magnetism between us was too much for me and I thought my skin would start sizzling any second now. I gently pulled away. "I do appreciate your saving my life and sticking by me, even though I drove you insane with my interfering."

We both turned back to the rail and Smythe laughed gently. "You really are a handful at times. But I also have you to thank for helping solve those murders."

"And Chris, of course. I couldn't have done it without him," I reminded him.

He nodded. "Of course. Chris is a bright fellow and he'll be a credit to any future employer."

I smiled. "Well, right now, he's coming in very handy, and he's a credit to me. I'm like a mother to him, you know?" I decided to confide in him. "Chris's mother never had much time for him."

"Ah yes, you mean the beautiful Elena." Smythe had met her in the course of his investigation of a suicide at our hotel about a year ago. "So where is she now?"

"Who knows? I think she's enjoying life in the rich playgrounds of Europe. According to Chris, she barely keeps in touch."

Smythe shook his head. "Her loss, I'm sure. And I assume she cleaned out old man Rourke?"

My body stiffened for a moment and Smythe shot me a querying look. "I wasn't privy to his settlement arrangements with her."

"So what's wrong?"

I played the innocent. "What's wrong with what?"

He smiled. "You've gone all uppity on me."

I hated it when he read me so well. "I have? Well, maybe it's because David's not 'old man Rourke', as you put it. In fact, he's younger than you, Smythe."

"Okay, so he's what... forty, forty-one?"

"Forty to your forty-four, if I remember your age correctly."

"Fine, so I'm forty-four. Big deal! I'm not in competition with him, you know. But you seem to think so."

This threw me. "It's not like that," I stated a tad too firmly.

Curious eyes regarded me. "But I guess at some stage it was?"

I raised my chin and looked out to sea. "No comment."

Smythe's hands suddenly reached out for me again, and this time he brought my body right up against his. I felt the hard muscles of his stomach and chest against my breasts and I turned to putty in his hands. My five-foot-nothing frame was at the mercy of his six-foot-three athletic build. I could have struggled, but didn't.

"What, no complaints, comments, or otherwise?" he taunted me. I simply gazed into his eyes with a passion I couldn't stem, much to my annoyance, and heard him say, "I've wanted to do this for a long time."

Before I could do or say anything, his mouth assaulted mine in a kiss that left nothing to the imagination. I opened up under him and his tongue invaded me while his arms tightened around my body, making escape impossible.

We kissed for a long time—meltingly, passionately, erotically—and I wanted the kiss to go on and on, never to end. I felt safe, loved. I was home. How would I ever kiss another man after this? I pushed closer into him, if that were possible, and felt his hardness against me. Images of us lying naked in his bed with him inside me invaded my mind. I instantly felt wet. I couldn't wait to have him.

"He's a good lay..." The statement flashed abruptly into my head. Amanda Wilson's statement, to be exact. She'd said this when describing Smythe's skill in the bedroom, only a few months ago. I froze.

Smythe sensed the change in mood because all of a sudden I was free of his arms, his eyes regarding me with confusion. "What is it?"

Anger overtook my other emotions. "You have the nerve to ask?" I took a couple of steps back from him. "How dare you kiss me after professing your love for Amanda just a few short months ago?" He went to answer, but I didn't let him. "You bloody men are all the same! Amanda didn't want you, so now I'm your rebound shag?"

Smythe seemed genuinely shocked. "What are you talking about? I thought I was falling hard for Amanda, but there was always something in the background that stopped me from—"

I put up my hands to ward off any excuses. "Please, spare me the explanation, Smythe. Whatever was *in the background* certainly didn't stop you from going to bed with her."

Now, he looked like he was going to push me overboard. He was onto me in a flash, his hands on my shoulders, trying to shake me into reason. "It was you, Ferrari! You, who was always in the background. I wanted *you*! Are you satisfied now? And who said anything about a rebound shag? We didn't even get to the bedroom, for God's sake! And believe me, when we do, it will never, ever be a rebound anything!"

I was awestruck. I had no comeback. I hated myself because tears of frustration started rolling down my face and Smythe saw them. So I did the only thing I could do, I pushed with all my might and sent him reeling a few steps away from me. Then, I ran away.

CHAPTER 19

My hopes of sleeping in were shattered with banging at my door early in the morning. I espied the bedside clock with one partly opened eye. 8.11am. Ugh!

"Whatever it is, piss off!" I yelled out with a croaky throat in need of water. I closed my eye again and shoved a pillow over my head.

The banging kept going. "Mia!" It was Chris's voice.

I raised my head off the pillow for a moment. "Go away!" I yelled out again. "I don't care if the friggin' ship's sinking. I need my beauty sleep. Now, be a good boy and buzz off."

"I found the username for Downes on the forum," he announced with persuasion in his tone.

Oh, he knew me too well! I bolted upright to a sitting position. "Wait a minute," I called out and heard laughter from the other side of the door. This had better be good, I thought as I dragged myself out of bed and went to the bathroom to pee, brush my teeth and splash water over my face. Only then did I feel relatively human.

When I started to open the door, an arm stuck through the crack holding a steaming cup of strong coffee and brioche. Then, the rest of Chris's body appeared with a wide smile on his face. He walked in and took a seat at the coffee table. He looked tired, but the smug glint in his eyes said it all.

I took a sip of the wonderfully aromatic coffee and a bite of brioche before I spoke. "Where's your coffee?"

"Been drinking it through the whole night. I didn't get any sleep yet. Too busy working while the likes of you was snoozing away." He grinned.

It was a good thing he said this with humour in his voice; otherwise, he would have worn the hot coffee all over where it hurt the most. My eyes went to the spot, and sensing violence, he crossed his legs. I smiled and joined him at the table. "Thanks for breakfast. So what gives that can't wait until I get up?"

"Man, I had one enlightening night," he declared in wonder, "full of deviant sex and depravation." He coloured a little despite his confident front.

"You're growing up too fast, Chris. And before I forget, if your father should ask, you did NOT take any part in this investigation. He'd sack me from my job if he knew I introduced you to hard porn!"

He laughed. "You're funny sometimes, you know? I'm my own man, Mia. Dad's really flexible with me."

"Okay. Okay. Just tell me what you found. You didn't wake me up so early for chitchat."

"Fine. Let's get on with it. You know how Cliff Downes was a plastic surgeon?"

I shook my head. "Can't recollect with all the doctors I met on this ship, but go on."

"Get this." Chris leaned forward in his chair. "His username is 'Abreast of Everything', just like the horse—plus his obvious love of boobs, I'd say."

I almost choked on my coffee. I coughed and spluttered for a few seconds while Chris watched me in amusement. "Want some water?"

I nodded and he grabbed a small bottle from the mini-bar fridge and handed it to me. I took a few sips before I could speak. "With the reputation he had, he should've called himself 'Pussy Fingers' or something to that effect," I stated with sarcasm. "But how did you find him?"

"I had to read through a huge number of Erotic Heart's posts," he explained, colour seeping into his face again.

"Hence the 'enlightening night of deviant sex'," I said, thinking about my own night of almost divine sexual pleasure. But I didn't want to go there right now.

Chris stood and got himself a bottle of water from the mini-bar. I felt like teasing him but didn't. The poor boy was probably getting very hot under the collar. It was one thing to read or watch porn on your own, but quite another when you had to relate it to someone who could be your mother. So I waited in silence until he composed himself.

159

He sat back down after drinking almost the whole bottle in one go. "I had to do a lot of cross-referencing to find him, but what helped was the name of the horse we got from Mrs Barry. You'd already found some of the others, but it took a while to find this one, namely because he had something with Erotic Heart in the earlier years. So I ran a search of Abreast of Everything's posts and compared his summary with Erotic Heart's. I almost missed it because they only shared one post."

My curiosity got the better of me when I asked, "And what was it about?"

Chris went bright red in the face. "Well... um..."

"Come on, Chris. You came in here boasting about your night of deviant sex, so spill it!"

He shifted in his seat. "Let's just say she gave him a tongue job he never forgot. He raved on about it on several other posts he exchanged with fellow enthusiasts."

"Is that all? So he gets a cool blowjob. Big deal!" I couldn't understand why Chris looked so embarrassed. After all, he was a young man of the world. He knew about these things.

"Um... no." His voice interrupted my thoughts.

I gazed at him as his eyes looked down and to the side while his chin subtly pointed downward and over his shoulder. "Oh no! Don't tell me! That is gross!" I exclaimed in a loud voice. "I'm eating here, you know!" I still held a piece of brioche in my hand, not sure if I should finish eating it. Chris remained silent while I took a few moments to get the gruesome image out of my head. "So the good doctor liked a bit of a sweep around his 'back door'." I couldn't find any other way of putting it without puking.

Chris nodded. "You got it."

"Does this woman have no self-respect whatsoever?" I launched on a new tirade. "I mean, she's really into such humiliating acts. I can't believe she boasts about them on the net. Who does that?"

"Some very sick puppies, I expect," Chris answered, his tone confident once again now he'd managed to get the message across. "And whatever you do, don't ask me about what they did with food."

I shivered. "Eew! Don't worry, I won't ask. I enjoy my food too much to lose my appetite forever. But this explains why Downes was naked. Maybe, the killer did something to humiliate him where the 'sun don't shine'."

"The doctor couldn't find anything, but perhaps the forensic people in Hawaii will find something in the nether regions of his back passage. So what now? We placed all the victims in the forum. I'd say this is definitely our common denominator."

I shook my head to dispel the image of something stuck up Downes's arse and brought my focus back to Chris. "Yes," I agreed. "You're right about that. What about Erotic Heart, though? Any luck tracing who she is?"

"Not yet, I'm afraid. I don't understand why she suddenly stopped posting."

"Because she finally came to her senses?" I suggested, even though I didn't believe it. "Albeit a little too late, of course."

"Either that or she dropped off the face of the earth," Chris offered.

"Okay. Let's assume she went to another ISP—she should still be posting to the forum, right? Plus the service she had before would still contain archived records of her account."

"Well, unless she's come up with a new username, she's not posting at all. As for archived records, yes, they should be there. But it all depends where the ISP stores its archives. Some companies do everything on one server; others may use several—each server having a different purpose."

"So you're saying they might use one server for active accounts and another for inactive ones?"

Chris shrugged. "It's possible. They can do pretty much anything they like."

I stood. "Well, it's the only lead we have at the moment; so get into their archives. You tracked all the others, but you couldn't track her. It's plausible she's in the inactive accounts." I finished my water. "Go get some sleep, Chris. You look tired." I noticed the dark shadows under his eyes for the first time since he entered my cabin. "We still have time before we reach Pago Pago."

Chris stood and followed me to the door as I showed him out. Then, he paused and turned to me. "What are you going to do today?"

Avoid Smythe like the plague, I thought. But I knew I couldn't do this altogether. "I'll update Dobbs and Smythe on what's going on. Oh, and one more thing, we assume Erotic Heart is a woman because she talked of her boring marriage, etc. Is there any chance it might be a gay guy, say someone like Enrico?"

"It could be anybody, Mia. Most people on the net like to invent new identities for themselves."

I frowned. "Well, see if you can find an account for Enrico Lotti. I doubt he's Erotic Heart, but I still want to know if he has an account in the cheaters' forum."

"Will do."

After Chris left, I jumped into the shower in order to help prepare myself to face the new day—and a new Smythe. Now, it was my turn to blush, and I was glad Chris wasn't here to see it.

~~~

I caught up with Dobbs and Smythe at lunch. They were sitting near the Deck Grill enjoying a burger under the sun. Smythe was in his bathers and Dobbs wore shorts and a short-sleeved cotton shirt, open halfway down his chest.

"Aren't you guys hot sitting out here?" I said on approach, averting my eyes from Smythe's athletic physique. Thank God I was wearing sunglasses so he couldn't see my eyes.

"Join us for lunch, Mia. It's nice and breezy here," Dobbs invited, taking a huge bite of his cheeseburger.

Smythe nodded hello. "Hope you slept well?" His tone was full of innuendo and I wanted to hit him. What if he'd shared with Dobbs the details of our romantic interlude?

I ignored his question and leaned over them. "I'm meeting someone for lunch," I told Dobbs, hoping this would make Smythe jealous.

It must've worked because he asked, "Where's Chris?"

"He's sleeping. He worked through the whole night and came up with Downes's username on the forum."

For a moment, both men stopped eating and gazed at me with surprise. "So we have a confirmed common denominator among the victims," Dobbs stated.

I nodded. "I'd say so. Chris is having trouble trying to identify Erotic Heart, though. He'll keep working once he's rested."

"They're doing a luau lunch at the buffet restaurant," Smythe tried to sound casual as he commented on this. But I picked up the inquisitive inflection in his voice. He was probably dying to know who I was meeting. If only he knew I made the whole thing up.

"That's nice," I said and glanced at my watch. "Well, gents, I have to go now. Perhaps, I'll see you at dinner." Before either of them could reply, I turned and walked away, knowing I looked terrific in a white see-through cotton dress with my swimmers underneath.

I ended up having a room service lunch in my cabin in case Smythe went looking for me. Let him wonder what I was up to. While I ate, my mind turned to Enrico. If Erotic Heart was to be believed, she was definitely a woman near my age or older. Enrico was too young to even remember what a lonely-hearts ad looked like. Of course, there was always the chance Chris could be right and Erotic Heart was someone inventing an identity—if so, it could be anybody. But all things being equal, my intuition told me Erotic Heart was genuine about her background and experiences. She didn't reveal much about who she was; but the idea of the forum was to share one's sexual experiences and not to give away the user's true identity.

Taking into account the cheaters' club as the common denominator among the victims, I ruled out the captain and Mike Yuen as suspects. At least, pending any additional evidence we might find. Their lives had been ruined by doctors—different doctors with different specialties—but we only had one killer. The CCTV had caught enough footage to enable us to confirm the killer was one and the same. And it was a 'he', which ruled out Martha Barry. This left Enrico as the main suspect. Of course, there could be other suspects we hadn't yet come across.

Enrico had access to information on the convention members, and he was known to all of them. Plus he kept the gossip going on about 'who might be next'—perhaps to divert attention away from himself. Could Enrico be the killer and Erotic Heart at the same time?

Although this was possible, it somehow didn't feel right to me. If Erotic Heart told the truth about her marriage, then gay Enrico did not fit the profile. Besides, those who had something going with Erotic Heart referred to her as a female in their comments. If Enrico truly was Erotic Heart, then he had the best disguise in the world, because nobody on the forum mentioned having a thing with a transvestite who went by the name of Erotic Heart.

As for being the killer, we now knew the person's gait and build from the footage we'd gleaned. Enrico was slim and lithe. He could have been a ballet dancer. The killer's figure was fuller and stockier, and the gait was all wrong for Enrico—unless he disguised himself with bulky clothing and walked more like a man than the waif he always projected in public.

I shook my head in frustration. Speculation always made me feel restless and it got me nowhere. Therefore, after a decent time interval of pretending to be having lunch with a friend, I made my way out of the cabin and went on deck. I felt rather clammy and decided to go for a swim; but first, I checked the pool area to ensure Smythe had gone. The last thing I needed now was to run into him again, and in my swimmers.

Thankfully, the coast was clear and I spent the next couple of hours swimming and sunbathing. It felt great to relax for a change. When I had enough, I noticed it was close to afternoon teatime. I was starving. So I threw the white dress over me and made my way to the back of the ship where I knew I'd find Professor Tully.

Sure enough, I found him at his usual table drinking lemon tea and eating his favourite strawberry tartlets. "Mia, what an unexpected pleasure!" He seemed genuinely pleased to see me.

"I'll join you in a minute, Professor," I said and ducked back into the restaurant to get coffee and a slice of carrot cake with lemon icing. "So how are you getting along?" I asked when I joined him.

"Feeling much better," he smiled. "It seems the sunshine and sea air agree with my health. But if truth be told, I think it's the remedial massages I'm getting from a lovely gal at the spa." He winked with humour, and I laughed.

"Well, I'm pleased for you. You seemed to be in quite a bit of pain when we rented the jeep in Vila."

The professor popped a tartlet into his mouth. "Those little jeeps are what I call 'bone-rattlers'. No suspension whatsoever. I was very tired that day after sitting in the jeep for so long, but I still enjoyed our outing."

I took a bite of my carrot cake and washed it down with coffee. "Mmm. This is excellent. Isn't it wonderful just eating and relaxing?" I didn't understand why I was in such a good mood—not when we had a murderer onboard, plus I was trying to avoid Smythe—but perhaps the professor was right and it was the sea air.

"I think this is what a holiday should be about, don't you?" he commented.

"Sure, except for..." I stopped just in time, but the professor was too fast for me.

"Except for the murders," he completed my sentence. "How is your investigation coming along?"

"Not much to go by," I replied, knowing I couldn't tell anybody outside of our group what we'd discovered. "I guess we're hoping the killer won't strike again and that we make it to Hawaii quickly so we can hand everything over to the authorities."

Professor Tully nodded. "Yes. That makes sense. Well, we'll be in Pago Pago soon and then onto Hawaii. Not long to go now."

"True." I finished my cake but still felt hungry, so I went back inside to grab a couple of cucumber sandwiches before rejoining the professor. "Despite the unsavoury goings on, how have you enjoyed your cruise so far?" I wanted to steer the conversation away from the murders.

The professor took a moment to respond and then a smile appeared on his face. "I'm tangoing."

"Pardon?"

"Tango—dancing the tango—just as I used to do with my Eden." He obviously saw the surprise on my face and went on to explain, "Eden and I used to belong to a ballroom dancing group when we were young, and we used to love the tango. Then, as my practice got busier, I had to give it up. Besides, by this time, my legs were not as strong and my hip gave me much pain."

"I'm sorry to hear that. So what happened with your dancing?"

"Eden kept it up. She liked to keep fit, and dancing can do that for you." His look seemed far away, probably reliving his younger years.

"And now you're tangoing again?"

He chuckled. "Yes. I felt much better these last couple of days and I noticed they were giving tango lessons on the ship. So I signed up. Mind you, I'm a lot slower, but then so are the biddies who come along to meet handsome men like me!"

I laughed. "You're a modest one, Professor," I teased. "But I'm glad you've found something you love to do. It just goes to prove you're never too old to do what you love."

His countenance turned serious again and I knew his thoughts were back with Eden and his younger years. Somehow, this made me feel depressed. Here I was, almost fifty, and I would never have the memories of someone I loved—at least, not someone who was the love of my life. I thought briefly of my cheating ex and the years I'd wasted on him. Life just wasn't fair.

CHAPTER 20

We sailed into Pago Pago at 7.00am and I stood on deck with Chris, taking in the panoramic view of clear blue waters against a backdrop of rocky hills and mountains. The weather was picture perfect and I was eager to go ashore.

"I don't see what the big hurry is, Mia," Chris protested, still half asleep.

I'd ordered room service breakfast for 6.00am and woke Chris with it, pushing him to hurry, eat, and get ready for our day out. I wanted to be off the ship before Smythe appeared.

The last couple of days we'd spent at sea, Chris worked hard to hack into the ISP archives to no avail. He seemed to be having trouble locating the correct server. The problem was compounded by the fact that we ran into rough weather and the satellite connection kept cutting out, thus making working online impossible at times.

While Chris kept busy working, I mingled with the convention members in case I picked up any useful information. At the same time, I ensured I only came into contact with Smythe when others were around me.

I could tell by the look in his eyes that he was trying to get me alone so we could talk, but I wasn't yet ready to face what had happened between us. So I kept busy onboard and always surrounded myself with people.

The night before we reached our port of call, Dobbs and Smythe discussed over dinner their upcoming meeting with the Pago Pago authorities. I heard them mention the meeting time of 9.00am. My plan, then, was to get Chris and disappear for the entire day the minute we reached land.

Now, as we stood on the Promenade Deck watching the ship being brought in and secured at the dock, I patiently listened to Chris's complaints.

"Man, I could've slept two more hours! I mean, who gets up so early?"

I sighed and ignored his latest protest. "What do you say we rent a motorbike?"

This got his attention. "You'll let me drive it?"

I knew I was taking a risk riding on a motorcycle with a young man who would probably speed, but I would rather ride with Evel Knievel himself than be stuck with Smythe on a romantic island. He was bound to catch up with me at some stage after meeting with the local authorities, but not if Chris and I rode around the island all day.

"Yes. You can drive us around," I responded to his enthusiastic remark.

He turned a suspicious gaze on me that made me blush with guilt. "Okay, what's going on?" he demanded.

"Er... nothing's going on. I only thought it'd be fun riding around the island seeing as in Vila we had to go rather slow because of the professor."

Unfortunately, it looked like he wasn't buying my excuse. Worse still, he was now fully alert. "Ferrari, I can smell the bullcrap coming from you, and it ain't good." He accused with a merciless look in his eyes.

I sighed and knew when I was beaten. Chris was not going to let this rest unless I coughed up. "Damn you, Chris! If you must know, I'm trying to avoid Smythe."

He rolled his eyes. "Is that all? When are you *not* trying to avoid him?"

"No. You don't understand... He... I..." The colour on my face must've turned a deep red when I caught the sudden look of realisation in his eyes.

"Oh, my God!" he exclaimed, a big grin on his face. "The sex site got to you. I knew it! And you and Smythe—"

Thankfully, anger came to my rescue. "It's not like that, you fool! What do you take me for?"

He turned confused eyes toward me. "Then, I don't understand."

I gave him a brief account of what Dobbs had told me about Smythe not interfering with my police application. "Smythe was very decent about the whole thing," I confided, "plus he took the abuse I threw his way all these years without saying anything."

Chris looked stunned. "Does this mean in future we're going to work together with him, and he won't stop us?"

Trust him to care only about future investigations. "How should I know?" I snapped.

Chris smiled now. "So, you two got cosy, huh?"

I examined my shoes, trying to find something fascinating about them. "Let's just say we had a weak moment," I finally admitted, and added when I happened to glance at his eyes and noticed his knowing gaze, "It's not what you think, so get your mind out of the gutter. We simply kissed. Besides, it's none of your business."

He looked at me with a touch of triumph. "Touché for when you were teasing me about my 'ladylove'."

"Fine. And now that you know, you keep your trap shut about all this. I don't want Dobbs in on it as well. I need to work things out with Smythe at some stage. I'm not sure what he thinks about the whole thing, plus I'm not ready to start anything with him."

"You know you can count on me, Mia," he reassured me, and I felt better. "My only regret is my dad didn't do anything sooner to win your love. His loss, I guess."

I pecked him on the cheek. "Thank you, sweetie," I said and he blushed. "Whatever did or didn't happen with David, you know I'll always be your friend and pseudo-mother."

He nodded, at a loss for words.

"Now, let's get out there and hire that bike!" I declared with a smile.

He didn't need a second invitation.

~~~

We spent the day touring the island, stopping here and there to explore a beach and buy souvenirs from quaint open-air markets we came across. We then went into town for lunch; and after riding to a few lookout points, we finally returned the bike and made our way back to the ship one hour prior to sailing time.

Dobbs and Smythe met us when we came onboard. I knew they'd been on the lookout for us.

"Where the hell did you guys get to?" Dobbs enquired, sounding put off. "I thought you were going to wait for us so we could spend the day together."

He looked rather disappointed, but I couldn't help it. I also noticed the frown on Smythe's face, and said, "We didn't know how long you'd be. You know how it is with these official things, so Chris and I decided to venture out on our own."

They seemed to accept my explanation even though Smythe still looked rather unhappy. "What did you end up doing?" he asked.

I'd pre-warned Chris not to babble about the bike as Dobbs would freak out and threaten to tell David Rourke. So Chris said, "We found a great spot for snorkelling and hired some equipment. It was really great."

Wow! The kid was beginning to take after me. I was impressed. "Now, if you'll excuse me, I'm off to shower. My hair's full of salt."

"We're meeting for dinner with the captain," Dobbs informed us. "After this morning's meeting with the police, we decided it would be better to expedite our way to Honolulu."

I remarked, sounding surprised, "He's going to change the itinerary?"

Dobbs nodded. "We'll talk later. Let's meet at seven in Horizons. I'm starving already and it's not even four."

I smiled. "Get yourself some afternoon tea. That'll tie you over till dinnertime."

Chris and I started to walk off, but Smythe stood in front of me. "Can I have a quick word with you?"

I saw Chris smirk and he and Dobbs went off toward the lifts, chattering in a lively manner. I knew I was trapped. "If this is personal, now's not the time. I'm dusty, sweaty, and tired."

His blue-green eyes pinned me to the spot. "You can't avoid me forever, Mia."

I sighed. "Later, okay? I promise."

A variety of emotions passed fleetingly across his face, and I thought he was going to keep me standing there until we had it out, but he gave me a half smile and let me go on my way.

~~~

We met for dinner in the a-la-carte restaurant and were seated at a round table behind black rattan screens for privacy. The captain, Garcia and Mark were already there having pre-dinner drinks with Dobbs and Smythe. When Chris and I arrived, I went straight for the chair next to Dobbs and sat down. Chris ended up sitting next to me with Smythe on his other side.

"Mia, Chris, can I order you a drink?" The captain greeted us with a smile.

"Just Pellegrino water for me, thanks," I replied, and Chris nodded for the same.

We chitchatted until the drinks arrived and we ordered our meals. Then, the captain turned to business.

"Under the circumstances, I decided to change our course. We'll still complete the trip as is, but I intend to put into Honolulu next so we have an extra day to deal with the authorities and offload the bodies. Then, we'll end the voyage on the Big Island."

"Can you do that?" Chris asked.

Mark answered, "The company reserves the right to change the itinerary as the captain sees fit. So yes, we can do that. In any case, we'll offer passengers free flights back to Honolulu for those who were originally going to end their voyage there."

"But they could stay in Honolulu once we arrive," Chris returned.

"Yes, but they already paid to visit the Big Island, so we're not going to cancel this for them."

"What about the extra day in Honolulu, are we going to sail faster to make up for it?" I asked the captain.

"Yes. As you probably know, we usually sail at a leisurely speed so we give the impression that we're cruising," the captain replied. "But the ship's capable of going much faster if need be."

Our entrees arrived then, and while we ate we reverted back to chitchat.

"Hey," Chris said to me quietly, "this means we get to go to Honolulu with Dobbs and Smythe after all."

"Yes, but don't go thinking they'll let us hang around with them while they're dealing with the authorities."

He shrugged. "I don't care about that. Let them deal with all the red tape. I want to visit Pearl Harbor."

"Yeah, me too."

"So if you let me rent a bike, we can—"

"Not this time, Chris. Honolulu has a lot more traffic than some small island in the middle of nowhere." He looked crestfallen, so I added, "But we can rent one of those big American Cadillac convertibles and drive all around."

His eyes shone. "Wow! That's even better."

"Let's just keep it between us, okay?"

He nodded and we joined the general conversation once again. "Captain," I said, "when do we arrive in Honolulu now?"

"Well, instead of the four days we were going to spend at sea, we'll make it in three. This'll give us the extra day for the stay in Honolulu."

The men then started discussing the procedure for handing over to the Honolulu Police while I turned back to Chris. "This is our last chance to catch ourselves a killer. You've got to find out who Erotic Heart is."

"I tried the satellite connection when we returned onboard and it seems okay now. If we get good weather from here to Honolulu, I'll have three days to work on it."

"Good," I replied, looking thoughtful. "In the meantime, I think we should try and flush out the killer."

"Are you crazy? That's too dangerous," Chris exclaimed.

A few faces turned our way and I shushed him. "Keep your voice down. I'll discuss it with Dobbs and Smythe, of course; but we have to do something if we're to catch this bastard before we get to Honolulu."

"And what about trying to work out if there are any future victims?"

I shrugged. "That's going to take more time than we have. But if you come across a name that jumps out at you, let me know. Mind you, even if we did get a few names, how do we know in which order the killer will get to them?"

Chris nodded. "You're right. Plus once the captain announces the change in itinerary, this'll put the squeeze on the killer. He'll surely strike if he still has unfinished business, so we need to catch him urgently."

I cocked an eyebrow at him. "My sentiments exactly."

Chris shook his head. "I don't like it, Mia. Besides, to flush out a killer you need bait, and who's going to be stupid enough to volunteer?"

~~~

"Daaaaarling, long time, no see!" Enrico Lotti sashayed toward me while I took a solitary walk on the Promenade Deck after dinner.

He wore white pantaloons and a cotton shirt, open all the way to the waistband of his pants. He had obviously been sunbathing because he sported a deep tan; and with his blond hair and green eyes, he looked like a sex god. No way he was the killer.

"Just the man I was thinking about," I said in greeting when he reached me, took me in his arms, and kissed me on each cheek. He obviously got over our little tiff, when I'd told him I wasn't going to give him any gossip.

"Why, you look positively radiant!" He admired me from top to bottom and flashed a smile of approval revealing his very bright and shiny teeth.

I was wearing white, like Enrico, in the way of an Indian cotton dress; sleeveless and with a ruffled skirt that felt like gossamer against my skin. I had gold-coloured strappy sandals on my feet and gold hoops in my ears. My light tan complemented my appearance.

"I've been looking for you, Enrico."

He put an arm around my shoulders as we continued to stroll along the deck. "And what can I do for you, bella?"

"Well..." I let the word linger for a moment. "How would you like to help me flush out a killer?"

The wide-eyed look he gave me, plus the parting of his luscious, cherubic lips into a beautiful smile, was his answer. "I'm at your command." He took a little bow for effect.

I stopped walking and turned to him. "I know this sounds like a stage production for you; but Enrico, you need to know—you'd be the bait." I felt I had to warn him lest he think we were playacting. With Enrico, one never knew.

He didn't even bat an eyelid, and I had to wonder at his sense of chivalry. "I will do this no matter what," he said while he picked up my hand and kissed the back of it in true gentlemanly fashion.

I told Enrico I would get back to him after I had a chance to put a plan together. He bid me goodnight with another kiss on each cheek and went on his way. I walked a little longer along the deck, but after a day filled with adventure I was ready to turn in. Therefore, I was totally unprepared when, about to reach my cabin, a door opened on the other side of the passageway and an arm stuck out, grabbed hold of my arm, and pulled me inside.

The door of the cabin shut and I was left leaning against it with Smythe standing in front of me. Talk about being caught between a rock and a hard place!

"What do you think you're up to? Let me out this minute!" I protested with as much indignation as I could muster.

"Not until we talk."

I knew from the determined tone in his voice I wasn't going anywhere until we had our discussion. I sighed and gave in. "Okay, if we must."

He relaxed his stance. "Can I offer you a drink?"

"No, thanks. Let's just get this over with." I didn't mean to sound so dismissive of the whole thing, but I truly was tired and my body craved for sleep.

"You snuck away during dinner," he accused with something like hurt in his eyes.

"Only because I came up with an idea to flush out the killer, and I had something to attend to."

His eyes flashed caution. "Mia, you're not to take any chances, do you hear? We're not dealing with an amateur here. Besides—"

"Hey, hold your horses, Smythe," I reassured him. "I have every intention of discussing it with you and Dobbs first. I was simply answering your question now because you accused me of sneaking out from dinner."

This seemed to have a pacifying effect on him, but not for long. He wore a frown when he said, "What is it with you? You can't deny that what happened the other night was one-sided."

He stood so close to me, I felt the current between us. But with everything that was happening around us, this was not the time to deal with our personal feelings. I wanted to process everything Dobbs had told me about my father, and I needed time to come to terms with my physical attraction for Smythe.

I took in his good looks, felt the sizzle between us, and knew I could make it easy for us by jumping into bed with him. At the same time, I was sure I'd regret it if things happened too fast. There were many unresolved issues between us at present and I didn't know how to proceed at this point.

I sighed with frustration. "Look, I don't have any answers right now. What is it that you want from me?"

Wrong question! But it was too late. No sooner were the words out of my mouth that his lips swooped down on mine and we became locked in a deep kiss too difficult to break. Not that I felt I wanted to break it. Besides, his arms were far too strong; his body too close; the excitement between us, too much. We didn't even talk except with our bodies. I gave in to the heady sensation of pure, unadulterated passion, and threw caution to the four winds.

I wasn't sure how we ended up naked in his bed or how what followed made me think I'd died and gone to some sexual heaven where orgasmic sensations were the norm. What we did initially was not make love but simply explore our raw sexuality. Our attraction for each other had been pent up for far too long, and now it exploded into being.

It took three times before we were able to slow down enough to a tender kind of lovemaking that brought tears of joy to my eyes. And this was how I finally fell asleep—in his arms, feeling safe, cherished, and loved.

CHAPTER 21

I opened my eyes and stretched languidly. My body was sore, but sated. I felt relaxed and rested, but at the same time in want of further sleep. Yet something at the back of my mind told me not everything was as it should be. Then, I became aware of deep breathing beside me and I turned my head slowly to the source, not wanting to disturb him.

Smythe was out like a light, sleeping on his side, facing me. I watched him for several moments as my horrified mind flooded with images of what had transpired during the night. I felt like screaming with joy, but also with alarm. As usual, I'd managed to get myself into trouble.

I had to get out of here immediately and seek the safe haven of my own cabin. I quashed my tumultuous emotions for the present and carefully slid out of bed while grabbing my discarded white dress, which lay in a heap on the floor. I slipped into it and looked for my undergarments. My panties rested on top of a lampshade and my bra lay over the plasma TV screen. I gathered them, together with my sandals, which I found in the bathroom, and softly made my way out of his cabin and into mine. I thanked my lucky stars the plastic key to my room was still in the small pocket of my dress and I hadn't lost it somewhere in Smythe's cabin.

Once inside, I tore off my garment and jumped straight into the shower, berating myself for being such a fool as hot jets of water almost scalded my skin. So much for my intention to wait and sort through my feelings relating to what I'd learned about my father and Smythe. In my usual impetuous fashion, I'd jumped head first into a world of erotic sensuality I'd never known existed. And I didn't mean the mechanics of it—it wasn't the sex and what we did, but how I felt when we did it. It was like everything in the universe fell into its rightful place the moment our bodies came together, and nothing else mattered.

I hated how I felt. It made me feel extremely vulnerable. It gave

Smythe power over me. I didn't want to feel this way. Not now, not ever. I'd learned the hard way in the past, and no man would ever have the opportunity to hurt me again.

I dried off from the shower and dressed in faded jeans, white T-shirt, and a pair of red Nike sneakers. I wore no make-up and allowed my hair to dry naturally while I grabbed the offending garments from last night and shoved them into a laundry bag. In the meantime, I debated whether to ring Chris in case he wanted to join me for breakfast even though it had only gone six. Before I could make up my mind, I heard a soft knock at my door. I knew who it was, but opened the door just the same.

Smythe stood on the other side, also showered, with still damp hair, and dressed in khaki shorts and a dark blue polo shirt. "May I?" he asked shyly.

I nodded, and he entered. I shut the door after him.

"What happened to you? I woke up and you were gone." He moved toward me and kissed me gently on the mouth.

I turned away, frowning. "This is moving too fast for me. You must see that. I never meant for last night to happen."

He nodded, albeit reluctantly. "That's what I thought, and why I came to apologise. It was my fault. You were trying to tell me you needed time and I attacked you instead. I was no better than Cliff Downes."

This brought a faint smile to my lips. "Yes, but at least your advances were welcome, despite my confused feelings."

He regarded me with warmth in his eyes and drew me gently into his arms. "I loved what happened between us. It's like nothing I ever felt before with anyone."

"Not even with Amanda?" I couldn't help myself.

He kissed the top of my head. "No. Not even Amanda. Amanda and I were merely consoling each other. I know this now."

I disengaged from the embrace and took a step back so I could gaze into his eyes. "Smythe, I feel the same way you do. But I still need time to process everything, and I think we should remain friends until this is all over. Once we're back home we can talk about it. Deal?"

He regarded me for a long time, desire in his eyes mixed with an emotion I couldn't put a name to. "Only under one condition," he said finally.

Now what? I thought. I looked questioningly at him and waited for his reply.

He suddenly smiled and said, "That you quit calling me Smythe. I think after what we've done I've earned the right to be called by my first name."

This was the last thing I expected to hear and I gave him an amused look. "Okay," I agreed. "But only when we're alone. I don't want the others to know what's been going on. So in public, you'll always be 'Smythe' to me."

He accepted this with a good natured, "Very well."

I sighed with relief. He understood and respected my needs. It was a good beginning, and one that should be celebrated with food. "I don't know about you, but I'm starving. Sex does that to me," I confessed.

He laughed. "Great minds think alike. Care to join me for breakfast?"

I nodded and we left the cabin together.

~~~

Smythe and I were eating in the buffet restaurant and chitchatting when Chris suddenly appeared at our table, startling us.

"Mia, I've been ringing your cabin since six. Where were you?"

He looked like he'd barely slept, but there was a glint of excitement in his eyes that set my heart beating faster. "Couldn't sleep so I came up here for an early breakfast and ran into Smythe," I told him, amazed at how easily the lie came to my lips. "It's obvious you found something, Chris. But by the looks of you, you need coffee and something to eat before you tell us. So off you go. We'll be here waiting."

Chris nodded and took off.

"Well, Ferrari," Smythe remarked with an amused grin, "already up to no good, I see. It's barely seven and you've already delivered your first lie of the day."

I smirked at his comment. "Better than telling him we shagged all night, Smythe." This took care of his teasing, but I felt good inside because it was the kind of friendly banter I wanted to have between us. And when he called me by my last name, he sounded so sexy it made me want to do things to him that wouldn't be deemed suitable behaviour in a buffet restaurant. I quickly shoved all sexual thoughts out of my head and psyched myself up for business.

Upon Chris's return with a plate piled high with scrambled eggs, bacon, grilled tomatoes, Italian sausage, and toast, I espied a sleepy-looking Dobbs walking into the restaurant. He saw me almost immediately and motioned that he was going for food.

"Dobbs just walked in," I said to Chris. "Let's wait until he gets here before you tell us what you found."

Chris nodded, too busy to talk, as he wolfed down his breakfast. Meanwhile, Smythe and I sipped our coffees in contented silence until Dobbs joined us, his plate similarly piled up like Chris's.

"So what's with the early hours?" Dobbs asked before tucking in like a man possessed.

I smiled. "I guess it's the thought of the killer having only three days left in which to finish off whatever it is he set out to do. I'm sure he's going to try to kill again. I discussed this briefly with Chris last night; and I think we need to flush him out before his next kill. Not only this, but Chris made some progress with his side of things."

Smythe said, "Regarding flushing out the killer, we need to discuss this in more detail before we agree on such a course of action."

"Of course, Smythe," I replied, pretending to be annoyed for the others' benefit. "It's not like I was going to go ahead without your and Dobbs's blessing. Besides, I've already got the bait all picked out." When I told them about Enrico volunteering for the job, they were stunned—even Dobbs stopped eating momentarily.

"The guy's a nutter, I tell you," Dobbs stated before turning his focus back on the food.

"Well, whichever way this plays out, we need to meet with Garcia and his men," Smythe said. "We have to be able to minimise the risk to all involved, especially if Enrico is bent on playing the bait."

I agreed. "Okay. Let's set up a meeting with Garcia and whoever you think should be there. Meanwhile, Chris, we're ready for you."

Chris had finished his food by this time and was onto his second cup of coffee. "I've been trying to do two things: find out Erotic Heart's true identity and check if Enrico belongs to the cheaters' forum."

"And?" I prompted.

"Still working on Erotic Heart, I'm afraid; but you were right about Enrico, Mia. He's in the forum as 'Deep Throat'; yet another one of the horse names Mrs Barry gave us."

"I knew it!" I banged the palm of my hand down on the table. "Something told me he was close to the group despite the fact he was turned down for that promotion years ago."

"You think he's the killer?" This from Smythe.

I shook my head. "No. Somehow, I don't think so. But he does have a love for the dramatic."

"So which thread in the forum did you find him in, Chris?" Smythe asked.

Chris grinned. "The men with men, of course."

Dobbs rolled his eyes and remarked with sarcasm, "What else did you expect?"

"Yes, but get this," Chris went on. "Not only is Enrico in the forum, but I managed to cross-reference two posts where he communicates with Erotic Heart."

"No!" I declared in disbelief.

"Oh yes!" Chris nodded emphatically. "And she had a thing with him, too."

Now, we all looked stunned. "You mean, like through the back door?" I said, trying to keep the conversation from getting into explicit sexual talk.

Dobbs, unfortunately, sabotaged my intent by exclaiming, "You mean she let him do her up the a—" He became aware of his surroundings just in time and cleared his throat. "I... er... I think I get the point."

"The answer is yes, Dobbs," Chris replied.

"Okay, so how does this change anything?" Smythe put in.

I shrugged. "I don't think it does. But what I do think is that Enrico knew about all the victims being in the cheaters' forum. This is what prompted him to spread the rumour of who'd be next on the list. At the same time, he's probably as concerned as us to catch the killer. I say he knows more than we do and he has a feeling he might be next."

"And why didn't the little bastard tell us this in the beginning to save us time? We might've been able to avert all those kills," Dobbs uttered with anger in his voice.

"Who knows," I replied. "Maybe it took him too long to figure it out and by the time he did, he was too afraid to come forward. This is why I think he's volunteered to be the bait. It's his way to atone for holding back information."

Chris's eyes shone when he spoke. "Just think, though; he might be able to tell us Erotic Heart's true identity. I mean, he did her... um... I meant to say, he had an illicit liaison with her after all."

"And," I added, "he may know who else from the convention group is in the forum. He could even know their usernames, which means we can pre-warn them."

"Let's get him in for questioning," Smythe said.

~~~

While Chris went off to continue with his work in case we didn't get any new information, Smythe arranged with Garcia to bring Enrico in for questioning. Dobbs, Smythe, Garcia, and I were present when Enrico was escorted by Mark Evans into one of the meeting rooms in the security office. Mark showed him to a seat at the round table where we waited and then quit the room, closing the door behind him.

Seeing as I knew Enrico best, I asked the first question. "Why didn't you tell us about Neurotic Erotics?"

Enrico had the good grace to look ashamed. "I'm sorry about that." He sounded genuine. "I wasn't sure until I put two and two together." He threw me a pleading look. "I was going to tell you all about it, Mia. But then, when you suggested I be the bait to flush out the killer, I thought it was a great idea. I didn't want to upset the other members by having you"——he swept both arms in a gesture to encompass all of us around the table—"asking a whole bunch of personal questions of them."

Smythe stated firmly, "So you simply let the murderer run around the ship, killing whoever he wants, and you turn it into a game of 'who's next'!"

Enrico looked down at his hands, which he'd placed on his lap. "It wasn't like that. When I realised what was happening, I was going to tell you."

"Do you know who the killer is?" Garcia leaned forward, his face serious.

Enrico sat back in his chair as if afraid. He undoubtedly felt cornered by all of us shooting questions at him. "No, I don't know. I don't understand the connection. Why is the killer after members of the forum?"

"We think it's a revenge thing," I answered, knowing for sure Enrico couldn't possibly be the killer. "What do you know about someone called Erotic Heart?"

He gave me a confused look. "Who?"

I sighed. "Good God, Enrico, you had sex with her!"

He cleared his throat and looked down at his hands again. "I did? When?"

Chris had told us the posts he found linking Deep Throat and Erotic Heart were five years old. "Sometime in 2008 or thereabouts."

Enrico's eyes flashed annoyance as he gazed at me. "How should I know who I saw back then? I happen to have a very busy sex life, you know! Besides, the club takes discretion very seriously. A lot of us wear a disguise if we don't want others to know who we really are. After all, we're all part of the medical community and we'd probably recognise each other."

"So you're expecting us to believe you had sex with a woman who was probably disguised as a man?" Dobbs stared at him with disbelief in his eyes.

Enrico shrugged. "I'm not into women generally. But if some woman dresses as a man, and takes it like one; who am I to argue?"

I felt like wringing his little gay neck for once. He made sex sound so cheap and sordid. But in his world, it obviously was. We were getting nowhere with him, and Erotic Heart's identity still remained a mystery. "Okay," I said, trying to control my temper, "can you at least provide us with a list of usernames of people in the forum who might also be on this ship?"

Enrico nodded. "There aren't many—only the ones I know really well. Remember, discretion is the key to our club."

"Officer Garcia, can you get some paper and a pen?" I asked. "We'll give Enrico a few minutes to write whatever names he knows. I say we reconvene in about ten minutes."

The others agreed, and while Garcia went in search of pen and paper, the rest of us moved into another office and waited until Garcia rejoined us.

"He's writing something," Garcia reported when he returned. "Not sure if it'll help, though."

Smythe said, "Meanwhile, Mia wants to put together this plan to flush out the killer. Mia?" He turned the floor over to me.

"Well, seeing as Enrico volunteered to be the bait, and the good news is he's part of this cheaters' forum, I say we get him to go around boasting to all who will listen that he made it with someone called Erotic Heart. He can drop a few hot comments about his 'unforgettable night with her'. You know; something that'll enrage the killer enough to go after Enrico."

There was silence around the table while the men thought for a few moments. Then, Dobbs commented, "So since we don't know the order of who is next on the killer's list, you're going to get Enrico to force his hand."

I nodded. "I say it'll drive the killer crazy to think this gay drama queen made it with his spouse, and he'll go after him."

Smythe concurred. "And I say we have nothing to lose. It may very well force the killer's hand. Of course, we have to keep surveillance on Enrico twenty-four seven. We can't risk something happening to him."

"I have three men at my disposal in addition to myself," Garcia offered.

"Plus there's Smythe and me," Dobbs put in.

"And me, too," I added.

"No!" Smythe uttered, turning to me with a protective look in his eyes. "No way am I putting you in the path of the killer. Look at what happened with Downes; the man practically raped you!"

I felt anger bubble away beneath the surface of my being. Just because we'd shared a night of passion didn't mean Smythe owned me. "Hey, this was my idea, Smythe! And I'm in, whether you like it or not!"

Smythe frowned, Dobbs shook his head at my outburst, and Garcia regarded me with admiration. "She's right, you know," Garcia said, making the other two turn on him while I smiled.

"You can't be serious, Jerry!" Dobbs protested. "I can't allow Mia to be exposed to danger."

Smythe simply fumed, but remained silent.

Garcia shook his head. "Gentlemen, gentlemen, don't worry. I didn't mean for Mia to take on surveillance by herself. There are six men altogether, so we'll do an eight-hour shift in pairs. Mia will be an extra, and can hang out with you two if you like."

Dobbs and Smythe looked mollified at this. "Very well," Dobbs agreed reluctantly, but not before he got the nod of approval from Smythe.

I felt like telling them all where to go, but thought it prudent to keep my mouth shut. Better to hang out with Dobbs and Smythe than be left out of the operation altogether.

"Besides," Garcia added with a smile, "I have a bit of an arsenal with me. Needless to say, those on shift will be armed."

I opened my mouth with the intention of asking if I would be given a weapon, but Smythe's hand covered my lips as he said, "Don't even think about it, Ferrari."

CHAPTER 22

Enrico came up with a list of five names, but I only recognised one of them—Dr Ken Gerard, Joy's husband, who was known as Sally Pox—yet another of the horse names given to us by Martha Barry. The name led me to wonder whether Gerard had bi-sexual tendencies; either this or he simply liked using a female username. The other four people were unknown to me, but they were all doctors who were onboard. It no longer mattered whether the usernames they utilised were linked to horses or not, what mattered now was that we could warn them, and at the same time entice the killer to go after Enrico.

We started to discuss the plan with Enrico and were joined by the captain, Mark Evans, and Mike Yuen.

"Mia," the captain said upon entering the security office, "Jerry told us about the plan, plus the fact we have another five members onboard that the killer might go for."

"Yes, Captain," I replied. "Aside from Enrico, there are five other doctors who belong to the club. We're going to focus on Enrico while we try to flush out the killer; but we need to warn the others."

"Mark and Mike will handle the other doctors. Plus a few of the crew working under Mark have volunteered to keep these people under surveillance while you and your group work with Enrico."

I gave the captain a look of gratitude. "That's great, thank you." I then turned to Mark and Mike. "This is excellent news, guys. We need all the help we can get."

Dobbs and Smythe nodded their thanks, too. "Great to have you join the team," Smythe said.

I noticed Enrico pout while the others talked in general about our surveillance plan. "Don't worry, Enrico," I whispered in his ear, "you also have our special thanks."

Enrico didn't look too happy about not being recognised by the group, but he would have to live with it for having withheld information earlier.

"We'll brief you in a while on the other five members," Garcia was saying to Mark and Mike. "First, we need to finish up here."

The captain and his officers withdrew and we turned back to Enrico.

"Now," Smythe spoke, "your job is to boast to members of the convention about your experience with Erotic Heart. Just don't go over the top, but drop as many hints as you can."

Enrico nodded, looking none too happy.

"We're going to keep you under twenty-four hour surveillance in case the killer comes after you," Garcia informed him.

This sparked off a reaction of indignation from Enrico. "What; even when I sleep?"

Garcia nodded. "Even when you sleep. This is why we're moving you to a stateroom, so your surveillance team can stay in the lounge room and give you privacy while you sleep."

"Can I have company?" Enrico had the nerve to ask.

I glared at him. "Keep your dick in your pants for once, Enrico. This is a serious matter. The last thing we need is to babysit two of you while you're going at it!"

Enrico seemed to shrink at my threatening manner and said nothing. I felt like hitting him over his ungrateful head.

"Okay," Garcia continued with a look of amusement my way. "I'll take Enrico so we can relocate him to the new room. Then, I'll meet you with Mark and Mike to discuss surveillance for the other five doctors."

Garcia motioned Enrico out of the office and Dobbs exploded when the door shut behind them. "We should let the killer get to that little mincing poof after all! He deserves it for being such an asshole!" Dobbs's American accent never failed to become more pronounced when he was angry, and I couldn't help laughing.

"Now, you don't mean that, Dobbs. Our business is to save lives," I teased.

"Hey, Ferrari, you were ready to clobber him over the head just now," he protested, looking agitated.

"Yes, but I wouldn't have killed him off. We need him too much."

"I'm off to grab a coffee," Dobbs announced grumpily. "I'll see you guys in a while."

Smythe laughed after Dobbs exited the room. "You two are so funny. Is this how you work at the hotel when you come up against a big drama?"

"It's usually me who loses her temper and Dobbs who calms me down. But I say in this instance, Dobbs has had enough. This killing spree's been too much for all of us. I think Rourke and Teppler owe us a real holiday after this is over."

"You can say that again," Smythe agreed. "In the meantime, I came up with my own way to calm *you* down."

His mouth took mine in a kiss that melted my limbs and left me clinging to him. Even so, I managed to break away and throw him a stern look.

Before I could speak, he said, "I'm sorry. I just couldn't help myself."

I took a couple of steps back to put some distance between us. "You promised we'd be friends, Smythe. Friends don't kiss each other like this." Then, I added with an impish look as I didn't want to hurt his feelings, "Besides, that kiss did nothing to calm me down. If anything, it had the opposite effect."

He beamed at the latter part of my admonishment, but then said, "I know. I know. I lost my head."

He looked forlorn when he apologised, and I wanted to take him into my arms and soothe him. But someone had to harden their heart—and it was going to be me. Thank God women were stronger and more practical than men.

~~~

Before the meeting with Mark Evans and his men, I ran down to check on Chris.

"Nothing as yet," he reported after I told him Enrico didn't remember anything about Erotic Heart. "But don't worry, I'll keep trying."

"I hope you can find something soon. It'll make it so much easier than trying to flush out the killer."

Chris glanced up from the laptop screen. "Yeah, but Mia, even if I do get an ID on Erotic Heart, it won't tell us who the spouse is unless the account is under joint names or just in his name."

I shrugged. "True. In any case, it would help to know."

Chris turned back to the computer. "I'm on it."

I left him to it and made my way back to the security office where the meeting was already in progress. Just as I walked in, Garcia was writing shift times on a whiteboard for both our surveillance group and the one Mark Evans would be heading.

"The first shift commences today at 3.00pm for both groups," Garcia informed us. "Enrico's going to start dropping hints at lunchtime. The convention members have a group lunch after their morning seminar; so we hope the killer will be among them. I'll take the first shift with one of my guys; then Phil, Guy, and Mia can do the graveyard shift in Enrico's stateroom from 11.00pm. You'll be relieved by two of my guys at 7.00am the following morning."

While Garcia discussed the shifts for Mark's people, I turned to Dobbs, who was sitting next to me, and whispered, "I guess we'll have to stock up on huge amounts of coffee to stay awake all night."

Dobbs beamed at me. "I just thank God we don't have to listen to Enrico humping away with one of his fairy friends."

I grinned and almost laughed aloud. The image that flashed into my mind of Enrico and a male lover was simply too much to bear—the situation in which we found ourselves, too surreal to contemplate. I was quite broadminded when it came to gay men, but I drew the line at having to listen to them going at it.

After the meeting, Dobbs and Smythe went off with Garcia to be assigned their weapons. I was left out of this macho bonding session but didn't care for once. I had no real desire to carry a weapon, let alone use one. So I decided to have a light lunch in my room and then catch up on my sleep in preparation for the graveyard shift.

An hour later, while I was drifting off to sleep, I vaguely heard Dobbs and Smythe going into their respective cabins, possibly to do the same thing. Tonight was going to be boring unless we got some action from the killer. Somehow, I doubted it. I couldn't see the guy coming up to Enrico's stateroom to knock on the door. It was already suspicious enough that Enrico had been allocated a new room. I only hoped the killer believed the explanation Enrico would be spinning about this—namely that his bathroom flooded in his old cabin and he was upgraded to a stateroom to compensate for the inconvenience.

~~~

I slept until after seven and then showered and dressed, ready to meet with Dobbs, Smythe and Chris for dinner before we got ready for our first shift. I wore comfortable khaki cargo pants and a black T-shirt, and I felt like some kind of a commando.

We met at the buffet restaurant and I noticed Dobbs and Smythe were similarly attired. Chris was in his usual shorts and T-shirt.

"I think we look a bit conspicuous, don't you?" I remarked to Dobbs.

Dobbs, who was already tucking into a full plate of lasagna, replied, "We can't very well turn up in our PJs now, can we?"

I laughed. "I guess not, even though you'd look so cute in a pair of horsey jammies."

His frown was enough to tell me he was not looking forward to babysitting Enrico; therefore, I should stop the teasing.

As it turned out, our shift wasn't quite so bad. Dobbs and Smythe played cards most of the night, just as they did at their usual poker night back home. I watched a movie and later read a book. We ordered room service twice: coffee and burgers at around two in the morning and a big breakfast at six. By seven, when we were relieved by Garcia's men, we were exhausted.

"Everything okay?" asked one of the security guards.

Smythe nodded. "Uneventful night. Enrico's still asleep. Anything to report from Garcia's shift?"

The security guard shook his head. "No. All's been quiet, including the surveillance of the other five doctors. Officer Garcia will be holding a debrief at 10.00am in the security office."

"Will do," Smythe replied.

We left Enrico's stateroom and made our way to the Promenade Deck to get a breath of fresh air.

"Man, that was a long night," I commented, stretching my arms over my head.

"That's what you get for insisting on being part of this team," Smythe admonished.

I knew he still wasn't happy I'd tagged along. "Well, too bad, Smythe. You're stuck with me."

Dobbs frowned at us. "Hey, you two, save the arguments for later. I thought you finally learned to work together."

I hid a smile. "It takes time, Dobbs."

Smythe winked at me when Dobbs turned away, then said, "So what now?"

"I'm off to get some shuteye," Dobbs answered. "Someone knock on my door at nine-thirty so I don't miss the debrief." With a wave of his hand, he left us alone.

"He's really cranky these days," Smythe observed.

"He must miss Eileen," I remarked. "And wait until she sees how much weight he's put back on. She'll positively kill him!"

Smythe grinned. "Let the poor man enjoy the holiday as much as he can, Mia—even if it means putting on a few pounds."

"I know. Dobbs can never resist good food, and he gets really irritated when hungry."

We stood for a while in silence, both of us gazing at the horizon. The sky was a light cerulean blue today while the ocean was its usual deep indigo.

After a few moments, I yawned. "I think I'll get some shuteye as well. What about you?"

His eyes danced with wickedness. "Is that an invitation?"

The look I gave him said it all.

"Okay, okay. I was only kidding," he placated me. "Want me to knock on your door for the debrief?"

"Yes, thanks. And if you don't mind, please check on Chris when you can. I want to know if he's made any progress."

"Yes, ma'am." He gave me a suggestive look, which said a thousand things, but he managed to control himself.

~~~

"Today, I'll get you guys to do the three to eleven shift," Garcia informed Dobbs, Smythe and me at the debrief. "I'll take the graveyard."

"Any news?" Smythe enquired.

"Nothing. But I don't expect such quick results. For all we know, the killer may not yet have heard about Enrico's exploits," Garcia answered. "Today might be different, though."

"Well, I hope so," I interjected, "because we have another day and night at sea after this one, and then we reach Honolulu."

We looked at one another in silence, all of us knowing that when we reached Honolulu the killer would certainly make his escape. For one, I didn't believe he was going to get to all the others on the ship. If anything, he'd probably get to them on land when we all went home. This made me remark, "You know, you have to wonder why the killer waited this long to get to everybody. Why now; why on the ship?"

Smythe answered, "Who's to say he waited? He may have left a trail of dead bodies back home that we haven't heard about yet."

The thought was sobering.

Garcia went on to cover a few other issues, and within thirty minutes we were out of the room.

"Let's meet for a late lunch and then go on shift," Dobbs suggested.

I nodded and turned to Smythe. "Anything from Chris yet?"

"He said something about finally having found the server he was after. Now, he's trying to break into it."

This raised my spirits a little. "Excellent. I'm off to snooze some more. I'll see you guys at lunch."

I didn't know whether Dobbs and Smythe needed to grab more sleep or not, but the moment my head hit the pillow, I was gone. It was amazing how working a graveyard shift mucked up one's biological clock.

I slept right through until a knock on my door woke me and Smythe's voice called out, "Mia, lunchtime!"

We had lunch at the Deck Grill with Chris, who was bubbling with excitement.

"I'm getting really close now. I finally found the right server, so it's a matter of cross-referencing the log-in times and dates and I should be able to ID her."

"That's great, Chris," Smythe praised him.

"Yeah, you should get a medal for this," I agreed. "If it weren't for your work, we'd never have come this far."

"I concur," Dobbs added with cheeseburger in hand.

Chris blushed. "Thank you, but it wasn't just me. Mia was the one who figured out the way to the cheaters' site. If she hadn't done that, we'd still be chasing our tails."

The other two did not deny it, and Smythe threw me a secret

smile. Then, he glanced at his watch. "Almost two-thirty," he announced. "Let's get ready to relieve the morning team."

We left Chris to finish his lunch and while Dobbs and Smythe went to retrieve their weapons from the security office, I changed into my cargo pants and T-shirt. Later, we met up with Enrico by the pool. The morning team left us and we hung around, sitting at different tables and having a cool drink or pretending to read while we kept an eye on Enrico, who was sunbathing. No one approached him, nor did we see anything suspicious.

After this, we were forced to hang around the stateroom while Enrico took a shower and a nap. Dobbs and Smythe played poker while I flicked through a glossy magazine, bored to tears.

Later, we dined at the buffet restaurant while Enrico and a 'friend' sat at a couple of tables away from us chatting and laughing every few seconds.

"If someone doesn't kill him soon, I will," Dobbs said through clenched teeth. "Who does he think he is; a pop diva? That we should have to hang around while he sunbathes or has dinner with one of his lovers. This is unacceptable!"

Smythe and I exchanged a glance before I said, "Hang in there, Dobbs. Only one more day and night and we reach Honolulu."

He sighed with frustration, but said nothing.

After dinner, Enrico and his boyfriend went for a stroll on Deck 13, which looked rather dark and deserted. Dobbs, Smythe and I held back at a fair distance in order not to look too obvious.

Dobbs complained again. "Great! He picks the darkest place, knowing the killer could shoot him from a distance."

Smythe and I remained silent. No good feeding Dobbs's frustration. Meanwhile, I turned to look down on Deck 12 through the stairwell rail. A movie was playing on a giant plasma screen, located high above the swimming pool. This was pretty much the only light we had, which filtered up to Deck 13.

We sat on the top steps of the stairwell leading to Deck 13 for ages, hoping Enrico would hurry up and stop making out with his boyfriend. I could just see the two figures engaged in a tight embrace and two heads coming together. I looked away. Then, I tensed.

My thigh happened to be touching Smythe's as we sat on the same step and he felt it go tense, along with the rest of me. "What is it?" he whispered.

"I think we've got company," I said in a low voice, enough for Dobbs and Smythe to hear. I pointed toward the stairwell on the other side of the deck, which also led up to Deck 13 from the deck below. A figure was climbing the stairs slowly in the dark.

Smythe patted my shoulder. "You stay here, Mia. And don't move."

I nodded.

"Ready?" Smythe said to Dobbs.

They drew out their Glocks and carefully began to move along Deck 13 and toward the figure, keeping low and out of sight.

The figure was definitely that of a male, similar in build to the killer's. This could be him. I took a peek over the steps and observed the person walking toward Enrico and his friend. I suddenly felt like screaming out a warning to him, but this would alert the man who was now rapidly making his way in Enrico's direction with something bulky in his hand.

With my heart in my mouth, I watched as the figure advanced. Then, when he was around twenty feet away from the embracing pair, I saw Dobbs and Smythe appear a few feet behind the figure.

"Stop right there!" Smythe suddenly called out, both his and Dobbs's guns pointed at him.

In that same instant, the movie ended and the credits scrolled on the screen in black letters against a white background; and with the light emitted from the screen, Deck 13 became clearly visible to everyone.

Dobbs and Smythe quickly put their guns down as Enrico broke away from his lover's embrace and ran toward the figure, which turned out to be that of a young crewmember holding a bottle of champagne in one hand and three glasses in the other.

"Darling Zane! We thought you'd never make it!" Enrico called out before he hugged the young man. Then, he turned to Smythe. "It's okay, he's one of us."

Luckily, no one on Deck 12 saw the commotion; and Dobbs and Smythe drew away quietly. As they came closer to me, I noticed the expression on their faces and thought, if only looks could kill.

CHAPTER 23

The next day was our last at sea before we were due to sail into Honolulu on the following morning. After a deep sleep as a result of the previous night's excitement, Smythe, Dobbs, and I met up for a late breakfast. I checked with Chris in case he wanted to join us, but he'd been up for hours and on a real roll so he ordered his meal through room service.

We sat in the outdoor area of the buffet restaurant that was practically empty as most people had eaten by now. Dobbs was making his way through a huge ham and mushroom omelette while I only managed a small portion of scrambled eggs on toast. Smythe had the whole works including Italian sausage and grilled Roma tomatoes. All of us drank from mugs of strong coffee.

"What shift are we on today?" I asked, knowing Smythe had just come back from meeting with Garcia.

"Same one—three to eleven."

"So this is it. If the killer doesn't make a move tonight, we'll never know who it is."

"We may have to follow this up back in Sydney, Mia," Smythe said. "Assuming the killer resides in Australia, that is."

"True," I remarked. "We don't even know where he's from. I remember Enrico telling me the convention has doctors from all over the place including the US, Canada, South Africa, and even India."

"Well, after this trip I'm not going anywhere else to chase up some demented killer," Dobbs chimed in. "I need a real holiday. Besides, the minute we put into Hawaii this ceases to be our job."

I frowned. "But after all we've been through it isn't fair to come away with an unsolved crime."

Dobbs said, "And you wanted to be a cop. I think Phil will agree with me when I say being a cop is often a thankless task, even if you catch the criminal. Half the time, they get a fancy lawyer who gets them off on a technicality and all the hard work you put in gets flushed down the toilet."

"Ouch!" I uttered. "Talk about cynicism, Dobbs."

"Hey, I spent enough years on the force to see this time and again. So did your father, and so does Phil."

I turned to Smythe, only to see him nod. "He's right, you know."

"Well," I stated, "I still would've liked to have had the option to experience life as a cop."

"Trust me," commented Dobbs with a full fork halfway to his mouth, "you're not missing out on anything special."

I rolled my eyes and decided to drop the subject. I really couldn't work out what was wrong with Dobbs these days. Perhaps, he was simply getting old. He was in his early sixties and obviously looking forward to retirement and being able to spend more time with his granddaughter in Hawaii. I was sure if David Rourke ended up opening a hotel in Honolulu, Dobbs would transfer there like a shot. The hotel on the Big Island was not practical enough for him, but based in his hometown, and near his daughter and granddaughter, would be ideal.

I sighed. If this went ahead and Dobbs transferred, I was going to miss him. He was like family to me—the only family I had since the death of my father. Of course, I still had Chris, who was like my son; and now, Smythe—well, at least as a friend. Beyond this, I couldn't think further.

I stole a quick peek his way while he ate and felt the blood rush to my face. The physical attraction between us was electrifying, but then I'd thought the same thing about David Rourke years ago; and later with Nathan, the evil ex. Sexual attraction was one thing, but living day in, day out with someone was quite another. After Nathan, I could never trust another man nor did I think I could survive another betrayal.

Smythe must've picked up on my vibes because he turned his gaze my way and threw me a warm smile that made me want to melt. And I thought hormones went out the window with approaching menopause. Boy, was I wrong!

~~~

We were back on shift at three and by eight that evening I'd had enough. I was fed up with watching Enrico flirting with his lover over dinner while we played nursemaid to him.

"I need some fresh air," I announced to my companions as I stood from the dining table. "I'll go for a quick walk and then check on how Chris is progressing. Do you mind if we meet in one hour?"

Smythe hesitated, and I knew he wanted to accompany me, but his duty lay in keeping an eye on Enrico. "Meet us back here," he said instead. "The way Enrico's going, he'll probably still be dining until ten."

Dobbs frowned. "Not if I shoot him first."

I threw him a smile. "Grumpy, grumpy!" I said and walked off with a wave.

The Promenade Deck was deserted when I went out and leaned at the rail to gaze into the night. We had a half moon, and in the silver light the ocean looked absolutely magic. I fleetingly wished Smythe was here with me. More and more, I felt my defences against him begin to crumble. I sighed. So what if the romance didn't keep going in our day-to-day lives? I could risk my heart once again. I'd survived hurt and betrayal before. I was older and tougher these days. Besides, if things didn't work out, I could always ask David for a transfer to another country—maybe even join Dobbs in Hawaii.

In my mind's eye, I flashed back to the night Smythe and I made love. It had been so intense that I now couldn't imagine going back to the humdrum life I'd been living since the break up of my marriage. Granted, I'd had a fling in between, but that meant nothing.

A door opened at one end of the deck, interrupting my thoughts, and I looked up. It was a young couple holding hands and occasionally exchanging a kiss. They strolled slowly past me, wishing me a good evening. I returned the greeting, and they walked the length of the deck and went back inside through another door at the other end. I was left alone with my thoughts once again, but I didn't want to revisit my feelings for Smythe. It was time to check on Chris and then return to my post.

I turned and walked in the same direction the couple had taken, but before I could reach the door it opened, and a man came out. I almost called out to him but stopped myself just in time, even though he'd already seen me and started to make his way in my direction.

Something wasn't right. The figure approaching me was that of someone fit and only a few years older than I. His steps were strong and sure. His face was the same. His eyes looked directly into mine, but there was no smile in them—only something tantamount to enmity.

My heart leapt to my throat as he lifted his walking stick to reveal a six-inch steel pick protruding from its end. Professor Tully did not need a stick to walk; he did not have arthritis, and he certainly wasn't in his sixties or seventies, as I had originally thought. He also had the exact gait of the killer—he *was* the killer.

"It was you all along!" I accused despite the cold fear permeating my body. "But why?" I was so surprised at his transformation that it never occurred to me to run in the opposite direction to make my escape.

He stopped a few feet away from me and uttered with venom in his voice, "Because she was a filthy slut! But she got what she deserved in the end."

I noted the ominous look on his face and realised he'd killed his own wife. He knew what I was thinking.

"Yes, I killer her," he confessed. "She betrayed me for thirty years. Yet, every day I was with her she acted the part of the perfect wife. But she was a sick depraved sex addict, and she couldn't help herself. If it had pants, she had to fuck it." He shook his head in disgust. "I think I must've been the only one who had normal sex with her, and she found it 'boring'; or so she said in one of her posts from that filthy forum she belonged to."

"You knew about the cheaters' club?"

"I knew everything: the personal ads she answered during the days before the internet, the online dating, the cheaters' forum, how she sneaked off to rut like a whore while on the pretext of taking tango lessons. I certainly knew everything!" His voice dripped pure hatred. "But she was careless, *my beautiful Eden*, and she was foolish enough to keep a diary, thinking I'd never find it."

I started to take minute steps backwards because I knew I was going to have to make a run for it, but at the same time I was mesmerised by this man—this killer, who meted out his own brand of punishment because his wife had betrayed him through their whole marriage. I could understand how it had pushed him over the edge. This happened all the time to people who were betrayed by those they thought loved them in return. Only not everyone acted on their hurt and anger; at least, not like Tully.

"But why put up with so many years of betrayal?" I asked; both wanting to know and also to keep him distracted while I took those miniscule steps in preparation for my escape.

"Because despite what she was, I loved her—and I lived in the hope she'd come forward and confess. I would have forgiven her anything, you know." For a moment, he rubbed at his eyes, in the process lifting his glasses; and I took another small step backward. Then, he continued, his voice full of anger. "But day in, day out, she lived her fantasies with these men—even gay ones like that dirty faggot, Enrico! I didn't know about him, but I heard the rumours yesterday." He shook his head as if he couldn't believe it. "What makes a prostitute like her want it up the arse?" His savage tone made me jump and I knew any moment now he would snap and lunge at me.

"Why did you say you had arthritis?" I knew the answer to this, of course; but I had to say something to divert him from his venomous thoughts, if only for a few seconds.

"It lulled her into a false sense of security while I started to hunt down her lovers. The arthritis gave me the perfect excuse to slow down and give up my medical practice. This way, I had more time on my hands." He threw me a knowing look. "Yes, I know you probably worked out by now this cruise isn't the beginning of my mission of revenge. The whole thing started after I killed her last year. I stabbed her through her black cheating heart with this very walking stick that I'm now going to use on you!"

I was still in time to make a run for it, but I had to know more. "What did I ever do?" I couldn't help sounding resentful. "I was nice to you, damn it!"

He looked me up and down, taking in my cargo pants and tight T-shirt that stretched across my chest, accentuating the shape of my breasts. "You're a slut, too," he spat out. "I've seen you on this very deck, first exchanging kisses with that officer and later with one of your travelling companions. You're a whore like the rest of them!"

"Hey!" For a moment, I didn't care about his threat to kill me; walking stick or no walking stick. "At least I didn't cheat on anybody! If anything, my own ex cheated on me!" What the hell was I doing arguing with a killer? I came to my senses abruptly. The guy was out of his mind. He wasn't going to respond to reason. I took another small step back, but this time he noticed.

"You're not going to get away from me, you bitch! If it hadn't been for you and your friends, I would've been able to finish off the job right here on the ship. But you had to stick your nose where it wasn't wanted, and now you're going to pay."

I turned to make a run for it then, but he lunged at me, bringing me down by taking hold of my feet. He was more agile than I thought.

I hit the deck hard, but protected banging my head by breaking the fall with my arms. The pain that shot through my left forearm was excruciating, but better this than be knocked unconscious so he could drive the steel pick through my heart.

I kicked out at his face with my feet and connected with his nose. He let out a yelp of pain, and I managed to stand up. But he was too fast for me. He followed and caught me from behind just before I reached the door. With a strong arm around my neck, half choking me, he dragged me away from the door and toward the rail. A thought flashed through my mind that rather than stab me, he would get rid of me a lot quicker if he simply pushed me overboard like he'd done with van Horn.

It seemed this was his purpose. He crushed my torso against the rail with his own body and winded me so much that I collapsed right into his arms. He then lifted me like I weighed nothing and brought my body up onto the balustrade. One small push and I would go hurtling down into the depths of the ocean, never to be seen again.

Just as he pushed, however, my right hand caught hold of the metal rail under me. He tried to pry my fingers open so I would let go.

In the meantime, I managed to wriggle out of his arms and my feet touched the deck. He suddenly let me go altogether and lunged for the walking stick instead, which was lying on the deck a few feet away. It took him seconds to retrieve it and run back toward me with the sharp pick aiming straight for my heart.

I tensed, knowing it was too late to step out of the way. With eyes closed, I waited for the piercing pain that was sure to put an end to my life.

A couple of seconds went by and nothing happened. Then, I opened my eyes just in time to see Smythe take a dive from the open doorway, tackling Tully out of the way and bringing him to the ground.

199

My legs collapsed from under me and I fell straight into Chris's arms while I watched Dobbs and Garcia overpower Tully as he struggled with Smythe. The walking stick went flying from Tully's hand, only to land a few feet away from Chris and me.

Smythe punched Tully in the stomach and winded him. He then stood and came away, letting Dobbs and Garcia turn Tully face down to cuff him.

Chris deposited me in Smythe's arms, where he knew I wanted to be. I was engulfed by Smythe and my body molded into his. He held me for a moment while we watched Tully being taken away by Dobbs and Garcia, and followed by Chris; who picked up the walking stick from the steel tip so he could preserve Tully's fingerprints on the wooden part.

When they left, Smythe swung me up into his arms. "You okay?" he asked with concern in his eyes.

I nodded and leaned my face into his shoulder. "Just a sore arm."

He reached with his head and planted a lingering soft kiss on my lips. "I thought I was going to lose you. I thought we were going to be too late."

A thrill of desire spread through me, but I controlled it. "How did you know where to find me?"

"Enrico left the restaurant early and I rang Chris's cabin, thinking you were already with him. He said you hadn't come at all. Then, he told me he cracked into the server and gave me the real name of Erotic Heart. It was—"

"Eden Tully," I said for him.

"Tully told you?"

"Not exactly, but he mentioned Eden belonging to the cheaters' forum, so I assumed he broke into her account."

"Her real name was Edina Vasquez Tully," Smythe informed me.

"Tully used to talk about her with such love," I returned sadly. "He killed her, you know; along with the others. You were right to suggest he might have left a long trail of bodies back home."

Smythe kissed me softly once more, probably so he could make himself believe I had survived the ordeal. I didn't stop him. I had come so close to losing my life that I decided to live for the moment. We kissed for a long time, passionately and lingeringly. When we came up for air, I said, "You didn't tell me how you knew I'd be here."

"Chris made the connection. He knew you and Tully were shipboard friends. And I figured you'd be out here because you mentioned you wanted to take a breath of air. I remembered you liked strolling along this deck."

I sighed with relief. "Thank God you guys arrived in time. I didn't know how much longer I could hold out. I had every intention of making a run for it but at the same time, I had to hear what Tully had to say. I never thought he'd be so fit, you know. I underestimated him. Some cop I'd make, huh? Besides—"

Smythe regarded me lovingly with his blue-green gaze. "Shut up, Ferrari," he whispered in my ear and held me tighter against him as he took the opportunity to put a stop to my chatter with yet another body-melting kiss.

Entry from Mia's Case Book

Case No 3 – The Neurotic Erotics Club

Upon arrival in Honolulu, Professor Tully was taken into custody by the local police. Dobbs had arranged for his contact in the force to meet the ship. While the men—Dobbs and Smythe, along with Mark Evans, Jerry Garcia and the captain—went to deal with the authorities, a number of police officers remained behind to take statements from members of the medical convention, the crew, staff, the ship's doctor, and Chris and me. A coroner's van arrived shortly thereafter to take away the bodies of Doctors Barry, Weinstein and Downes to the morgue.

David Rourke and Edward Teppler flew into Honolulu from the Big Island and while Teppler waited on the ship to confer with the captain upon his return, David Rourke escorted his son and I to a luxury hotel in Waikiki, where he booked us in for a few days' rest before we were due to fly back to Sydney. He also booked rooms for Dobbs and Smythe, telling us we needed a well-deserved break. David then flew back to his hotel project in Waikoloa with the promise he'd see us upon his return to Sydney in a couple of weeks.

Chris and I slept for most of that day, absolutely exhausted from the long hours we put into the investigation while onboard the ship. Dobbs and Smythe came back to the hotel in the late afternoon, also to rest. In the evening, we had a catch-up session over dinner.

Smythe told us Tully made a full confession. Aside from those he killed onboard, he also murdered six of his wife's lovers back in Australia, plus he killed Eden in 2012—hence the reason we couldn't find any recent posts from her on the cheaters' forum. Considering the nature of the crime and the fact that all the victims were Australian, the professor was to be extradited to face charges in his home country.

Upon inspection of Tully's papers, the police confirmed his age at fifty-five years. This fitted in with Tully's story that he met Eden at university and they later married, and stayed married, for thirty years. I had been convinced the professor was older, especially because of his white hair and his complaints about the arthritis. Tully confessed to pretending he had arthritis to throw people off, but the white hair was natural—probably premature greying as a result of the betrayal he suffered at the hands of the one he loved.

We never learned why someone as passionate as Eden—or Beatriz Edina Vasquez, as was her formal name in the old passport Tully still carried with him as a reminder of happier times—had decided to marry someone as conventional as Tully. We could only surmise Eden wanted the financial stability Tully could provide, but still live out her fantasies and assuage the desires of her Latin nature with other men.

The Neurotic Erotics Club was the brainchild of Dr Bertrand van Horn. Many of the doctors in his circle wanted to satisfy certain sexual fantasies and desires, which they couldn't very well do at home. Discretion within the club was the order of the day. If discovered it could mean the end of the members' career if they were found out. So rather than belong to intimate dating sites, they decided to form their own club; and only members of the medical and health sector were admitted after scrutiny from van Horn and a couple of his closest colleagues.

Enrico Lotti, having been a doctor once upon a time, was an avid member of the club, especially within the gay medical community, which was still frowned upon, as he later found out when he was passed over for promotion on account of his partner having been diagnosed as HIV positive. Despite Lotti choosing to leave his medical career, he kept up with the club's activities and remained very much an active member.

After five days of total relaxation time in Waikiki; and even though I fought hard to resist Smythe's charms and failed a few times, we flew back to Sydney and returned to our respective routines. Dobbs lost his grumpy demeanour the minute he was reunited with his wife,

Eileen. Not only this, but Eileen was so happy to have him back that she didn't even scold him for the extra pounds he packed on.

Chris returned to university and kept working as a casual waiter in the functions department of the hotel, where he also resided in the Penthouse with his father. David remained with the hotel project in Waikoloa and then began negotiations for the takeover and revamp of a hotel property in Waikiki. This brought my fear to the fore that Dobbs, my good friend and father figure, might decide to return to his homeland to be closer to his daughter and grandchild.

Smythe went back on the job as Detective Sergeant with the Kings Cross police. He was later offered a promotion to the position of Detective Inspector. This meant he would take on more of a supervisory role at the station and limit his time out on the streets. He accepted the position and told me it was high time for a change. Like Dobbs, he felt sometimes being a cop was a thankless task. Besides, he'd seen enough violence in his career to the point where he now wanted to take more of a backseat role within the local area command.

I suspected he accepted the job because he hoped we could make some kind of a life together if he worked in a safer environment. He knew how difficult it was to live with a cop who was always out on the streets, especially in an area like Kings Cross—Sydney's red light district. But the whole case of Tully and his revenge of Eden's betrayal left me feeling numb. I'd only been divorced from Nathan for three years; and after an eighteen-year marriage, the last thing I wanted was to become involved in another relationship. I still felt the sting of Nathan's betrayal and constantly questioned the meaning of romantic love. People always professed to love one another only to end up splitting up, hating, or even killing each other when things didn't work out.

I didn't feel ready to commit to anyone just yet. Besides, I wanted time to think about my father and why he led me to believe Smythe had been responsible for my not getting into the force. I loved my father and missed him every day, but I also needed to forgive him.

Smythe and I ended up falling into a close friendship that constantly tempted us to take things into the bedroom. I managed to put a stop to this most of the time, but not always. After all, I'm only human. Smythe took it well and remained patient. I knew he wanted more of a commitment from me, and he figured if he wanted to be with me long term he would have to wait until I was ready. If he remained constant, there was the chance we may end up together. At the same time, he knew there were no guarantees. I made sure he understood this because I didn't want to trap him into thinking he and I would become a permanent item.

We were both fully aware of the well-known saying: "If you love something, set it free; if it comes back, it's yours. If it doesn't, it was never meant to be."

One thing I did agree to do, however, was to call him "Phil" whenever we were alone.

THE END

About the Author

Sylvia Massara is a multi-genre author based in Sydney, Australia. She loves to dabble in wacky love affairs, drama, murder, sci-fi (or anything else that takes her fancy) over good coffee.

Born in Argentina from Italian and Spanish descent (with a bit of Swiss thrown in) and transplanted to Australia at age 10, Sylvia describes herself as a bit of a "moggie" cat by way of mixed pedigree. She is also a citizen of the world as she has travelled widely throughout most of her life and she's the proud owner of three passports.

From a creative perspective, Sylvia has been writing since her early teens and her work consists of novels, screenplays and freelance writing. She has also dabbled in acting on and off, songwriting and even had her own band during her teens/early 20s where she performed at various venues.

As with most authors, Sylvia draws on her varied experience from the often puzzling tapestry of life. A few years ago Sylvia resigned from the human race because she discovered the animal kingdom was a much nicer place to be.

Currently, Sylvia lives with her cat, Mia; and always vicariously through the many characters in her head. Occasionally, Sylvia ventures into the world of humans, and she cherishes genuine friendships as they are a rare find.

Sylvia has recently released her 7th novel, The Stranger, a sci-fi apocalyptic romance with moralistic issues that involve the fight of love vs evil in the cosmos.

Please visit the author's website to keep up with her latest novels or to contact her at: www.sylviamassara.com

About Massara's Novels

The Mia Ferrari Mystery Series

Playing With The Bad Boys

A woman plunges ten floors down an atrium and lands on a baby grand piano in the luxurious Rourke Hotel Sydney. The police rule this as a straight case of suicide; but 48-year-old hotel duty manager and wannabe investigator, Mia Ferrari, thinks otherwise.

As Mia sets out to unravel the mysterious death and prove the cops wrong, especially her archenemy, Detective Sergeant Phil Smythe; she comes up against an unsavoury cast of characters who will do anything to shut her up. But with a little help from her friends, Mia will not stop until she unearths the truth.

Mia Ferrari is a "wiseass", older chick with determination and an attitude, and she never takes "no" for an answer.

The Gay Mardi Gras Murders

Mia Ferrari, smartarse, older chick, super sleuth, is back in her 2nd murder mystery, and this time, she is up to her neck in drag queens, a rare diamond with a curse and murder most foul against the backdrop of Sydney's world famous Gay Mardi Gras.

A female impersonator is found dismembered in her hotel suite bathtub, and a rare diamond worth twenty million dollars is gone. The Gay Mardi Gras is fast approaching and Mia Ferrari, senior duty manager of the exclusive Rourke International Hotel Sydney, has to juggle a bunch of drag queens, a number of fabulously handsome gay men, a transsexual with a dark mystery, a young cop with sex on his mind, a close friend from the UK who is having marital problems and a mounting body count.

As Mia pits her investigative skills against her archenemy, Detective Sergeant Phil Smythe, to solve the case, she not only becomes embroiled in the life of the people around her, but it looks like she is the next target for a serial killer with a grudge against gay men.

The South Pacific Murders

It's a well-known fact that wherever Mia Ferrari goes trouble always follows, and going on a holiday cruise to Hawaii is no different.

A killer is on the loose onboard ship. A number of doctors from a medical convention are being murdered one by one. The captain of the cruise liner asks Mia and her travelling companions to take over the investigation while the ship is in the middle of the Pacific Ocean toward its final destination. A secret sex club and horse racing bets are the only clues that can uncover the identity of the killer, but will Mia be able to solve the mystery before the killer strikes again?

Join Mia and her friends, plus her sexy detective archenemy, on a cruise to murder, mayhem, and sizzling hot sex.

Science fiction romance

The Stranger

The Stranger is a sci-fi apocalyptic romance with moralistic issues involving the fight between love and evil and its repercussions.

Rhys is on a mission on Earth in order to determine Earth's destiny, but his judgement is in danger of becoming clouded when he meets and falls in love with Carla, a human. The balance of life on Earth depends upon Rhys's recommendation to the League of Galaxies. But how will Rhys choose between his mission and his love for an Earthling? Rhys is forced to weigh up the collective evil on Earth and its causal effect on the greater good of other life in the universe against the love he has for one woman.

This is not simply a tale of love between two beings but a story of the unconditional and sublime love, which is the force that drives the cosmos.

The Stranger was dedicated to the Loving Memory of David Bowie.

Romance

Like Casablanca

What does internet dating and Casablanca have in common? Nothing, unless you go to Rick's Cafe and find out what antiques dealer and dating blogger, Cat Ryan, is up to.

Cat's doing research for her internet dating blog gig, and the place she chooses to meet her many dates is at Rick's Cafe in Sydney. But what of its disturbingly handsome owner, Rick Blake?

Cat wonders what he thinks, seeing her with a different male all the time. What's more, why does this bother Cat so much? It's not like she wants any involvement after her recent break up with Josh, her cheating ex. Besides, it looks like Rick is trying to get back together with his ex-wife, Denise. So Cat decides to play it safe, but her heart has different ideas.

The Other Boyfriend

Sarah Jamison is on a mission to find a boyfriend for Moira, who is her lover's partner. And Sarah's best friend, Monica, comes to the rescue with the perfect solution. Enter the enigmatic Mike Connor.

Monica is sure that Mike will sweep Moira off her feet, leaving the way open for Sarah to be with her true love, Jeffrey.

Sarah hates Mike on sight despite the fact that her body tells her otherwise. He is a romance novel "hero-type" who is smug and full of himself. But the only way to accomplish her mission is for her to work with Mike so she can be together with the man she loves.

Jeffrey has promised her that the minute he can end his platonic relationship with Moira, he will be with Sarah for good; but he is having trouble letting go of the wretched woman, and Sarah feels her time is running out. She is terrified of the pending big "M" (menopause), and seeing as she's just turned forty, and her hormones are driving her to do insane and desperate things, she is sure that it is not too far off into the future!

So here she is, building a multi-level marketing business in Taiwan, and struggling with it all: a stranger in a foreign country, away from her mother and friends back in London; a reluctant lover; a drop-dead gorgeous man who might have ulterior motives for helping her, and finally, a business that seems to be dwindling.

Sarah is doing it all in the name of love and the last chance to have a family, and if this means scheming and working with the devil himself, then she will do it! What she doesn't take into account is the fact that instead of getting closer to her goal, Sarah's feelings take a turn, and she finds herself increasingly thinking about the very man she despises the most – "the other boyfriend".

Contemporary fiction - drama

The Soul Bearers

Partly inspired by real life events, this is a story of courage, the gift of friendship and unconditional love. The story involves three people whose lives cross for a short period of time and the profound effect which results from their interaction. Alex Dorian, freelance travel writer and victim of child abuse, arrives in Sydney in an attempt to exorcise the ghosts of her past. She shares a house with Steve and the disturbing Matthew, a homosexual couple. Alex finds herself inexplicably attracted to Matthew, and she must battle with her repressed sexuality and her fear of intimacy. Matthew, extremely good looking and an inspiring actor/model, lives with Steve, who is dying of AIDS. Matthew has his own battle, that of dealing with the rejection of his socialite parents, and facing a future without his partner. Steve is the rock to which the troubled Matthew and Alex cling as they examine their lives and beliefs. Steve finally dies, but his legacy lives on in the strength which both Matthew and Alex find to face their own pain. Alex learns to love again, thanks to the gift of friendship from Matthew; and in turn, with Alex's love and support, Matthew learns to forgive the past and move on to follow his dream.

This beautifully told story explores the true meaning of unconditional love--for both one's self and for others. Readers of "The Soul Bearers" will come away with a deeper understanding of human relationships and of what it means to truly love without condition.

Made in the USA
Las Vegas, NV
29 January 2022

42581565R00118